firewater
A GREEN NOVEL

BY EDWARD STONE COHEN

Firewater is the first selection of the *Akashic Rural Surreal* series.

Published by Akashic Books
Editor: David Shirley
©2003 Fritzi Cohen

ISBN: 1-888451-43-2
Library of Congress Control Number: 2002116774

Akashic Books
PO Box 1456
New York, NY 10009
Akashic7@aol.com
www.akashicbooks.com

firewater

A GREEN NOVEL

BY EDWARD STONE COHEN

AKASHIC BOOKS
New York

NAHCOTTA MANIFESTO

When Ad Hoc Coalition for Willapa Bay, Nahcotta, Washington, takes over the Oval Office of the White House, it will issue by executive order a series of immediate reform programs to begin leveling the playing field in North America. The Nahcotta Manifesto is a first step in that process. Ad Hoc Coalition's own programs for clean water and a clean and safe environment can benefit from these simple, logical, and direct actions:

• Ban all government, military, and industrial pollution on America's coastlines. (This would specifically and immediately benefit Ad Hoc Coalition for Willapa Bay.)

• Cut off electricity to all missile bases and bomb-building facilities. (This would be important in shifting emphases away from the war-making syndromes that sap the intelligence of every new generation.)

• Massive land reform to redress takings from native peoples. (This is critical if we are to reexamine original stewardship and future land use.)

• Provide nuclear suppositories to nuclear business leaders and bureaucrats. (This will enable said personnel to "turn their brights on" whenever they need inspiration for work.)

• Require corporate executives and stockholders to personally taste-test their own agribusiness chemical products before sending them to market. (This would save Ad Hoc Coalition much time, energy, and scarce money.)

• Order the military to grow its own food, along with a surplus for those who can't grow their own. (We hope that they would grow naturally and organically and share with others.)

• Redirect federal policy to provide food surpluses to Americans rather than for export. Available supplies of surpluses could be sold or distributed regionally to all in need. (This would eliminate the wasteful food stamp programs, along with the enormous subsidies received by the grain companies for their $5.00 boxes of cereal.)

• Run the entire Federal Government—starting with the Pentagon—on a strict 9-to-5 schedule. No document would be able to leave any department without the Secretary's personal review and signature to assure accountability. (This would be critical for revitalizing and simplifying government.)

• Audit the U.S. Treasury to find out where everything went since WWII. (This would be an important step and provide work for a lot of unemployed bookkeepers.)

• Put a moratorium on building prisons, with savings going to education, health, and social rehabilitation. (Build schools, housing, hospitals, and clinics—not prisons.)

• Provide full employment for all, with millions of workers trained to meet the human service needs of society. This could be funded from the appreciated wealth gained from pairing down and eliminating the unessential government and military procurement that costs the country trillions every decade.

Good leadership will dynamically transform a basically dense, boring, bloated, corrupt government/industrial/military complex into a streamlined, creative, responsive, vital social resource with the stroke of a pen. We can do it. Much of the static, day-to-day political, business, and government action of the country will be transformed with far-reaching positive consequences for the people. Immediate steps can be taken to free the country from the intransigent yoke of government/military/corporate power's business-as-usual maneuverings.

Right now, our organization, Ad Hoc Coalition for Willapa Bay, is poised, with a little help from our friends, to set new policies for Southwest Washington State and the Northwest region that can lead to banning agricultural chemicals, as well as synthetic pesticides and herbicides, from our estuary and other coastal areas. With a little more seed money, Ad Hoc Coalition will memorialize the funding in low-budget, community-based research and development, education, and advocacy to reach our chemical-free estuary goals.

"Big Foot"
(after Neruda and all the others)

My giant feet crush your heavenly sweet body;
Your fertile ripe fields sink from my oppressive weight,
And the forests splinter between my toes.
Your oceans wash away in abject fear to let me by,
And your silent volcanoes suffer, wondering why
They cannot speak against me.
My feet laugh at you, Nicaragua, as they plunge
Deep into your heart.
Just wait until I put my shoes on
And you learn the taste of leather.

Kiss me, Bigfoot.
Kiss my ass.

January 20, 1988
(Goodbye Reagan Day)

Urbanchuk

"URBANCHUK'S ON HIS WAY HERE, BOSS," Harry whispered into the telephone, pulling his chair around so that he could monitor the view from the big picture window in front of his desk. The landscape beyond the window stretched to the south, across the deep, shit-brown tidal flats, the brackish pools of water, the low-slung oyster reefs, past the tangled marsh grasses down below. The sky had darkened from the constant downpours, and a dark new clump of storm clouds was brewing to the south.

Something dark and unsettling was brewing inside of Dr. Harry Teitel as well. The guy was really acting strange, far more anxious and paranoid than usual. The truth was, he was freaking out, and he knew that he was freaking out. And I knew that he knew it. And from the way he looked at me, I could tell that he knew that I knew it, too. He just didn't seem to be able to do anything about it.

The whole thing was starting to make me feel very nervous. Something was clearly wrong here. Harry looked way too tired and way too desperate, like he could lose it at any moment. I looked across from him and searched my friend Millie's eyes to see if she had noticed it, too. She was sitting at the opposite side of his desk, correcting some paperwork for him, her angular seasoned face and grayish wolf-green eyes focused on the sheets of paper strewn across the desktop. It didn't take long for me to get her attention, however, and to see that she saw it, too. She looked first at me, then at him, then back at me, and I could tell right away that she was as worried as I was that Harry was about to come apart at the seams.

Millie gave me a knowing little smirk that seemed to say: *"Our resident doctor/director here at the fish lab is a total mess goner. He's acting like a piece of shit sliding down the hill into the bay."*

The two of us passed the time like that for a few minutes, signalling each other telepathically about our worries concerning the inevitable tumult to come. Telepathically *and* sympathetically, I might add, since Harry really wasn't a bad guy, as far as bosses go.

I knew that it would be difficult to protect myself and the rest of the interns if the director was shoved out. Millie might even be forced out, too, in spite of her undeniable importance to and knowledge about the lab. She'd been at the lab for more than twenty-five years, somehow lasting through eleven directors in the process. Harry had actually lasted the longest of any director—twelve years—but it was beginning to look, from his recent behavior, like his days were numbered. This was definitely the worst I'd ever seen him. And if Harry blew, there'd be problems for everyone, especially us interns. But, hey, for all I knew, it might just have been hemorrhoids. No need to panic until we knew for sure what was up.

Suddenly, Millie jumped back from the desk where she had been working and looked desperately toward me as Harry lurched over to the edge of the platform, just above Rupp's desk, and vomited right down into Rupp's open briefcase. It was a total disaster. Rupp was still out on the flats, thank goodness. We all sat there in stunned disbelief, totally knocked out, as Harry continued to vomit down from the raised platform stage that housed his office right onto the workspace below. Rupp's belongings were completely covered in dark, green bile, but the vomit continued to pour out of Harry. Though Harry's convulsions didn't stop, the vomit finally did, as he began to labor with rough, gasping spasms of dry heaves, his body still dangling wretchedly over the platform railing.

I was totally flabbergasted. I mean, what a disgusting display. I looked out toward Stop 8 where Rupp and three of the interns were busy picking up specimens. I could hardly see them in the rainy haze. All morning, the outer-perimeter fencing and everything beyond it had been obscured by a dense, heavy fog, even during the brief periods when the rain had temporarily subsided. Before things exploded inside the office, I had been waiting for Harry to send me out after the crew so that they didn't get stuck out there and waste any of the lab's precious overtime allotment. Harry normally had this thing about overtime, especially the past few weeks. But now, in his present state, I wondered if Harry would even think about it.

Suddenly, a lightning flash cut through the haze and illuminated Rupp, along with the others, out near the steel barrier fence. Rupp was crouched down and trying to apply to his aging shoulders the harness from the sled that we used to haul in the specimens. Egg-sized raindrops and hailstones pelted the poor guy from every direction, smashing unmercifully into the mudflats and everyone and everything near them.

Needless to say, these endless July storms made it difficult for any of us to work out on the flats. But we were having a clam shortage this morning and badly needed three buckets of clams to continue our work in the lab. The clams had been a lot harder to find lately, since they were mostly dead and the ones that weren't dead weren't reproducing according to schedule. There had been a lot of mortality on the flats. Harry insisted that it was only a temporary aberration for the estuary, but most of the interns agreed that the clam people had been badly overusing the tidal flats and that we were all paying for it now.

In response to this little emergency, I had sent out three of the younger crew with Rupp, who was the most experienced employee in the lab. They all carried five-gallon buckets, pulling the lab sled through the mud to where we thought there might be some usable clams.

* * *

Ruppert Leonard Emerson was an older man, probably in his late seventies, but very well preserved for his age. Everyone called him Rupp. He loved to work, and he loved to talk about all the work he'd done during his life. He bragged that he'd been working ever since he'd been a little kid. He had worked, at one time or another, in grocery markets, in a rendering plant, in a chicken-processing factory, just to name a few. He had worked to support himself, his family, his neighbors, and his friends. He'd worked at various times in the government, in the press, and in the private sector.

Rupp claimed that he'd even worked for a while in the place where they'd started making Jell-O. He especially liked to talk about that experience. He called it his guns-and-butter days. He described how he and his coworkers took the hooves of animals and melted them down into gelatin. Some of the gelatin went into Jell-O and some of it was used to make explosives.

Rupp had worked during the New Deal for a lot of different organizations with names that were acronyms. Leon Henderson, another old guy who worked at the lab, had also worked a lot during the New Deal. Leon was a colorful character and sort of a gentle, homespun economist. Leon was a little younger than Rupp, I'd guess, probably in his mid-seventies. A really wonderful old guy, he reminded me a lot of my granddad.

Rupp and Leon loved to list all the places they'd ever worked, and they especially loved to recite those old New Deal and wartime acronyms, the

ABCs of government and business, Rupp called them. In World War II, for instance, they were both in the WPB, the LRC, the TRB, and the "yu no vut," as Leon liked to say. During the Korean War, they'd pushed papers in the Commerce Department. Strangely enough, the two of them had apparently worked for the Labor Department during the Vietnam War in the very same building. They hadn't realized it at the time, though, and both thought it very strange that they never ran into each other. That would have been kind of unlikely, I thought to myself every time I heard the story, since they didn't know each other back then. I didn't say anything, though. No point putting a damper on their reminiscences. They were both such nice old guys.

* * *

A bad thing happened a few months ago. Rupp suddenly became very ill. He had been out doing some harvesting, searching for oyster drills over in the western mud flats. One of Rupp's main jobs was to pull the sled full of specimens back into the lab. It could be quite an ordeal, depending on the day's load. He did it without complaining, though, each time literally bending over sideways to get the leverage to pull the sled through the thick mud. As he trudged past, colonies of ghost and burrowing shrimp would retreat into their cavernous underground tunnels. No matter how many shrimp were killed, though, each time the sled butchered up their beds, there would always be plenty more to take their place. At least, that's what Harry said. Rupp and I weren't so sure.

This time, Rupp spent nearly eight hours out there between tides, only returning with five specimens from the oyster drills. Harry had asked for an even dozen, though, and was plenty mad when Rupp came back with only five. But Rupp could hardly stand up by the time he made his way back to the lab. He was tottering around the office, the dark mask of his face streaked with yellow. Something was definitely wrong.

Harry stood up on the platform and announced the results to the rest of the lab.

"I can't stand this," he moaned. "We're being decimated by this critter, and you people seem to just be farting around out there and then claiming that you can't find any. I know they're out there."

Millie looked over at me with a frown, a deep crease forming across her brow, as if to say, *"What's going on with Harry? He knows the bay's a dead zone. The guy must be going bonkers."*

Meanwhile, Rupp was still trying to steady himself. He leaned against the wall in the back as Harry lashed out at the rest of the workers. I could see that he was really ill. Millie walked over to where he was leaning, took his arm, and helped him to a chair beside the aquarium, near where we stored the fibula.

In the days that followed, none of us could find any more oyster drills, no matter how hard we looked. After a while, Harry seemed to get the point and finally lightened up on the tirades. I thought that the matter was closed. Then Rupp started getting even sicker. He was out for nearly two weeks. At first, Harry acted more concerned about Rupp's health than the missing oyster drills. I knew, though, that he was getting more and more worried about what he would say to the front brass. I mean, even I knew that he couldn't submit a report with a baseline of five oyster drills.

Millie had already typed an initial draft of the report a couple of days earlier. When she was finished, she held it up for all of us to see.

"Harry," she cautioned, "if I were you, I wouldn't send this in. You haven't got any baseline to speak of. You need a lot more than five oyster drills for this study. We ought to wait until Rupp gets back. Then he can go out again and try to find the rest."

What could he do, though, I wondered, with the state people pressing for the report?

Meanwhile, I stopped by to see Rupp and find out when he was coming back. The old guy lived about a mile from the lab in a little cabin off the road. He was able to greet me at the door, but he didn't look well at all. He was gaunt and fragile; the lines of his face had deepened into sad distress since the last time I saw him. He told me how awful his recent illness had been. The whole thing was apparently just terrible. He told me that he'd been diagnosed with colon cancer. Now, he'd have to undergo a colostomy, which would keep him from returning to work for at least another month.

"I ate too much white bread," he said, trying to make sense of it all.

When Rupp finally did get back to the lab, everyone was really glad to see him again. We were all disturbed by his condition, though. He had lost a lot of weight; his tall, thin frame looked even more string-beanish than usual. His skin had taken on a jaundiced, yellowish cast, and he just didn't look right to me at all. But he showed up with his bucket and his rubber gloves, and he seemed to think that he was ready for work. Just standing there by my desk, though, I could see that Rupp was starting to turn from yellow to green. Really, by anyone else's standards, the man was not in good working condition. He should have been excused.

Harry had other ideas, however. He gave Rupp a once-over and said, "Good to have you back on the team, Rupp. Make sure you get those little oyster drill fellas in here today so we can finish the report. Please bring your sled back to the shed when you're finished."

I loved Rupp for what he did and how he did it. He was a very gentle man. He had been around the lab for about five years when I first got there, and he had trained me to be the lead intern. He had been in some think tank before joining the lab, a follow-up to some top-secret work that he'd done for the government during the 1930s. Still, management regarded him as a low-level, blue-collar worker, probably for payroll reasons. He really should have been running the lab, if the truth were told. It would have been great. People would really have worked hard for him and without a lot of complaining. As things were now, it was just another job for me and the rest of the interns: get food money, get back to college, get graduated, the usual.

Dr. Harry Teitel? He was okay, too, I guess. But recently, he had been extremely worried and unhappy. Some bad stuff was going on that apparently had something to do with the unfinished lab across the road, which was supposed to have been completed last winter. I was only planning to work at the lab for another eight months, and I was glad that I would be leaving soon.

But it was really a mess, I'll tell you. And it seemed to be getting worse and worse in the days since Rupp returned to the office. It had been particularly rough on Rupp. The pressures were just coming too fast for him, especially in his present condition.

Since he'd gotten back from the hospital, he'd been working full-time for two weeks, dragging the sled across the tidal flats. The sled was weighted down with specimens from the specified areas where Harry wanted us to work. It was too much for an old guy. Rupp was always completely exhausted by the time he got the load back here. And couldn't make it out to the clam and oyster beds and back without having to change and empty his colostomy bag at least once, right out there on the flats. But if he couldn't work the flats and retrieve the specimens, he wouldn't get a paycheck. No paychecks meant no rent, no food, no medicine, more suffering, a short painful future, and finally oblivion with a busted gut. Not exactly a pretty picture.

According to Rupp, his present circumstances were nothing compared to some of the things that he and his coworkers at other jobs had endured in the past. He could be extremely poignant and persuasive when describing working conditions. He told us some really grisly tales about his experiences with the meat processing industries. He'd relate in graphic detail how the cancerous chickens would come down the conveyor belts, the workers struggling frantically to clip off the wings and other diseased portions. The way Rupp described the experience, it all sounded like a grotesque parody of an old skit on *I Love Lucy*. The picture popped in my mind of Lucy and Ethel in their bloodstained smocks, straining futilely to yank off the cancerous portions as the putrid chicken carcasses raced past them and began to clog up the line.

Rupp said that it was pretty easy to tell which parts were cancerous because of all the lesions and sores on the chickens. As long as all the affected parts were removed, the rest of the animal could be packaged and sent to stores as parts. The legs and necks usually went to the Soviets, and the feet were shipped off to China. It was a perfect freebie for the company.

Rupp claimed that he'd never since eaten another chicken, but I don't think his eating habits were anything to brag about. He was and always will be a white-bread man. But he really did hate chicken. I mean, I don't think he really hated chickens, per se. But he hated what chicken had become, and the people behind the chickens made him want to puke. He wanted the other workers to feel that need to puke, too. He wanted them to puke right on their bosses and to puke right on the cancerous chickens going by on the conveyor belt. And he wanted them to puke right on the stockholders. It was the only way, he insisted.

Rupp liked to tell me about an action he had once led in a Maryland slaughterhouse to protest something called the one-and-a-half-second rule. He always started laughing whenever he talked about it. He called the whole thing Campaign Sicken, a reference to how people in Delmarva mispronounced the word "chicken." Rupp had thousands of Sicken stories, and everyone in the lab loved hearing them. He told them all the time in the office when he wasn't out on the flats, and it kept us all giggling as we worked. And when we weren't giggling, he had us all gurgling in disgust. Rupp was especially concerned about the effect that something called Larvadex was having on chickens and people who ate them. According to Rupp, there wasn't a chicken left in the country that hadn't digested the drug. Larvadex and its components were all over the place, he said.

* * *

Things got a bit dicey in the lab when Harry summoned us all one day to a special "workshop," as he called them. The topic of the workshop was Rupp's recovery from colon cancer. Harry ruled the lab and almost always got his way. Harry basically used the workshops to announce changes about office policy and other decisions that he had already made. We were given the chance to discuss the new policies that he announced there. But it was already a done deal, no matter what we had to say, and everyone knew it. It was virtually impossible, given Harry's background and authority, to challenge any of his decisions. After all, he claimed that he had trained under a famous rocket scientist named Edward Teller, an experience that had apparently made Harry world-famous himself. His German accent, his scientific credentials, his power over all the lab research—there was really no way for us to resist. We normally just did our jobs and abided by his decisions.

This workshop was a little different, however.

We gathered in the middle of the main office where the interns had their work desks and tables. Harry stepped down from his platform and took the armchair to the left of the storage closet. The lab staff all adjusted their chairs to form a circle around him. From opposite sides of the room, Millie and I swiveled our respective chairs to face the center of the circle and each other.

Harry always started the meetings with a briefing about some new research plan he'd concocted or discovery he'd made. Last week, he'd announced that he would soon disclose his plan for new gene research that would allow salmon to jump higher up the ladders at Bonneville. This was good news for both consumers and taxpayers, Harry informed us, because it meant that we no longer had to worry about removing the dams to save the salmon. This was a perfect example of how science could mitigate politics, he explained. It was just one of the many unanticipated bonuses provided to nature by new scientific research.

Today, though, Harry didn't seem to be in control. He looked even more exhausted than usual, and he was slobbering all over his clothes. He must have been under a lot of stress, I thought. It probably had something to do with that unfinished lab; after all, this old one was about to bite the dust.

Harry looked around the room at all the interns and the office staff. The only missing person was Rupp.

Millie took the opportunity to point this out to him. "But Dr. Teitel, Ruppert Emerson isn't here," she said, loud enough for everyone to hear.

"Well, Millie, I sent Mr. Emerson on an errand. I don't want him to hear this until we can make a decision, have a consensus, figure something out. But here is the problem. I'm very concerned and have put in a lot of time thinking about this. I've lost a lot of sleep. I really don't want Rupp to lose his job. We need Rupp. He pulls his weight. It's a tough call. I'm really not sure what to do. It's really agonizing to make a decision. But, as you all know, Rupp has been ill, and he's still got some problems."

"Cut the crap, Hank!" Millie interrupted him. "What the fuck's going on here? Talk straight, Doc. Stop giving us those simple out-of-the-ass rationalizations. I can't stand it anymore."

Millie slumped back in her chair in mock exhaustion, fanning her face with one hand and smirking over in my direction at an angle that Harry couldn't see.

"Calm down, Millie," Harry countered. "I'm sure it's not that bad. Maybe we can get them to change their minds."

"Them? Cut to the shorts, boss!" Millie shouted, jumping up from her swivel chair. "Tell us the truth for once, huh!"

She was really getting hot. I hadn't seen her this way since her poor old dog, Sparky, was run over by a bulldozer heading down toward the bay. The machine flattened Sparky as he slept and then just kept going. "Hit-and-run is a euphemism for what happened to Sparky," Millie would tell us later. "This is crush-and-go." She vowed that she'd get justice. "I'll kill those dickheads to get even," she had wailed, wrapping Sparky in a blanket and putting the dog in the back of her truck. Poor little Sparky looked disturbingly like a large pizza with all the toppings and condiments. It was obvious that Millie was still carrying over some of her unresolved anger and grief about Sparky. I don't think I'd ever seen her so livid or outspoken in the office.

In spite of Millie's spirited response, the other interns sat silently at their desks, mindlessly twiddling their pencils, their vacant stares pleading indifference. They were used to having her voice the office concerns for them. Millie, who was about forty-five, headed the local AFSCME. She had been calling the shots on benefits and working conditions for the past ten years. We all pretty much took her leadership and advocacy for granted, I'm sorry to say.

Millie threw me another glance when Harry wasn't looking. She could tell that she was really getting to him this time. He just sat there in his chair, looking confused. Suddenly, he choked on something and ended up in a coughing fit. He erupted into five or six deep coughs before he could even raise his head to look at us. He appeared as if he were choking to death. The truth was, Harry was staring straight ahead at his immediate future. It was coming, and coming fast, though none of the rest of us knew it yet. I could definitely tell that something strange was going on, though; that was for sure. One of the interns tried to hand him a glass of water, but he waved it away at first. His coughing and choking quickly grew worse, however, and he was soon waving at another intern to give him the water. We sat there in silence while Harry chugged down the contents of the glass. Once finished, he handed back the glass and then just sat there, breathing heavily.

The first intern, whose name was Ralph, was standing back in the shadows, obviously uncomfortable about what had transpired. Why had Harry been so particular about the person from whom he received the water? Ralph was a new intern here. Maybe that was it. He'd only been here for about a week and was still receiving the official treatment for new interns, shit work every day. He got nothing but the worst stuff to do, worse than anyone. He had to keep emptying the buckets placed under the toilets because the sewage pipes under the building were all busted. In the past, the work team had included the seven interns, with me as their team leader and trainer; Rupp and his buddy, Leon; another old-timer named George, who was studying the origins of salmon hybrids and who we could only get to go outside one afternoon a week; and Millie, who wanted to be with us in the worst way but was usually preoccupied maintaining the business office of the lab. We divvied up the work so that each of us shared all the tasks. Whether it involved taking out the shit buckets or tracking green crabs and zebra mussels, we shared it all equally. We all believed in the principle of "one for all, and all for one" and did our best to live it out in our work. But now Harry had started to introduce more specialization into our work responsibilities. Specialization weakened the generalists and destroyed morale. That's what Rupp always said, and I agreed with him.

Finally, Harry regained his composure and started talking again. He was hoarse, though, from all that coughing, and still seemed to be choking from time to time.

"They're saying up at the fisheries that Mr. Emerson is not permitted on the tide flats because . . . because . . ." Harry's voice faltered. He began to whimper. ". . . because his wastes may foul the estuary."

Harry looked as if he hadn't gotten any sleep in days. His necktie was crooked, and his collar had come unbuttoned. He probably hadn't changed his shirt or shaved in about a week. The guy was a mess. I looked around at the other interns. They looked totally numb. I knew the numbness. I suppose in his own pathetic, wishy-washy way, Harry really was worried about Rupp. All the worry in the world wouldn't help Rupp at this point, though. It just didn't seem fair, to Rupp or to the rest of us. This place would really fall apart without the guy. And what would happen to him without this job?

Leon Henderson asked Harry if there were any alternatives. Could Rupp work closer to the lab, for instance, so that he wouldn't have to trek so far in the rough weather with his loaded bag? Could he be reassigned to deskwork until his health improved? A couple of the others offered to share some of the monitoring work with Rupp, if that would help. But none of it was enough, and we all knew it. Like everyone else, I was worried about keeping my own position at the lab. Rupp was being fired by co-option, and if we let it happen that way, then we were all to blame. No one would complain, though, because our jobs were so insecure. Any one of us would be terminated at any moment, we all knew, if we put up a stink. Only Millie had the guts to speak up. She had somehow lasted longer than anyone, with all the scars and calluses from years of fighting and infighting.

Despite my reluctance, I finally decided that the moment had come.

"I agree with Millie," I said, just loud enough for Harry and the rest to hear me. "It's really unfair to have this meeting without Ruppert present. We should wait until he's here."

Harry looked at me, his face twitching like he was suffering from some type of Parkinsonian affliction. His teeth were grinding audibly. He didn't answer me outright. "Okay," he said, vaguely, "let me think about it." That was pretty good, I thought, a small start, if nothing else.

Harry seemed to be wrestling with the possibilities when the telephone rang. He took the call at a nearby desk, and we all sat in silence while he listened to the voice on other end, hardly saying a word himself. When he hung up the phone, he looked up at us and scowled angrily. The expression on his face reminded me unpleasantly of the reactions on the faces of my classmates in Victoria Hall at Evergreen College, when everyone on the sixth floor ate too many bananas—and then went a little bananas themselves, during the shit-ins. Something was definitely wrong.

Leon tried to continue his questions, but Harry waved him off.

"We've got a crisis, my friends. First, the new lab isn't ready. We have to wait for the new diurnal to put the roof back on. The current legislature just isn't going to pay for it. They seem to think we can get enough money from a community fundraiser or a garage sale to get the roof fixed. After that, it's anybody's guess."

Harry paused for nearly a minute, looking at all our faces, trying to catch something. He finally grimaced, opened his mouth, and spoke again.

"Dr. Urbanchuk is going to be here earlier than planned. It's going to be quite a squeeze in here. I want your total support in making his tenure here a success. The National Academy of Sciences is very pleased with the selection."

He rubbed his eyes and collapsed into the chair where he had been sitting before he took the call, his energy totally spent. He looked as if he might croak at any minute.

"This isn't about the lab and Dr. Urbanchuk," Millie said, as soon as Harry had finished. "It's about us here at the lab and all the work we gotta do. Dr. Teitel here doesn't get it. We're goddamn slaves. And it's not even quality work that we do. It's just shit work. And if I might say, it's your highness' little brown derby, you and your goddamn butt-hole buddies. And then you take Rupp and rip his heart out. And you do it secretly. You send him on some phony errand to get you some fucking pizza, and you tell us he can't work here anymore. Well, it's you guys who stunk up this bay, not Rupp!"

"Millie, I won't have you talking like this. I was being completely honest about the pizza. This is a scientific laboratory. And we must have standards. Our science must come first. Don't you realize that?"

Harry was starting to sound desperate.

"Yes, Harry, I do realize that," Millie replied, with great emphasis. "It's about us, the workers. You and Dr. Urbanchuk, you have these big salaries. You have all these degrees. You have all these discoveries. You're the management, the big decisionmakers, the big talkers, giving off all this green-slime environmental crap."

I watched Millie in awe. She was really taking off.

"And totally fuck you, Harry. And you can fuck the pizzas, too. And you can fuck your goddamn buddies who really stink up this bay."

Millie paused, but not for long. She stood, arching her slight frame so that her face was less than a foot away from Harry's. She stared him down for at least a minute before she began again.

"I don't give a shit about you or Dr. Chuko. You're both total assholes. You'd better give Rupp the break he deserves or I'm going to the union. And don't start giving me that green crab shit, either."

"Millie, please," interrupted Harry, trying to get control of things. It was a futile exercise, though. Millie's adrenalin must have been spilling all over her body. "Can't you see that I'm doing my best? I can't sleep. I can't work. I feel terrible. Anyway, you can't go to the union. You're management."

Millie wasn't going to fall for that. She was the office manager, alright, the one who figured out how to get things done around here, even with our low budgets and demoralized, underpaid staff. She'd been here a lot longer than Harry. Way back during the war, her job had been to hand out ration stamps to the people who lived around here. She was tough and smart and she made things work. A real manager, alright.

But Millie made it clear to Harry that she wasn't going to be roped into siding with management on this one.

"What fuckin' management is this?" Millie snapped back at Harry. I thought she might explode with anger at any minute. "You can't even protect our best workers. What you feel and how you feel, Harry, is irrelevant. It's time to get some backbone. Or the next thing you know, you'll be out of here on a gurney bed. Elena's going to be turning your bedpans for the next twenty years at the rate you're going."

I thought Harry would faint dead away at the mention of his wife, Elena. I didn't think she really knew what was going on around here, but every once in a while, she did drop off her husband at the lab and pick him up after work. She drove an old, white '49 Packard, and we could hear it chugging over the hill a couple of minutes before she arrived. The two of them still seemed pretty affectionate as a couple, I guess, though they had been together for many years. Harry's quiet years, I figured. She worked about ten miles from the lab at a Costco near the tribal offices, where she did a lot of checkout and stocking work. I couldn't believe that Millie would bring her name into this, no matter how pissed off she was.

I looked around the lab. Most of the staff was just standing around in silence. Maybe they were all worried that their jobs were on the line. If Rupp went, it was probably the beginning of the end for everybody. Soon, the rest of us would be out on the street. That must have been what they were thinking. I wouldn't really mind if it ended that way myself. But with the others, it was different. Some of the interns had families, babies on the way, car payments and Visa bills, the whole thing. It made sense that they would be worried now.

Harry and Millie were almost at each other's throats now. Millie screamed right into his face.

"Harry Teitel, you little fart squirt, show us some guts!"

Harry was withering under the attack. He slumped back into the chair and answered her weakly.

"Millie, you wouldn't be talking like this if it wasn't for Sparky."

Millie's face turned bright red and purple, all at once. Harry was being intentionally cruel now, I thought, bringing poor little Sparky into this. It had only been a little more than a week since Sparky was mashed and mangled by that bulldozer, after all. I was beginning to get really paralyzed by all the heavy emotional warfare going on between Millie and Harry.

"I want this meeting called off," said Millie, a bit more calmly now, though clearly shaken by the Sparky comment, "until Rupp gets here and the whole thing can be aired openly."

She then turned her chair back to her desk and began to rummage through her purse, finally pulling out a Kleenex and wiping her eyes. Leon went over to the desk, put his arm around Millie, and tried to console her. I just sat there, sort of numb, the way I sometimes got when the stress really built up in the lab. I guessed correctly that the meeting was over.

The interns sagged back into their respective chairs and began to correct their paperwork. The venomous anger from Millie and Harry's confrontation was still in the air, though, and I wanted out of there. I had to get a quick dose of fresh air and sanity. Harry had returned to his desk on the platform, his head slumped over his latest scientific report. The guy was looking worse and worse.

I was still feeling pretty numb when I left the lab some time later to retrieve the specimens from the flats. I really hated getting the baby salmon. I couldn't stand it, in fact. This was probably the tenth time I had been forced to do it this year. I hated that their little lives were interrupted before they really ever got going, with so many of them mashed up in the equipment. I wished we could have just left them alone out there, to be what they were and to do what they were meant to do. I hated doing this to them, but I went ahead and did it anyway. Just like I always did.

It wasn't just me who had to retrieve the baby salmon. Every intern had to carry buckets of them into the lab for branding every season. We took turns. There was a special part of the lab where the salmon were branded before they were re-released into the rivers and streams throughout the area. It had been going on for years, but there hadn't been a single report so far of a single fisherman actually catching one of the marked salmon. If one of the branded salmon was caught, the fisherman was supposed to take it to the nearest fish station for inspection. The notices were posted throughout the area. You got caught with one of those branded ones and, pow, you were in for some big-time trouble. Maybe even prison. Or so they said.

We could only catch the baby salmon in the summer. I carried a very light net and a couple of buckets. The whole thing was completely ridiculous. I had told Harry that I had noticed that most of the babies were punctured and ripped apart as they went through the branding machine, that they were dying right and left.

He always answered me in the same rough, condescending way: "So, little Vrhoda," he would start in with his fake German accent. "Vos is dat qveschun?"

"And vos is dat?" he might say later, as he looked over my shoulder at my paperwork.

In addition to the fake German crap, Harry would also sometimes use pigeon English when he talked to us. He did it to everyone in the lab, whenever he wanted to avoid some prying question or to get out of offering advice. Harry would also fall into the whole German routine whenever he talked to the senior officials who monitored the lab from time to time. He could really get obsequious with those guys. It could get pretty nauseating after a while. I'm not even sure that he knew what he was doing at times. And I never understood why he did it.

Eventually, though, Harry usually got to the point when he was talking to us about lab matters or retrieving the specimens from the flats.

"Your job is to get the fish specimens and not to ask questions about methodology," he would say sternly. "You're wasting your time and mine asking questions and looking for answers. In our science, there are no answers. The logistics of our research make it extremely difficult to carry out with precision; we have to expect some degree of mortality with the salmonids. We're trying to change the way we do things. I've worked hard to uphold, even to raise, the high standards of this lab. And the industry standards are getting tougher."

And once he got going on a point, like the mangled salmonid issue, you couldn't get him to stop until he was good and ready to stop.

"For one thing," he would pace up and down the lab, making sure that he had our full attention, "we're trying as fast as we can to get the new salmon-branding equipment. I've seen the new equipment, and it's pretty amazing. Believe me. The salmon are herded into tiny tubes."

He pointed to a small easel set up near the front of the stage and rapped the diagram with his pointer.

"We can push pins through the microscopic orifices and brand the baby as it swims by through the tube. Very little mortality. The salmon really like the tubes, too. You know, Rhoda, we proved that last year. They love it because they know they are part of an important mission. And, Rhoda," he would say, turning my way for emphasis, "it can be operated by one person. You could run it yourself, my dear Rhoda. Anyone can."

Well, the lab finally got the new branding equipment, and Harry never let us forget all the strings that he'd had to pull to get it. When the installers showed up in their big trucks with the new machines, Harry made a point of coming to my desk and announcing that the lab now possessed a special new machine that would save the salmon stocks from extinction.

"My little Rhoda," he said at the time, "it doesn't come any finer than this. You can save your little naturalist fantasies for your Greenpeace buddies at Evergreen. I'm personally flattered that we've been chosen for this assignment."

As he said this, a small rush of anguish passed through my body and seemed to bog down in my arms, which became, at least for an instant, heavy and immobile at my sides. I had been holding a pencil in my right hand, and it just seemed stuck there. I felt totally paralyzed by Harry's aggressive words. The other interns, pretending to be engrossed in their paperwork, could feel that something was happening. Everyone finally stopped their work and looked over at Harry and me. They all knew how much I cared about those dead salmon babies. We had discussed the issue again and again in our staff meetings. What right, I continually asked, did we have to mess with nature? But it was too late now. We were all trapped by our training, our quest for credentials, our professional privileges. We were stuck in this mess. And the mess was a lot bigger than we were.

Dr. Teitel would listen for a while before breaking in to say something like, "C'mon, kids. Let's stop this nonsensical talk. Stop setting up shibboleths. We're the best science has to offer these days. We're here to do a job. We can't really help who we're working for. It's not our fault. Someone's got to take hold and do it if we're ever gonna get the results we're looking for.

"Our mission is to bring advanced knowledge and solutions to problems to the public. We apply our knowledge to the problems at hand. For instance, a big problem right now is that Atlantic salmon are escaping from fish farms up the coast. This threatens our entire native salmon stocks. What happens when they mate, the Atlantic and the Pacific salmon? It would be catastrophic. Our economy here will suffer dire consequences if the native salmon gene pool mixes with the Atlantic salmon gene pool. We need answers. How can we mitigate the results? That's our special duty as scientists. We have agenda-oriented research. We need to find the best way to protect our salmon stocks. It's a privilege and a duty to serve our country."

Buzzozzi

BUZZOZZI LAY THERE IN THE EARLY DAWN LIGHT, contemplating a new tautology that had struck him a few hours earlier during an awakened encounter with his own fiery brain matter.

What's the difference between a headtrip and a mindfuck?

The question kept recurring. Buzzozzi tried to make it go away, telling his brain that it could wait until office hours, but it kept coming back, over and over again, leaving him with a slight neuralgia on the left side of his forehead.

He still had twenty billion neurons in there, he figured, though he was losing them at a rate of about 10,000 a day. Within a relatively short time in human history, he would die of a programmed brain death if something didn't give first. His brain, his intellect, down the tubes, nothing saved for anyone's particular benefit, his life a tiny spot of sunlight flashing a millisecond. Every time he hit a stoplight, Buzzozzi would silently calculate, there went one more IQ point, siphoned away into some eternal rolodex.

The occipital jolt flashed again. Buzzozzi felt for the spot and pressed his thumb to the pain, the first self-help step in treating the emerging condition. It wasn't good; the stress piling up, the work content was so massive and grisly, so disgusting, that any human being would sag under the depressing weight of knowledge. It could be that Bhopal did it. He felt for his beard, now five days in the making. It seemed to be growing faster than usual. His troubles, he knew, were growing as rapidly and as inexorably as his whiskers. There was so much work to do just to catch up. Everyone kept telling him to rest, that he was taking on too much at once. But there was just too much work to be done and too many questions to be answered. And too many things seemed to be getting more and more difficult. How much longer could this go on?

For one thing, the crank calls were really starting to get to him. Carbide must have figured out what he and the Chief were up to. They probably had hired a telephone bank somewhere to make crank calls and slow down their work. Buzzozzi had gotten so many crank calls lately that he stopped answering the phone almost completely. The last two times that he had actually answered, however, it was that fucking asshole Teller on the other end, trying to do a number on him. Teller and his sacred fucking space marbles. He needed his space marbles. That was all the guy could talk about.

Suddenly, an idea occurred to Buzzozzi. Was it possible that Teller had been making the crank calls, and not Carbide? The throbbing head pain temporarily subsided, and he smiled in the dark. At least he had managed to relieve the symptoms for a few moments, even if he couldn't relieve the vast depression in which he'd been floundering for days. How could he find his way out of the darkness and misery that were draining the joy and energy from his life like a gigantic bloodsucker attached to his heart? All he could really do now was scratch the surface of the malaise, maybe just scrape some of the surface shit away.

Buzzozzi hadn't felt this type of despair too often in the past, fortunately. Maybe the questions he was trying to answer right now were just too massive for the human brain to consider. As a man of science, he had always felt competent to handle the big ones, like identifying, once and for all, the difference between peristalsis and perestroika. That had certainly been an awesome wrestling match in the struggle for truth. But now the questions had become obsessions, blowing his brain out like landmines. He never knew, from one moment to the next, when he would step into another tautological explosion.

Right now, though, Buzzozzi just lay there, staring up at his ceiling. He was tired and depressed, but at least he had been reasonably productive. He had completed all but the finishing touches of the Bhopal report within ten days of the disaster. He felt some real pride in that accomplishment, of course, but more than anything, he felt disgust. Bhopal was the worst thing that he had ever seen. And he wasn't through with it yet. He still needed to wrap up the report.

The Chief liked to have the research done quickly. He wasn't one for sitting around and waiting; he appreciated Buzzozzi's fast research and that he didn't try to offer the typically lame excuses and diversions that others often used. You could be sure, though, that those sick fucks at Carbide didn't want Buzzozzi to finish his report. Not now, not ever. He wouldn't be surprised if they were doing the crank calls, after all. The ruins were still smoldering in his head, figures wandering across the barren landscape with no eyes and no prospects.

A sliver of light slipped through the Venetian blinds, disrupting Buzzozzi's dark vision. It was still too early to move his carcass off the mattress. And why would he want to move, anyway? He was alone. He spread his left arm across the bed sheets and pillow next to him. Alone, utterly alone. And he's been that way for a while now. It seemed like months since Lavey had left for Minneapolis to take care of her mother.

Buzzozzi couldn't remember when he'd heard from Lavey last. He'd check the mail when he got back to the lab this morning, before heading over to Skankerville. Maybe one of these days he'd find a letter.

The car was gassed up; his valise was packed with a clean set of clothes. He still had to decide whether to shave, one of the great questions of Western man, before or after the trip. Could he really show up at Skankerville unshaven?

Another conundrum settled in, and Buzzozzi felt apprehensively for his cock. It was still there, thank God. Given all these questions rising up in his head like long lost orgasms, how could he even be sure anymore that he was still attached to his diviner? Buzzozzi lay there motionless, thinking of the last few weeks, searching for a handle on all the strange and disturbing events. The Bhopal report, at least what he had completed of it, was already packed for the trip to Skankerville. Once he'd smoothed out the report's rough edges and handed it to the Chief, he'd probably just be given some new, cockamamie assignment right away. That's the way it always happened. He shuddered with the thought that he might be handed the Waco assignment. He really didn't think he could handle that one now. Whatever he did next, Buzzozzi knew that he badly needed some rest to recover from Bhopal. Hopefully, the Chief would see that, too.

The images of all the maimed bodies rose up in his mind again. Resigned that he couldn't squeeze them out of his mind, he decided to work it instead. He pulled out the report and began to pick it apart for the umpteenth time. He still wasn't sure about some of his wording, especially the part of the introduction that described the background for and intention of the overall document. He kept reviewing the passage in his mind to see if he had it right.

1. THE ISSUE

Developing countries are particularly vulnerable to industrial crises. However, industrial accidents such as Bhopal are not just an Indian, or even a Third

World, problem. Industrial disasters of this magnitude are currently waiting to happen throughout the world, both in the form of "mini-Bhopals," smaller industrial accidents that occur with disturbing frequency in chemical plants in both developed and developing countries; and "slow-motion Bhopals," UNSEEN CHRONIC POISONING FROM INDUSTRIAL POLLUTION THAT CAUSES IRREVERSIBLE PAIN, SUFFERING, AND DEATH. These are among the key problems that we face in a world where toxins are used and developed by those who have not bothered to fully anticipate the harm that can come from their use or abuse.

Buzzozzi kept working over the "slow-motion Bhopal" passage. He had marked in caps the words that he couldn't quite get right. Now, looking back at it, he was uncertain and worried that the Chief would start questioning him about the "slow-motion Bhopal" concept overall.

Buzzozzi could just hear the Chief now: *"Isn't the whole world really a giant Bhopal ready to blow?"*

This time, however, the Chief's concerns turned out to be more pragmatic and politically motivated, no doubt a reflection of his new position within the campaign.

"You're telling me what it is," the Chief had caught Buzzozzi by telephone just before he left for Skankerville, "but you're not ready to say how to get rid of it. I give up. I've got to see which way the votes are going. Billy, I'll see you at Skankerville Saturday p.m. Gotta go, Scout. By the way, did you hear about the new American pastime?"

"You got me, Chief."

"Bill, it's called 'Swallow the Leader.'"

Buzzozzi laughed nervously. The Chief signed off, and Buzzozzi hung up the phone in disgust. Maybe Monica was entitled to a little privacy, too, Chief, he thought to himself. Why couldn't everyone just leave the girl alone? With everything he had seen in Bhopal, Buzzozzi was absolutely bewildered by the current goings-on in Washington, where everyone wanted to talk about who was getting into whose pants.

"Swallow the Leader." The Chief's words still lingered in his mind. Buzzozzi was disgusted, alright. But what could you do? That was the Chief for you. That was the way he had always been, and nothing was going to change him now.

Buzzozzi began to reread his document, trying to remember the sequence of events that had inspired what he had written. When Carbide blew up, the Chief had instructed him to get over to Bhopal right away. It had taken him three days to make his way to the blast site. He could tell he was getting close when he began bumping into more and more blind people staggering around the streets, the juices from their eyes now caked in streaks on their paralyzed faces. Rescue workers were swarming in from everywhere, everyone trying their best to do something, but it had been too late for most of the people he saw there.

In his report, Buzzozzi had emphasized the ongoing nature of the problem. The "slow-motion Bhopals" were everywhere. They could be big, or they could be small. Love Canal, for instance, was just a tiny one, minuscule compared to some of the others. Richland was nothing, comparatively; Chernobyl, a medium-burn. There were different dimensions to each new horror. He knew that. But how slow were the slow ones, anyway? As slow as molasses? As slow as an Amtrak passenger train shooting across the Rockies? There had been quite an argument during the investigation about whether the "slow-motion Bhopals" should be listed for all to see. Wouldn't it just result in widespread panic, with no real solutions in sight? There had also been numerous predictions about when the "mini-Bhopals" were likely to explode. Or whether they would simply attrit into the ongoing, low-level "slow-motion" mode. The Chief, of course, now wanted it all out in the open, the whole thing, the whole pile of shit that Carbide had unleashed when Bhopal blew.

It had been quite a job pulling this report together, Buzzozzi felt. Ten days were really not enough. It was such a rush job that it made his brain sore.

Buzzozzi tried to tell the Chief that he couldn't keep up this pace—it was just maddening—but Shelldrake wouldn't hear it. He never did. No sooner had he finished one investigation than the Chief would hand him another. Buzzozzi's brain flashed again on Waco, the tanks crashing through the walls, spraying cyanide gas into the buildings, the anguished screams, the fires, the total wipeout. If he absolutely had to do Waco, then that would be the end, Buzzozzi reasoned. When was all this murdering going to stop? Buzzozzi lay back on his bed again, completely knocked out, fatigued and weakened by the sickening realization that the experiment in democracy called America had ended long ago—and ended in failure. And democracy wasn't the only thing that had failed. Between his tired legs, Buzzozzi's diviner was motionless, curled up, un-nurtured, its yoni off in Minnesota, a waste of good testosterone now pushing out his whiskers.

The whole thing was relentless. They wouldn't leave him alone. And he had so much to do.

Buzzozzi knew that he'd better get up before the whole thing started again. Lurching up out of bed, he pulled on his shoes and began to lace them, suddenly realizing that he'd forgotten both his socks and his trousers. If only Lav were here to help him keep things in logical order. She had always been a master of detail, preparing his daily outfit in logical, conservative sequence so that Buzzozzi could pretty much dress by the numbers.

Buzzozzi undid his laces, pulled off his shoes, and flipped on the television to check out the weather news. It promised to be a nice, balmy July morning, with some minor disturbances near the ocean, left over from the massive winds and hailstorms that had recently hit the area near Astoria on the central coast. Now, the front was striking hard on the Oregon and Washington shorelines, battering coastal towns like Wheeler, Seaside, Ocean Park, and Klaloch.

People who had been caught outside in the storm had later reported that it felt like being hit with hundreds of golf balls. There had been numerous concussions, lots of people with knots on their heads, and lots of unconscious bodies littering the roadsides. Many people had apparently ignored the warnings, which had been broadcast on television and radio. It was always that way, though. People had to get to work and go shopping, get their kids to school. Houses throughout the area had reportedly been pierced by icy projectiles from the storm. Hospitals were overflowing.

The hailstorms had been striking for more than two weeks now, virtually every fifteen minutes in some places. The forecasters blamed the whole thing on *el niño,* but Buzzozzi was starting to get suspicious.

"You can't push this one off on poor little Jesus," he thought out loud.

Buzzozzi needed to speak with Reba Dickerman. Apparently she was suspicious, too. Her latest call to him had been a bit mysterious, actually suggesting that the incessant storms hitting the coast could be part of a larger conspiracy to disrupt the Chief's presidential campaign.

Buzzozzi hadn't talked to Reba about it directly, but the voicemail message she left had really concerned him. The Chief had also learned, according to Reba, that more tarbabies were coming in soon. What were they to do? Buzzozzi sat on the toilet in dismay, pondering the situation and brushing his teeth. He wondered if it all was really just a ruse to disrupt the campaign, or a really substantive threat. He should probably call Karpinski. Or maybe Remus. One of them would know the score.

Buzzozzi could feel the rumblings of his large intestine from the methane buildups. He laughed aloud as his bloat exploded into the porcelain bowl. He sure as hell wouldn't be heading back to the Slurp & Burp any time soon if this was the way you ended up, blowing your guts out. The news wasn't all bad, though. He noticed that his headache had suddenly disappeared, immediately following the violent wrench of his bowels. What a discovery! His headache was apparently caused by the gas pressure. Another medical breakthrough. It must have been one of those desserts at the S&B.

The tarbabies hadn't been the only troubling development that Reba had mentioned in her long monologue on his voicemail. If, as Reba reported, rogue droppas had really cut off an elk's head, taken it for a souvenir, and left the body by the roadside, then that was some really bad-ass business. Nighthorse was the first name that popped into his head. But it was hard to believe that even he would let himself get involved in something like that. Lots of people had seen it, though. If the Chief's people couldn't get the elk's head and body back together pretty soon, Buzzozzi knew, things could get really bad, really fast.

Soon it would be too late, and the tribes would roar. It would probably represent the end of the tenuous truce that the tribes had worked out with the whiteys. All hell would break loose. Well, it would be up to the Chief to figure out what to do. Buzzozzi would see him at Diehard and deal with it then. The Chief would listen to Buzzozzi's suggestions, as he always did, and then come up with some mincing little word dance to make everything sound much simpler and easier than it was.

"Remember our goal, Bill," the Chief would say. "We must make peace with the white man."

When Buzzozzi was done with his potty and his toothbrush was safely tucked away, he took a long shower. After that, he went to the phone and dialed up the lab. He wanted to see which of the droppas had gotten loose, but he couldn't get through. It was Saturday morning, of course, and everyone was probably streaming over to Diehard. He finished dressing, downed a bowl of Cheerios and some organic espresso from Guatemala, and turned off the television, but only after watching some additional footage from the hailstorms on the coast. Something funny was definitely going on.

The telephone rang again, and he hoped instinctively that it was Lavender. If he could just talk with her, get her to listen to reason, get her beautiful yoni back here where it belonged. It wasn't Lav, though. He immediately recognized the voice of Edward Teller on the other end. He could tell from the guttural speech, like a bad Hollywood actor pretending to be a Nazi general. Ed Teller, however, went on like he was the real thing. The poor sonofabitch just couldn't stop.

"Dr. Buzzozzi, I really need to talk to you. You've got to help me."

Teller was pleading, sobbing, drooling into the mouthpiece, his gutturals churning like shickelgrubbers hard at work.

"Listen, Ed," Buzzozzi responded as patiently as he could, "this is the tenth time you've called me in two days. The Chief says you should take your space marbles and shove them up your ass. And stop the cranks, Ed, or I'm calling the cops."

With that, Buzzozzi slammed down the receiver, grabbed his suitcase, and dashed out the door. He didn't have much time. If he hurried, he could still make it to the fish lab by nightfall. He hadn't thought about where to stay. If he made it before the lab closed, he'd just barely have time to check out Dr. Urbanchuk, visit with the interns, try to find Ruppert Emerson for the Chief, and gather the goods from Millie about everything else. It would be easier than Bhopal, in any event. Cleaner, less fuss and muss, and probably no dead bodies lying all over the place, no survivors coughing their guts out. The lab would be a piece of cake by comparison.

When Buzzozzi got to the car, he checked his briefcase to make sure that he had the most recent draft of the Bhopal report. He'd review it as he sped toward his destination.

Dr. Urbanchuk

TODAY, HARRY TOOK AN AWFUL FALL. A crushing demise. He didn't know what hit him. I could tell all at once, though, that he was a total goner.

It started with his arriving late to the office. Elena's Packard got a flat over at Gloomy Pass, just south of the lab. Gloomy Pass was on the ocean road and rose about two thousand feet before descending into ocean meadows and then winding down a dirt road leading into the parking lot of the lab. We were on a spit of land that had been left over by the university when seafood research grants gave out in the 1950s. The Feds had taken over, leaving a generous science endowment to forestall the collapse of the fishing industry in the Pacific Rim. The lab's job was to provide a get-up-and-go, cutting-edge program that would keep the country competitive with all the foreign fishing fleets that passed along this corner of the Northwest, grabbing up virtually every fish in or out of sight. We had to grapple with all manners of fish diseases, like roundies, ich, and topfloat, not to mention genetic malfunctions due to oil spills, pesticides, and other toxins in the ocean and bay waters. The steady infusion from the now-radioactive Columbia River wasn't helping things either.

Elena and Harry finally made it to the lab on a doughnut furnished by a gas station up at Endlow, but the Packard was on a definite slant by the time it reached the parking lot. Tempers were short. After Elena drank some tea and consulted with Millie, she left for work, and Harry retired to his desk up in the front, fielding the morning calls. He was very tense.

After a few minutes, Harry hung up the phone and turned around, first facing me head-on and then looking up and down the rows of desks at the intern staff. He was just about to open his mouth when the door swung open, a rush of rain bursting through the portico. Papers from the desks blew everywhere.

As the interns bent down to pick up the blown papers scuttling around on the floor, a stranger made his way through the door. Everyone saw him at once, apparently, or felt his presence, even if they weren't looking in his direction when he came in. Everyone froze.

I knew right away that it was Dr. Urbanchuk. I was shocked by his appearance. At first, I thought the strangeness of his appearance must have been an effect produced by the raging storm outside, the giant dark clouds barging into our inlet, crowding their way right up to the laboratory door. Out of the dense cloud bank, he appeared before us. He had on a standard yellow rubber raincoat and black hip boots. But something was obviously wrong. I looked over at the interns and then up at Harry. I flashed back to my desk and glued my eyes to my paperwork. But there was no way to escape the fact that Urbanchuk was in the lab. Suddenly, I felt myself trembling uncontrollably. I held tightly to the side of my desk to stop the vibrations. My insides felt like they were turning to goo. I thought that at any second my body would collapse into a gelatinous mass on the floor. I was supposed to be completing the time charts for the interns. Payday was next Monday, and I had to get the time charts and check requests in to Euphrata or no one would get paid. But I was beginning to doubt that I would be able to finish the paperwork without caving in. The guy was scaring me shitless. I kid you not.

The paychecks on which I was supposed to be laboring weren't very much, by the way. We were virtually unpaid interns, trying to get degrees in oceanography and related disciplines in the schools around the area. The "chump change" that the lab paid us reminded me unpleasantly of a waitressing job I once had over in Olympia at the downtown Holiday Inn. I had to show up for breakfast each day at 6 a.m. and didn't get paid squat. I had wanted to be a marine biologist back then, so I regarded all the hard work as a means to an end. But now I'm not so sure. Working here at the lab hadn't done a lot to convince me. The job was a joke, to put it kindly. I stared at the numbers, trying to concentrate, to pull myself together, to keep my mind off the ominous new presence in the office, and I noticed that Leon Henderson had been out there on the flats for a total of ninety-five hours this pay period. Harry was going to be furious, all that overtime on top of our other budgetary problems. Right now, though, I suspected that Harry probably had other things on his mind.

I shivered as I felt Urbanchuk walk past me and up the stairs to the platform where Harry made his office. He didn't waste any time crossing the floor over to where Harry was staring out the window, trying to act as nonchalant as possible, I suppose. Otherwise, why would he possibly be staring out the window at a time like this?

By now, Urbanchuk had taken off his yellow raincoat. The man was a true homunculus, and a devilish little one at that. He was wearing a zoot suit, the coat tightly buttoned over a typical Northwest beer belly. Had it not been for his clothes, he could have come from anywhere. I suppose my first guess would have been West Virginia, though I'm not sure why.

Urbanchuk's belly protruded well below the line of his shirt and his T-shirt. The guy was a real pig. A total dick-do. On his head, he sported a baseball hat, which he left on even after he arrived in the lab. His long, black, greasy hair was combed back and swept out from beneath his cap. From what I could see, it looked as if he had a collapsed pompadour glued to his scalp. At any rate, I was glad that he chose to leave the hat on. At the front of his cap was the emblem of an axe crossed with a hammer. Urbanchuk didn't look the slightest bit like a carpenter, though. On the front of his zoot suit, I noticed an emblem with a reversed lightning strike, crossed with one of those long, spiked maces that you would use to smash in someone's head—if you happened to live in the twelfth century.

He really was a tiny little squirt, that Urbanchuk. I noticed he was wearing elevator shoes, though they didn't do him much good, height-wise. He was also very thick, nearly twice as thick as most people you'd meet. From the look of things, he was thick where it counted, too, if you know what I mean. He sported a gigantic bulge in the front of his pants that didn't look like it was going away any time soon. When we first talked about it, Millie claimed that it was nothing but a big codpiece. That had been a mistake on her part. After the first time that Urbanchuk exposed himself, he made sure there were no mistakes, displaying it openly around the lab for everyone to see. Millie and I had fled the lab that day in sheer horror, and she had later taken me out and treated me to dinner at Troia's. She apologized for her mistake about the size of Urbanchuk's penis and said that she hoped that her misanalysis wouldn't cause any hardships for the other workers. She had flipped a quarter across the table at me.

On this particular occasion, however, Urbanchuk's penis was still safely hidden away in his pants as he made his way toward Harry, who was still staring out the window toward the mud flats. When Harry finally turned around to face Urbanchuk, who was now standing right behind him, chills rippled through his body. His legs began shaking like cornstalks in a tornado. The time had finally come for poor old Harry. He'd never been up against anyone or anything like Urbanchuk before. None of us had. Hopefully, we never would again.

* * *

That was pretty much the long and the short of it with Harry. Urbanchuk shuffled right in, knocked him out of the lab, and took his job away from him. Urbanchuk was the guy that Harry had been talking so much about, the wonder scientist who was credited with finding verniculous and scramosis in the shellfish beds off of Bellingham. Urbanchuk had also claimed, at least according to Harry, to have tested a chemical that could save oysters from the oyster drill. It was even rumored that he had found a way to recapture the Atlantic salmon escaping from the sea-farm pens off British Columbia. Every day, Harry had bragged to us about Dr. Urbanchuk and the new research division that was coming to the lab. How could he have known he would have been swept away by its arrival?

In the end, it was a septic tank that had done Harry in. Harry had certainly done everything in his power to keep construction going on in the new laboratory across the road. Apparently, the work had been stopped because the architect hired by the state to design it had completely forgotten about the need for a septic tank and had run the sewer pipes right into the bay instead. Harry had reassured us that the ecology and agriculture people would work things out in time to complete the lab before Urbanchuk arrived. But the new lab wasn't finished, wasn't anywhere near being finished, and Urbanchuk was pissed. I mean, how could someone of his stature and skills do research in a place like the current lab? How could anyone at all, for that matter?

Meanwhile, Harry was frozen in fear at the sight of Urbanchuk, completely oblivious to the telephone that was ringing off the hook beside him on his desk. Urbanchuk clearly wasn't amused.

"Harry," he yelled at the top of his voice, "get the phone! Pick up the goddamn telephone!"

Urbanchuk had worked his magic on Harry, alright. The poor guy was scared shitless. We were all scared shitless. Urbanchuk's surprise appearance had abruptly transformed our normal, crappy research jobs into a state of total fear, anxiety, and panic. My guts were knotted and churning inside me, about to start gushing their contents into my rubber boots at any second. Intestinally speaking, this was even worse than eating Pringles potato chips and having their olestra cooking oil dripping out of my ass. Those things really didn't deserve to be called potato chips. I swear; it was a mockery of potatoes. But this was much, much worse than eating Pringles. Reality itself was right down the toilet, along with my intestines. Something big was definitely happening in the fish lab.

Harry snapped to attention and bent down to pick up the telephone. He held the receiver to his ear for a moment, nodding but not saying a word, and then turned and held the receiver toward Urbanchuk.

"Dr. Urbanchuk," he said as calmly as he could, "you have an emergency call."

I watched as the new man stared right through Harry and toward the flats that stretched out beyond the window beside his desk. Urbanchuk just stood there, neither speaking nor accepting the phone, until Harry suddenly realized that he was waiting for him to surrender his desk. Harry immediately jumped from his seat and scuttled into the corner. Urbanchuk took his seat ceremoniously. He lifted the receiver from where Harry had left it and then slowly wiped the mouthpiece and earpiece on his sleeves, with a look of obvious disgust. Urbanchuk finally put the receiver up to his ear, listened for a few moments, scowling in our direction the whole time, and then barked at the person on the other end of the line, "I want three more here on Monday. And don't bullshit me, Bob."

Urbanchuk listened a while longer and then hung up the telephone. He stood and turned to study the room below him. At this point, only seven of us were in the lab; the other three were still out in the field. Urbanchuk just stood there above us with his grim, unforgiving countenance. The rain and hail were beating down on the roof furiously. I wanted to look over to where I knew Harry was cowering in the corner, but somehow Urbanchuk's gaze locked straight in on my eyes and froze me where I sat. I couldn't break his grip. The guy was so ugly and scary that the room itself was shaking with fear and disgust, along with everybody in it. All except for an intern named Brett, who had his head on the table, apparently fast asleep. Brett was narcoleptic, though. In times of extreme stress, he always fell asleep. There was nothing he could do about it. And this was definitely a time of extreme stress. Somehow, Urbanchuk didn't seem to notice him, or to care.

I looked back at Millie, who was eyeing both men. The two were now mortal combatants, and I didn't like Harry's chances at all. I signalled for the interns to come out, but Urbanchuk glared them down and they stayed at their desks. Forget about work, though, I thought.

Urbanchuk just stood there triumphantly, smiling now, gloating in his complete control of the lab. His meaty hands were pressed mirthfully against his belly. He looked us over. I suddenly realized that he was staring right at my breasts. It was awful. I was really afraid for everyone, not just myself. The whole place was caving in.

"My name is Dr. Bill Urbanchuk," he finally addressed us. "I've been assigned to handle research here. I'm the new research director. You can call me Dr. Urbanchuk."

He looked over at Harry, who was still squatting in terror in the corner, and then back at the rest of us.

"He's outta here. Pack your bags and hit the road, Mac."

Urbanchuk pulled up Harry's chair, sat down, and looked down toward where we were sitting. Except for Harry, who was still crouched in the corner across from Urbanchuk, everyone was cowering down in the office pit, looking up at this new monster that had somehow found his terrifying way into our lives. I swear he was the ugliest, scariest, most disgusting thing I had ever seen. He was short, squat, and grotesque, and his dead, empty eyes were now fixed unwaveringly on my belly button. I swear, he was freaking me out.

And it wasn't just how Urbanchuk looked, either. The guy gave off an odor to match his appearance. It wasn't exactly the smell of death, but it was pretty close to it, sort of a moldy, putrid, fart kind of smell. I noticed that his eyes had once again wandered up to my breasts. Thank goodness he was still up there on the platform where Harry's desk was and not down here near me. I swear that if his stubby little fingers had as much as touched me, I would have vomited right in his face, so help me God. The guy really did make me sick. I have no idea how I kept from throwing up all over the place as it was.

After staring around the room for a while and ogling all the women to his satisfaction, Urbanchuk once again addressed the lab, his voice now a dull monotone.

"You can tell right now that your new research director is not a happy camper, and I'll tell you why." Though he didn't raise his voice at all, you could tell that he was really furious. "The new lab is supposed to be ready. It was supposed to have been ready three months ago. I only agreed to come here if I could get a free hand with my research. I expected a new lab, and look what I got. A rotten piece-of-shit lab. A bunch of namby-pamby interns with brains for assholes."

Urbanchuk looked directly at me, and then turned on Harry.

"And look at that dork hiding over in the corner. The great Harry Teitel." Urbanchuk cleared his throat and spat a huge gob of phlegm into Harry's ashtray. "Come over here, worm boy."

I noticed that Harry had smuggled a phone over to the corner and was trying to dial someone. The situation was definitely hopeless, though, as far as Harry was concerned. If I'd had any doubts about it before, I could tell now that he was a goner.

"Get over here, worm boy," Urbanchuk repeated. "Get the fuck off the telephone and get your sorry ass over here."

My eyes switched quickly back and forth between Harry and Urbanchuk, like I was watching a Ping-Pong match. In spite of Urbanchuk's continued abuse, Harry had somehow persevered and had finally reached his party on the phone. I didn't know who was on the other end of the line, but, all at once, Harry became hysterical, his face red and contorted as he babbled incoherently into the receiver. Suddenly, Harry began to flap his arms at his side like a bird, the receiver still pressed to his ear by his shoulder. It was a very strange moment, to say the least. To my surprise, Urbanchuk just sat back and let him go on like that for a while. He actually seemed to be amused by the whole display.

It occurred to me that I hadn't been out to help the interns with their specimens. The three of them were still out there on the flats, and it was really beginning to get dark outside. A real monster storm must be brewing this time, I thought. Normally, Harry would have been bugging me about bringing them in already. Right now, though, he was huddled in his corner, hugging the telephone to his miserable chest and gasping for breath. Urbanchuk seemed to have forgotten all about Harry for the time being, as well as the rest of us, and was leafing absentmindedly through the papers on Harry's desk. After looking briefly at a document, he would then tear it up and throw it into the trash. Meanwhile, the clouds outside the window by Harry's desk were getting heavier and heavier, and I knew that at any minute the three interns would be pummeled with hailstones and heavy rain. The worst of the storms had been settling in at about this same time every day. We'd been having them for the past couple of weeks. Mercifully, most of the storms only lasted for about ten minutes or so, but if you were unlucky enough to get stuck out in one, you could really get pounded senseless. I knew I'd better do something before it was too late.

I walked quickly outside the front door and up the front deck and rang the old cowbell that we kept there for such occasions. It didn't do any good, however. The interns were too far away from the lab to hear it. I knew that I could use the FEMA death machine, the powerful horn that they'd installed to alert the general population in case of real emergencies; its powerful staccato blasts were enough to wake the dead. That would certainly get the interns attention and tell them to get their asses off the flats as soon as they could, a full-dress FEMA event with serious consequences if they didn't comply immediately. It seemed like a pretty drastic measure, though, even with the heavy storms coming in. I wondered if Harry would want me to warm up the FEMA machine, just to show Urbanchuk and the rest of the staff that he was still in charge. Or was Harry too gutless for that?

At any rate, I knew that if I didn't hurry up and get the interns off the flats, Urbanchuk would do a lot more than ring the FEMA alarm. I'd probably be fired. Or worse. I stuck my head back in the office for a moment. Harry was still cringing in the corner, but I decided on my own that I'd better get going right away. I got my gear, came back to my desk, and began pulling on my boots and hipwaders. Urbanchuk was staring at the back of Harry's head. I could feel him drilling his radar right into Harry's brain. Or maybe I was just imagining it. I suddenly remembered that Rupp still hadn't returned with the pizzas. Where could he be? He doesn't now yet about Urbanchuk. Or about what's happened to Harry. Or that he's lost his job.

I figured that the best thing I could do for myself, as well as the interns, was to get out of there as quickly as possible. Get some fresh air. With that fart-like smell from Urbanchuk, it was getting grosser and grosser inside by the minute. I was gagging. Everyone was. I sat at my desk trying to pull on my boots, which weren't exactly cooperating. It wasn't their fault, though. I was so scared and nauseated by Urbanchuk that I couldn't seem to do anything right.

"By the way," Urbanchuk had lifted his eye-beams from Harry for a moment and was staring in my direction, "I understand one of the crew here is prohibited from working in the beds. I want to see Mr. Ruppert Emerson immediately."

I went outside and walked up the dirt road next to the lab to see if Rupp was coming back from the new Pizza Hut. There was still no sign of him. I had to find him quickly and then get the interns in from the flats. I walked down toward town in the general direction of Shorty's, where I knew Rupp hung out a lot. A barrage of hail splattered the ground, and I stopped under a cedar tree and waited for things to settle down again. I thought about the poor guys out on the flat. I thought about the big blowout at the lab. I thought about Rupp, the best damned worker we had, getting canned like this.

The hail finally stopped, and I felt totally alone as I made my way toward Shorty's, hoping desperately that Rupp would be there. I was starting to cry. I couldn't help myself. Fortunately, there was no one on the street to see me. The clouds erupted again and the wind started blowing the hail in every direction. I was bruised and battered all over, but somehow I kept going, trying to make the last few steps toward Shorty's. Once there, I told myself, I would find Rupp. Then the two of us could head out the back door and down the hill toward the flats to find the other interns. To my right, I could barely made out the outline of the lab up the road. I wouldn't be seeing it for long, though. Heavy, black clouds were descending upon us, and the storm seemed to be getting worse and worse. I was really starting to lose it. I felt totally deranged. If I could just talk to Rupp, I thought, and just have a few moments at Shorty's to get dried off and get myself composed.

The weather had other ideas, however. All at once, one of those really big mammas settled in on top of us. Huge hailstones began pounded the ground unmercifully. I could barely see past my nose. I made it inside what I thought was the back door of Shorty's just as the bottom fell out of the sky. The rain and hail blasted down against the glass windows and the roof. It sounded like a battle was going on out there. Brushing back the hair and moisture from my eyes, I realized that I wasn't in Shorty's at all. In all the confusion from the storm, I had somehow stumbled back up the hill and found my way back to the lab. I couldn't believe it. I worked feverishly to gain control over my increasing paranoia. Up on the platform, Urbanchuk was shouting something at the staff, but it was impossible to make out what he was saying above the roar of the storm. He held a telephone receiver in the crook of his neck, while he smoothed back his oily, black ducktails.

Outside, the hail was beginning to slack off. I gripped my eyes tightly shut and made sure my raincoat was securely fastened. I did my best to squeeze every thought of Harry and Urbanchuk out of my brain as I bolted back out the door. I still had to find those other interns and get them off the flats before things got really bad.

.

Firewater

SHELLDRAKE PULLED OUT ANOTHER PINT OF VODKA. He started to polish it off all at once, then changed his mind and put it away in his desk drawer. He began signing papers again. His self-imposed deadline to finish this current batch of land-title documents was 6 p.m., one hour after the tribal offices closed and all the clerical staff had gone, but he seemed to be fighting a losing battle with external delays and his own impatience to get back to the bottle. He'd hold out on the bottle, though, until he finished processing these last five claims. He had already received a series of calls during the past week from lawyers in Seattle, Boston, and Canada wanting to know when the latest batch of claims was going in. Many of the properties belonging to the tribes were divided by the territorial boundaries of Canada and the Estatus Unitus, and there were countless property disputes—and countless lawyers. The Queen of England herself claimed title to the properties in Canada.

It was all such a load of crap.

"I'd like to push a swizzle stick up Thatcher's butt," the Chief said to himself. "That's all it would take. Reagan could pull it out with his teeth, which is about the level of ass-sucking he's been doing with the Iron Clit lately."

As he looked around him at all the evidence piled up on his desk, the Chief was struck by the sizes of the new piles. The original pile was getting smaller, but other new piles were somehow getting larger all around it. In fact, some of the new piles had spilled over from Shelldrake's mammoth desk to a conference table that divided the large office into two sections. Obviously, the claims were coming in a lot faster that the Chief and his staff could process them. There must be a bottleneck somewhere, he reasoned. Something to consider, at least.

Every day more and more documents came in, as the tribes processed more claims for lands. Shelldrake worried from time to time that the claims would swamp the office. He also feared that he would never finish his work in time. The Bureau of Indian Affairs deadlines were fierce, worse than the ones from the VA. You missed your appointment at BIA and you had real shit to settle. If you had any self-respect, they'd say, you'd be on time. The Christian ethic of promptness, thought the Chief, of being places and doing things at precisely the right moment. What a load of crap. Jesus had apparently died at the exact moment he turned thirty-three years old. Not a second before. Not a second after. Just look what I have to live with, he mused. All this religious shit really screwed up the calendar.

And what difference did all the deadlines make when it came right down to it? The BIA never accepted the validity of the claims anyway. But organization was beginning to make a difference. With the sudden success of the property-rights movement, the BIA couldn't really afford to ignore their claims anymore.

We'll outwit and outsmart them until the only way they can hang onto their lousy jobs is to clamp their rotten teeth onto us and hold on for dear life.

Such were the Chief's thoughts as he watched one pile of documents rise three feet in less than two hours.

* * *

Shelldrake's day was already crowded with the usual meetings, conferences, and other indicia of effective, goal-oriented organization. Numerous staff meetings were called this week to work on potential campaign strategies and appointments. The offices were buzzing constantly with new visitors and new demands.

With rumors circulating about his forthcoming presidential campaign, people were all over him, trying to get his attention and vie for his favor. The Chief was having a hard time setting priorities for speaking engagements. There were so many requests, and there was just no way that he could keep them all. The campaign hadn't officially begun, but he was already feeling its effects. If you're running for higher office, he thought, you've really got to concentrate if you're actually hoping to get anywhere. But you can't leave the people behind, he reminded himself.

Tomorrow, he was scheduled to make a fast trip to Skankerville, across the Cascades, to meet with the Diehards. That would be even more time out of his already-impossible schedule. His number-one priority right now, he knew, was to move this river of paper along in the office and with it the tribal land-reform program. It was time to get it all back.

"I'm shit out of time," he protested to Walker Nighthorse, the emissary from the Diehards who had shown up out of nowhere Tuesday morning with a couple of peewee troopers.

Nighthorse's visit had left the Chief gaping and confused. The Chief had heard about the short men before, but he had never actually seen one up close. He noticed an odor like rotten rat farts when they came through the door, but the air seemed to clear a few minutes after Nighthorse and the two somethingorothers settled into the office. It may have helped some, of course, that the windows were open and the exhaust fan was turned to high.

The short men's heads were too large for their bodies, the Chief noticed at once. Yet they weren't dwarfs, and you couldn't really call them midgets with big heads. They were something else entirely, and they were definitely from elsewhere. They looked to the Chief like strange, little bigheaded geeks, dressed like bodyguards in Anne Taylor designer army duds. They both looked a bit jaundiced, too, with a yellowish tint to their complexions. They could just be Asians, though. The Chief couldn't say for sure.

"Look, Chief," Nighthorse said, dragging a couple of extra chairs in front of Shelldrake's desk, then motioning for the ugly little men to sit down. Nighthorse sat down in the middle chair, facing the Chief, a little guy on each side of him.

Nighthorse had failed to make an appointment, as usual. Personally, it didn't make that much difference to the Chief, but his schedule was really loaded, with all the claims, his basic management responsibilities in the office, and the campaign coming up. There was also the staff to consider and their ongoing demands for compensation time amidst the immense load of work the campaign had generated. The girls had asked for more time to themselves over the lunch hour, and the Chief had recently approved a forty-five-minute break starting at noon. They liked getting out in the fresh air. It was easier to put up with the musty, moldy air of these old, rotting-out temp buildings if the staff could take a break once in a while. Any other leave time would really be impossible, though, considering the circumstances. It was bad enough that Barb let Nighthorse through when time was so short. But what could be done? The Chief couldn't stall his top advisors. The truth was, Barb had done everything she could to keep Nighthorse out. But if Nighthorse couldn't get in to see him, who could? The Chief knew that Barb and the others were doing their best to protect him from intrusions so that he could get his work done. But maybe they were starting to get a little too protective.

Whatever the office manager's inclinations, Chief Shelldrake was usually accessible, particularly for his native compatriot, Walker Nighthorse.

Safely installed in the office, Nighthorse immediately began his appeal to the Chief.

"We really need you over there," he implored. "I've been commissioned to bring you an invitation on Saturday noon at the opening of the summer Diehard summit. You're the keynote."

After profusely apologizing for the intrusion, complete with little royal bows from Walker's geeks, Nighthorse grabbed his chair and pulled it up even closer in front of Shelldrake's desk.

Shelldrake Plays Along

I NEARLY CHOKED UP MY BREAKFAST from the rat-fart stench they were giving off, but I decided to play along. Nighthorse appeared to show no ill effects from his association with his little gladiators. He leaned toward me and whispered, "Look, Chief, I admit, we got some problems here. I need about ten minutes to show you what we're trying to do. Can you spare the time? Barb says it's the girls' lunch break, and you're on a horrific schedule. Just give me a few minutes."

He went on and on like that until I nodded okay. He got close, way out of range of the two guys, and looked me right in the eye. I could see that Horse was at his serious best.

I had never seen one of these little guys before, and Horse barging in with them the way he did required an explanation. So I asked him. "What about the little guys? They're sort of smelly."

Nighthorse nodded in agreement, but he didn't answer my question directly.

"Frankly, Chief, the Diehards want to know what it's going to be like after the way it is now. When are you going to rip the assholes out of the armaments companies? What can they expect from life now that you're on the move? Basically, Chief, you've got to go there to save us."

Horse sounded sincere up to the last line, which seemed a little obsequious. It was alright, though, compared to a lot of the self-serving shit I'd been hearing lately. I kidded him a little about it. I told him that the room started stinking the moment he came in. "Do Churd and Choad like fresh air?" I asked. But those two little soldiers didn't pick up on it at all.

Nighthorse said that it might have something to do with the fact they hadn't taken a shit in four days. He laughed out loud when he said it, but I could tell he wasn't kidding.

"I'll tell you about it," he said, "but first I need to tell you something else. I saw a great demonstration over at Middle Reservation. Potex did a new one, but it may have killed him. He barfed up an MX missile. I saw it with my own eyes. I couldn't believe it at first. But a bad thing happened. He convulsed afterwards, went into shock, and is in a coma. Mel. Remember Mel? Well, Mel became a shaman a few years ago. Before that, he couldn't hold down a cough drop. He took a name, a code name, Potex, and he began practicing. Well, yesterday, he did it."

I hadn't been paying that much attention to that part of the campaign, frankly. Nighthorse had more to say, so I listened. I had to. Nighthorse's genius could bring permanent reform to the country's military forces.

"Between Potex and Borker, I think we have the missiles under control. I still think we should turn off all the electricity to the bases. Right off. It should be your first order of business."

I couldn't disagree at all with that.

Then Nighthorse lightened up a little, and we gave some typical greetings back and forth, like: "Chief, how's your old wazoo?"

We then pulled out a few old bad lawyer jokes and passed them around, like: "Why do lawyers wear neckties?"

We ended up our greetings with a few choice Jack in the Box jokes, like: "We cook the living shit out of our burgers."

Nighthorse and his little deputies sat in front of my desk. I could hardly see the little guys behind the piles of documents. I moved my chair to scan the strange men, the oddest and most unique soldier dollies that I had ever seen. Nighthorse shot me a knowing look. Or did he? You never knew with Nighthorse. The man bullshited a lot.

The little guys with Nighthorse hadn't laughed at any of the jokes. I figured that they probably didn't understand what Horse and I were talking about. Between the piles of paper, they looked like a blend of Borneo and Manchuko. Maybe they were models for outdoor wear at Costco. Maybe they were Edward Teller Mengele models of the modern man. They were probably about four-feet-two, I'd guess, and they were wearing the latest in special GI designer uniforms. I had seen some of these outfits before, in Honduras and Guatemala, where the locals are always dressed to kill, so to speak. These two wieners, I wondered, what's their connection to Nighthorse? Who dressed them up? The two were loaded with armaments. Each had Glocks up to their armpits. Bandoliers of ammo covered their chests and grenades drooped in their laps. They had on the standard military protocol, though with proportionally smaller rectangular plastic wedge badges, black with white lettering. Horse watched me staring at the two little men. They were like identical twins. To be more precise, they looked like exactly the same version of identical twins.

"So how do you do, Churd and Choad?"

No response.

"Listen, Nighthorse, I've heard some of these guys are around. But if they're Churd and Choad, then I must be Queen Kristina."

"You know, Chief, you have to be careful around them. The guy told me they know their own names."

"Horse," I said, "their connection with you notwithstanding, your pals need to leave their appliances at the front door."

"I met Churd and Choad a few days ago up in Boise," Walker started up. "The dealers were showing off their new hardware and software at the summer solstice conference. You know, Shell: gun trade and barter deal, guns and butter day. I was over there last week. I think I had just called you. Yeah, I remember. We were trying to figure out who's making all those crank calls."

I recalled the conversation. We thought it might be Eddie Teller again.

"Anyway, Horse, get on with it. What are you doing with these dwarfs? Or should I not dignify them by calling them dwarves?"

"Well, Chief, the way I see it is this: I think these little gnomes are the software. To their credit they're very attached to me; they follow me everywhere I go. Shell, they don't seem to have much of a sense of humor, but they don't eat much. You know how you can do two or three Big Macs? Well, we stopped on our way over at Burgerville. I got a small one, and they split one between them. But, Chief, I'm getting some funny vibes. I think they could be killers."

Nighthorse walked over to the window and looked down onto the lot. He came back and stood next to the desk. Choad was sitting to my right, motionless. He could easily have passed for a live dummy. Churd was to my left. There had been a lot of experiments with live dummies lately, and this might well have been the newest technique. They were going to hit us with this now, along with the tarbabies. That was all we needed right now.

Durka informed me this morning that a fax had come in from the sign people. The corporate hairball was the next one. Durka said that they were brief. She spoke at length with them on the pace of our national signage campaign. The sign people are near Drainsville, a short way from Avtex. Everything west of Drainsville, I kept thinking to myself. Every telephone pole in the country up to Drainsville had my picture on it. I needed to be briefed regularly on trouble spots in the campaign that I might have to deal with personally. Fuckin' unbelievably fast work. And, of course, Avtex was enveloped in a corporate hairball. I almost broke out laughing. I told Durka to find out how large a corporate hairball it was—medium or giant sized? For a moment, I was too preoccupied trying to imagine the scale of corporate hairballs to hear what Horse was saying to me.

Suddenly, he stood up from his chair dramatically. I saw that he was building up to tell me something important, and I focused back in on what he was trying to tell me. From my past experience with Horse, I figured that it was probably going to be something bad.

He pointed his flash blink toward the window, walking slowly over in the same direction. He obviously didn't want to talk in front of our little guests, Choad and Churd.

"Hey, Shell, look at this," he said nonchalantly, like he was hoping they wouldn't hear him, and then started in on a completely different topic. "So far, in two days, I've spent just $1.05 on the two of them for food."

I stood up and joined Nighthorse at the window. I followed his gaze down into the back of the black pickup parked near the dumpster. A pack of dogs had gathered around it. A crowd of people had gathered, too.

Oh, shit, I thought, as I saw the head of a buck elk, cleaved off and resting near the rear of the truck bed, the bloody neck stump dangling over the back gate, dripping a steady pool of red onto the asphalt.

"Jesus, Horse, where did you get that thing? And where's the rest of it?"

"I know, Chief. It's really bad. It happened so quickly. I couldn't stop it."

Nighthorse teared up a little as he said this. The two little guys were watching us now. Trouble was hitting big-time.

"Tell me what happened."

"Well, it's like this," Horse started, trying to compose himself. "We're coming from Boise on the interstate, not too much going on, and on the right, we see this guy on the side of the road acting like he's out of gas. I pull over, and he tells me that he's hit a huge elk, maybe twenty years old, a really huge mother. His truck is wrecked. I put a call in right away. and he climbs aboard, takes one look at these guys, and says, 'Hey, which of these guys is Ping and which is Pong?' And then he starts laughing.

"'Hey, man,' I said to him, 'you must be doing some good scanning, because that's exactly what their names are, Ping and Pong. I just don't know which is which either.'

"'Well,' the guy says to me, 'I don't know much. But there seem to be a lot of these around here now. Someone told me that there's quite a few in Utah.'"

"Horse, cut the commentary," I interrupted. "Get down to it, man. Who cut off the elk's head?"

"They did, Chief. They wanted a souvenir."

I took a closer look at our small guests' solemn faces. They were neither cherubs nor putis; their olive-green complexions would have been the envy of ghouls. Whatever they were, they were making me sick. I might not be able to tell the living from the dead if I had to be around these guys very long.

At any rate, I suddenly realized that I was being inhospitable. I pushed the intercom and said, "Barb, we need some refreshment for our guests. Guys, you want some radiator?"

I usually offered our office guests our regular libation, a particularly potent radiator blend from Columbia Valley. It wasn't the best, since it was sometimes made in old radiators, but it was better than nothing. Nighthorse nodded, and the two little wiener faces beamed up at him.

"And, Barb, come in and show the guys where they can store their pieces. And bring some of the Quillicut goat cheese and saltines. And, Barb, I think we got some Hamma Hammas in this morning from Billbob. And don't forget the Tabasco."

That was the way it started yesterday. Barb took the two guys out and deposited all their stuff, including the handgrenades. They poured out water glasses full of the radiator and drank it straight down. Nighthorse continued to make his case about the Diehards. Barb brought in some trays of Hamma Hammas on the half-shell that Billbob had brought over in the a.m. when he drove over from Hood's Canal.

According to Nighthorse, there would be more than five thousand Diehards at the meeting, and they wanted to hear it from me, the Chief himself. It was all very flattering, of course, but, like I said before, Nighthorse was a well-known bullshitter. He said that the Diehards were becoming more desperate and could blow any moment, though he couldn't say for sure whether they were going to implode or explode. But now was the time for leadership and direction.

As Nighthorse saw it, there was unaminity among the Diehards about only one thing. "They want to see and hear Chief Shelldrake for themselves. And the sooner the better.

"You know you're going to have to make this trip at some point," he continued, raising another glass of radiator, "that is, if you're going to keep your campaign plugged in."

Reba brought in another bottle of radiator, and Nighthorse poured a little more for his disciples.

"Chief, hear me out," Nighthorse said. "If we can win this campaign, we can begin to change some basic behavioral patterns in this country and for sure in the military. I want to show you something."

Nighthorse had been working on a military policy task force for the tribes. He had always maintained in council that the heart of military strength was the discipline of each soldier.

Nighthorse stood and in a low but determined voice barked an order to Churd and Choad. They both got up from their chairs, lazily, clearly bombed out, but still attentive to his instructions. "These guys come from Idaho or Montana," he said, turning to me, "from a tribe of Laotians who came here after the Tet Offensive. They're not much, but they can take orders, and they grow some good poppy up near Boise."

"Atten-hut!" he barked at the twins, and then turned back to face me. "Now look at this, Chief!"

The two little guys leaped up from their chairs and stood ramrod straight. I couldn't get over how tiny there were—just over four feet, and maybe seventy-five pounds, if that. They stood there for a moment.

"At ease, soldiers," the Horse finally instructed, and the two guys slid to the floor and, with acrobatic coordination, adopted fetal positions in one swift movement, knees locked to their chins, eyes closed. They laid there, perfectly still. A few moments passed, and they continued to lay prostrate on the floor.

Not bad, I thought. Where's Dickerman? She's got to see this. I pushed the intercom to get Barb, but there was no answer. She was probably busy. She was always busy this time of day, getting ready for the late-afternoon finale.

Mercetemps

"WE WERE TRAINING THESE PUPS for the modern arm," Nighthorse continued his explanations to the Chief. "I mean, Shell, not we, but the country, the government, whomever. The people I met on the other side say this is the way of all the research now in military administration and discipline. If you can get a lot of guys who don't eat much and don't have to carry packs, well, you get what you have here. MTs. See their arm bands? MT. Well, that could mean a lot of things, I realize, but the Boise guys I met say it means *mercetemp*. They bang these guys out pretty fast; they're already selling squad and platoon sized units to the Pentagon. The government is planning to use them for running law enforcement, crowd control, prisons, you name it. These little guys are the latest. Watch this."

Nighthorse put his drink down on the edge of my desk and reached for his briefcase. The little soldiers had been working on the oysters one minute and taking sips of radiator the next. Now they were sprawled out motionless on the floor, their faces still silent, grim, pale. Churd and Choad, huh? Someone over in Montana sure did have a sense of humor, the Chief thought to himself.

"When you come over to Skankerville on Saturday," Nighthorse continued, "you can see what's going on at the armory. If they can do this with these guys, why can't we retrain the joint chiefs and top brass when we get to D.C.? We might even be able to remove some of the more disturbing behavior traits that have been programmed into soldiers over the last five thousand years. I'm no scientist, Chief, but I can tell you that over at Boise, I saw in one demo twenty of these guys lined up in a row, all in fetal positions. Like little babies. They called it 'the Pablum Division.' By the way, Chief, you really ought to send Buzzozzi over there. It's really weird."

Nighthorse reached deep into his briefcase and brought out a couple of small objects.

"We have two choices now. When I say, 'Parade Rest,' they will either start sucking their thumbs or this pacifier." He reached down, put the pacifier near Ping Choad's lips, and uttered, "Parade Rest." Ping's lips pouted just enough to feel the tip of the rubber nipple. He then drew it into his mouth and sucked contentedly. Pong made a spontaneous insertion with his thumb. Nighthorse sat back down in his chair, and he and the Chief watched the zoned-out little guys sucking away in babyland.

"This is revolutionary," Nighthorse continued, raising his glass. "Don't ask me how it works. These little fuckers are all over the place. I don't even want to tell you how I got the two of them."

While the two little guys remained at "Parade Rest," Nighthorse told the Chief just that. They had apparently been a giveaway of sorts, some kind of test drive or free start-up offer.

Exhausting the dwarf issue for the moment, the two men discussed current politics for a while, along with some of the themes that they'd be using in the Chief's campaign during the coming months. Nighthorse recounted some recent military maneuvers.

"Remember Borker? He says he can spit on an MX missile and disarm it for forty-eight hours. Borker will be there on Saturday."

Nighthorse held up another item from his briefcase. It was a cork. He inspected it, smelled it, and then aimed it like a tiny telescopic sight at Shelldrake.

Before Nighthorse could speak again, Shelldrake pushed the intercom with another assignment for Barb.

"Barb, see if you can find Dickerman. Tell her Nighthorse is here." He put down the phone.

Nighthorse was clearly eager to continue. "I already showed Dickerman how it works, Chief."

"Okay, you got me," said Shelldrake. "Don't tell me that they'll cork up their butts on command." He laughed. "I guess that's what I'm smelling. Right, Horse?"

"Right, Chief, exactly right. On command, either Ping or Pong will install one of these in his butt. The current military thinking is that soldiers these days take too many smoke and shit breaks. This is all classified, I was told, but they're working toward the development of, if you haven't already guessed, totally synchronized shit breaks to save time during marches. As much as thirty percent of the delay in every maneuver is due to poorly timed shit breaks. Take these little guys. They don't eat much. With their plugs in, they can march for several days without building up much poop. And look at this." Nighthorse pulled a tiny penlight from his breast pocket. He flipped it over the desk to Shelldrake. "Push the button, Chief."

Shelldrake pushed the button, and a series of three lights flashed. "I guess this means that they've got their plugs in."

"True enough, Chief. Three lights means that they've had them in for three days. And look, they haven't even begun to stink yet."

Nighthorse was wrong about that part, the Chief thought. He must have left his schnozz back in Boise. The little guys were really stinking.

It took forever to get Ping and Pong out of the office and Nighthorse had to carry out one of the little bozos on his back; the other he dragged across the floor by one leg.

"You keep the ordinance," Nighthorse instructed as he left. Shelldrake could see that the whole outer office was staring at this freak show. "When they gave me these little guys, they didn't even ask for a receipt. Can you imagine that?"

Nighthorse revved up his pickup truck in the parking lot outside the Chief's window, his tires grinding and throwing gravel as he and his little friends sped out of sight.

Shelldrake Servicing Land Claims

SERVICING THE PAPER was merely a question of division and grading, like sorting or grading beans or oysters or golf balls, for that matter, as the Chief had done when he was a little boy. He and his friends had once found thousands of golf balls after a truck carrying them had crashed into a ditch near the reservation. Sorting and selling those things had kept the gang supplied with trading cards and smokes for quite a while.

But these were legal documents, not oysters or golf balls, based on exhaustive title searches, legal briefs, judicial decisions, and all the long waits in between. Shelldrake knew that his work was merely one link in an endless chain, yet another administrative task to be completed before the Native American claims could be forwarded down the line, first for the Governor's signature and then on to Uncle Sam. In the end, after the documents had been thoroughly passed around, everyone was still pissed off at what they were getting, if they got anything at all.

In order to maintain his momentum, the Chief began signing with both hands. He felt like he had developed carpel tunnel syndrome, his wrists and shoulders aching under the enormous weight of his task. Shelldrake finally stood up and stretched. He burped, belched, leaned into a farting position, and then let go of a big one. The office shook and the pictures vibrated on the walls. The walls of the outer office began to shake, too, as the staff preparing to leave for the day were suddenly hit with the impact. The Chief could hear the fast talk of the girls, hurrying out of the office before the stench sank in. Shelldrake laughed. The women had somehow escaped.

As the Chief came out of his momentary pleasure, he fixated on the furniture. This Hepplewhite stuff was for shit, he thought. He picked up a long sidetable and moved it closer to the desk so that he'd have room for some more stacks when the xeroxing started again. The space wasn't bad.

Typical BIA temps left over from World War II. Japanese interns had once lived in here. Not bad at all by BIA standards. The Chief's old friend Bob in Mud Bay used to bring oysters over to the prisoners. Boy did the Japs love oysters. Maybe even more than the locals.

The Chief managed to reach the mantle over the fake fireplace, found an ashtray in the gloom, and picked out a couple of choice roaches. He lit up near the window. Parting the government-issued Venetian blinds, he could see out into the courtyard and the mall beyond. It looked as if almost everyone had gone home. He did see one guy over near a small fountain flapping a blanket, apparently sending smoke signals to a second guy whom the Chief could just barely make out over in a parking lot near the Costco. Shelldrake strained his neck, trying to get a better angle to read the smoke. Shit, there was Mud Bay Bob's kid, Billbob. He was the one who had brought the Chief those nice Hamma Hammas. The Suminoes he'd brought weren't bad either. The Chief couldn't quite make out the message that Billbob was sending, probably another bumper sticker slogan. *"You're going to eat shit and love it,"* was one of his recent best. The Chief couldn't quite decipher this one, though.

Rising above the Costco, the Chief saw the irridescent halo of smoke and debris from the regional landfill. Beyond that were a few plots of no-till farmland, leading past a few small hills and a golf course, toward the reservation. Above the arc of light from the smouldering landfill, the Chief could see the faint beginnings of a second glow, the early illuminations of the tribal casino and pachinko parlor. The neon lights cast a rising yellow glow against the reddish, late-afternoon July sky. The lights of the pachinko parlor went on automatically every day at this time. Passengers on the Amtrak trains that sped down the coastline each afternoon could reportedly see the lights from a distance of thirty miles.

"We now have the first pachinko parlor on any reservation in the United States," Shelldrake mused. "Christ shit, where do we think we're going?"

The Chief took a huge draw from the roach, leaving only a glowing ember wedged between his thumb and his index finger. He raised the last remnant, drew the haze of smoke into his nose, then killed the cinder with his index finger, pulling one last, delicious flume into his smeller. He realized that he had been looking out the window too long and needed to plow back into the paper. Taking one last look toward the Costco, he noticed that the lot was now empty and Billbob was gone. A slight haze remained from the smoke signals, but he could no longer see the embers from Billbob's makeshift message center.

The Chief stretched some more and returned to his pile of paper. He noticed a couple of large paperclips on the rug and bent down to pick them up. Dropping them into a cup on his desk, he sat down again, more clerically minded now, or so it seemed. He could stop himself, though. With his left hand, he opened the drawer where he kept his vodka. He took a generous swig. This time, he left the pint on his desk near the lamp, which he then turned on to offer a little more light to his task. In another two hours or so, he'd be finished for the week and another batch of land claims would be heading down to the Governor for his signature.

"Soon, there'll be a brighter world for all my Cheyenne and Appollusa friends," he mused, taking another gulp from the bottle. "If we can do enough of these, we'll get this part of the country back from the non-native invaders, all the whitey assholes out to kill us."

He picked up the pint and looked at the label. *"Spudka,"* it said, *"made from distilled spirits."* He liked the word Spudka, he thought, because of the international intonations. He knew the shit was all the same. You couldn't even get good booze anymore. What were you to do when it was all basically government-issue anyway? But, hell, there was always radiator.

The Chief heard the familiar noises from the secretarial pool, signalling incoming faxes. He could actually hear the paper sliding out of the machine. *More fucking wallpaper,* he thought. He turned back to his pile and once again applied his moniker to the bottom sheet. Usually each claim was two pages, but occasionally you'd get three or four. The Bureau of Indian Affairs had asked that each claim be kept to one page, due to the Paperwork Reduction Act of 1986, but some of them spilled out into second, third, and fourth dimensions. And then there were the attachments.

The Chief had to write his name four times on each document, and two more on the affidavits. His writing was getting a little scratchy.

BIA wanted all original documents. *But then we'd never see them again, would we?* reasoned Shelldrake.

When he had refused to give them the original deed to land under Sioux City, Iowa—which had been discovered by Queen Raging Shiningbull's family in their great-grandmother's trunk—BIA warned, in a long memo to the region and then down to Shelldrake, that copies alone would not be enough to verify the claim, and that anyone refusing to supply originals could face long prison terms and heavy fines.

In the councils, Shelldrake had heard countless theories about how to proceed with these land claims and whether to turn the originals or just copies into Indian Affairs in Washington, D.C. It all came down to one thing, the most militant of the tribal theorists reasoned. The millions upon millions of stolen hectares had to be returned to the native peoples before there could be further settlement with the white man.

Others argued, though not persuasively, in the Chief's opinion, that the tribes should be careful not to rock the boat too much. Maybe they should at least try to trust the good ones at BIA. The tribes didn't want to lose their precious food stamps and bingo licenses, after all.

The Chief had heard versions of all the different positions for many years. His compromise position was to get all the claims in at once but only to give BIA copies of the deeds. The originals were stored in different places inside the tribal mountain, where the BIA people and their militia asshole friends could never get near them.

"Tear another asshole in those BIA fuckers," thought the Chief. "Kick their lying butts out of there. They couldn't stop lying, anyway, about what they were doing to us. We'll give them the papers, and if they don't like it, tough shit all the way around. All they'll do anyway is fart their brains out to Congress, lying to them, too, kissing the asses of a bunch of wiener dorks who have the temerity to say they represent us. I say, bullshit on five thousand smallpox blankets.

"Even a half-assed Indian knows that the white man will make the deeds to land owned by the native people disappear whenever he can get ahold of them. They'll shred the shit out of them. They've turned us all into felons anyway with all their laws. No intelligent person can follow these laws. As soon as you get to know one law, some other law will be introduced that will cancel the others out.

"But BIA only wants originals, no copies. After BIA verifies that they're true originals, then they'll make a copy and charge us a dollar per page. We don't have to pay in cash, they say; it'll all be debited against the tribal accounts. The greedy bastards will xerox us to starvation. Well, fuck that. The typical shit from the government. All our tribes are just part of BIA's annuity anyway."

The Chief was really working himself up now. The Spudka was pretty smooth. That, along with the dynamite shit Dickerman had recently scored off someone at the reservation, made the clerical work relatively bearable. But all this paperwork was really just a gigantic farce to keep the people down. Papering the world with legal definitions was the white man's seemingly nonviolent way of stealing everything after they've basically killed you all off to start with.

"That's another reason why you know you're an Indian." The Chief took another swig. "The paper trail is just another dead end road into whitey's pocket."

The Chief's bitterness had subsided slightly by the time he polished off the pint. He heard the doorknob turn, and he put the bottle aside and tried to sit up straight. He heard a light knock on the glass door at the same moment that a young woman entered the room, an unfurled fax in her hand.

The Chief had hoped for a moment that it would be his niece Cheryl. She had been working in the offices for three years and now headed up the clerical crew that was accumulating the documents for the land claims. But he could see that it wasn't Cheryl, it was Barb. And he could tell by the way she looked that it was urgent.

"Chief, come outside immediately!" she barked, before he had a chance to say anything. "Come outside and see what we've got here."

Barbara

BARB WAS THE OFFICE MANAGER. She had been here, working at my side, for more than ten years. There was no bullshit with Barb. She really ran the office. She worked the shit out of people. I liked that. It was my own style. You've got to get the most out of the workers, or else you end up with your typical dark-age clientelism. And the workers have to get the most from you, or else they might just as well go pick bananas. There's a very strong work ethic here.

And Barb? When she called, you went.

I had just gotten back to work after Nighthorse left with the two little guys. He had one on his back and was dragging the other out of the office on the floor by one leg. They were totalled. I rearranged the chairs and went back to work. That was when Barb came into the room and told me that she had something to show me out in the parking lot. I told her I'd be right there. But first, I went into the crapper for a few minutes and gave one to the gods.

When I returned, a new stack of faxes sat in the inbox. I couldn't remember when they were brought in, but it had to be after Nighthorse left with his new buddies. I was really only in the can for a few minutes. When I checked the new claim acreage against the wall maps behind the desk, I saw we had one for half of Montana.

I must have forgotten about Barb for a minute. Outside in the parking lot, she was screaming obscenities and telling me to get with it. She was getting louder and nastier out there every minute. Finally, I stuck my head out the window and saw Barb and Lois fiddling around over at the dumpster, peering in. I caught a glimpse of what looked like little feet sticking out of the top of the container. *Oh, shit!* I thought, as I exited the building through the side door and rushed down the emergency fire escape that descended straight into the parking lot. The staircase was pretty rickety, but I managed to get down without any mishaps.

Nuzzling in beside Barb and Lois, a couple of local dogs had wandered upon the scene and were sniffing around the dumpster. I got up closer to where Barb and Lois were examining the bottoms of the little guys' feet. Four tiny little feet just sticking right out of there. The size-6 combat boots were gone, and their feet were a purplish-yellow color. It looked as if they had drunk too much radiator.

Barb was in a rage. Her contorted face contrasted uneasily with her ample shape. The woman had a really nice set, if I haven't mentioned it before, and they were heaving against her whale totem T-shirt. She was pissed, alright, and I could understand why.

"Why is it our dumpster is always being used by other people, and then we have to pay to get it to the landfill?" Barb was practically in tears. "It's really unfair when you're trying to recycle and someone else is too cheap to use their own dumpster."

I could see that Barb was raising a serious policy question, but I had other fish to fry right now. I remained silent as the three of us peered into the dumpster for signs of life. The Glocks, grenades, and ammo belts were gone. Walker Nighthorse was nowhere to be seen, of course; his black '72 Ford pickup was also out of sight. I thought I could still hear him revving up shortly before Barb came into my office, right before I went into the crapper. But maybe I had just imagined it. The Anne Taylor designer outfits were smeared with barf and blood, and their little mutant faces bulged out hydrocephallicly. Lois had donned a pair of rubber gloves and was trying to push one guy's feet further into the bin so she could close the lid.

"Alive or dead," she said, "we don't want the rats to get them. It will really be a mess then. It's starting to stink already."

Barb gagged involuntarily. Her eyes were turning red. The dogs pissed on the dumpster and trotted away. Through clenched lips, she finally announced to Lois and me, "We can see what's up in the morning." She pulled off her gloves, threw them in behind the guys, and then shut the lid. She went over to a nearby hose, drenched herself, and scrubbed her hands with gravel from the driveway. The elk's head was gone. Hopefully, Nighthorse was going to take it back to its body so that the poor fucking elk could find some peace.

"You and your fucking friends, Chief." Barb was Barb again. But her speech was funny. I finally noticed the black oval of her mouth. Her mouth had lost its ivories.

"Barb," I asked, "Where are your teeth? What's going on here?"

Barb's face was red and swollen. Waves of tears poured down her cheeks, her precious water dripping incessantly onto the parking lot. She mumbled something and pulled up her dress, and I suddenly realized what had happened. I bent down to take a closer look. Without further ado, I helped Barb remove her teeth from her lower orifice and get them back where they belonged. Before I knew it, she had composed herself and started back in again on me and the campaign.

"You and your fucking friends, Chief." Barb was Barb again. "How did they even get in the front door?" Her contorted face twisted and tore the space between us to bits. "How can you keep this campaign going when you waste time with these total dorks? Durka's trying to keep you on the beam, and she's going to shit when she hears about this.

"And you know, goddamnit," she screamed, "I even went over to Costco to get you the Tabasco for your fucking oysters!"

I watched the pain in Barb's face. I knew she meant business. I nearly melted in her awful contortions.

Is this what politics does to someone? I asked myself. "Okay, Barb, Lois, what do you want me to do? Should I take them to the dump in *my* rig?"

There was nothing left to say. I still had a lot of ground to cover upstairs. I turned back. I had to take another crap, and quick, so it looked like the Barb and Lois discussion was over, at least for the time being. As I started to mount the stairs, I heard Barb's voice behind me, sounding almost apologetic. I turned to face Barb, whose contorted face was now mottled up in emotion and nearly in tears again. At least she had her teeth back in place, so she wasn't just wagging her gums at me. I was really glad that I was able to help get her teeth back where they belonged so quickly, rather than go through the protracted and frustrating ordeal of trying and failing to find them somewhere on the floor in the office.

"Chief, I'm so sorry. I forgot to give you a message when you were with Nighthorse. That guy Teller called again. I told him that you were busy and you couldn't talk. He said to leave a message. He talked to Buzzozzi. He said Buzzozzi refused any deal on space marbles. You should call. He wants you to leave space marbles alone. If you stop his space marbles, he's going to be really upset. He sounded really pissed. I'm sorry; I forgot to tell you with all this other nonsense."

"That's okay, Barb," I said. "I guess you owed me one. I guess we're even now."

I went back upstairs to finish my work. I thought about Teller, about the age we were in. Teller could beg 'til his nuts fell off. The whole thing was going, going, gone.

Cheryl

CHERYL HAD STARTED WORKING at tribal headquarters as a legal paraprofessional intern from her college in Olympia. Cheryl was one of Shelldrake's nieces by marriage. Durka always claimed that her own ancestry led back directly to Massasoit. Shelldrake never understood where Cheryl fit into the chronology, but he loved having her around the office. She was sharp as hell and felt his own suffering. And Cheryl was beautiful, like Pocahantas, his women-watching friends always spilling their juices everywhere she went.

"Hi, Chief," Cheryl squawked, as she made her way across the room to the front of Shelldrake's desk, holding the gossimer fax message in front of her body. "I've got one this time," she said with sort of a sad moan, her long, blondish hair swinging around over her breasts. Cheryl's body, her intelligent face, and her sultry manner drew the Chief into yet another sensual eruption, one more massive reltne. Shelldrake secretly and hopelessly craved this twenty-year-old beauty who ran the office pool.

Actually, the Chief's desires weren't as big a secret as he might have suspected. Cheryl knew exactly what was happening to him as he watched her, and she also knew that he couldn't help the way he felt. The women in the office knew that the Chief was a beautiful caged-gorilla of a man, locked away in his own private zoo, looking out through the bars at all the lovely females passing by, even though he could never touch them.

Throw me something, girls, the Chief often thought to himself as Cheryl or one of the other young women would walk past him. Durka would throw him something, alright, and it would probably be a knife in the heart. *Most likely, she'll throw it into my balls,* Shelldrake mused.

Cheryl cherished the moments alone with the Chief, when she knew he would be eruptive. But they both knew that there was business to do right now. She stood there transfixed by the face of her leader, his rumpled clothes, his five-day growth of beard, his big, gap-toothed smile, as big a gap as Oliver North or Bobby Lee Inman. But the Chief was a lot better looking than that chipmunk asshole, Inman.

Cheryl looked down at her leader, who was staring right back at her through his hazy blue eyes, as blue as a coyote's scream in the night. Alcohol is the curse of our nation, she thought, admiring Shelldrake's countenance. It would be a crime to ruin a face like this. Cheryl knew that the Chief had been dipping into the Spudka more often than usual lately, with all the pressure from the campaign and the land claims.

"Durka says she thinks you're working too hard," Cheryl informed the Chief, "and she wants you to come right home when you're done here. I'll drive you home. She says that if you don't get there by 7, all you're getting to eat is salal cakes. And she said she'd be happy to stuff them up your butt."

The Chief sat still, staring at Cheryl standing there with her uncoiled fax. The fax must have been six feet long, a paper serpent caressing Cheryl's bod. The Chief sure did envy that fax. A split second passed, and Cheryl lowered the fax down, just a little, revealing the length of her torso to Shelldrake. He noticed her nipples pouting through her Evergreen College sweatshirt.

"I still have a lot of work to do," he told her, trying to get his mind back to the business at hand. "I've got to speak to the Diehards tomorrow afternoon. I'm opening their Freedom Day rally."

"You're really going to Skankerville?"

Cheryl could feel the Chief responding to her. The pull from her nipples was so strong now that she could feel the skin on her forehead begin to tighten.

"Chief," she said, "the fax is from Greenland. Dickerman said that you need to see it immediately. The Pentagon is up there trying to corner the lichen markets. They're after our food supply."

The Chief stared at her longingly as she read him the fax news. In his face, competing with his desire for her, she could see the concerns of all Indians, everywhere. She could see the destruction and ruin of all the tribes, the humiliation, the starvation, the smallpox and syphillis, the forced marches, the scalping of women, the slaughter of the buffalo, the enslavement of children. And now, when there was so little left, the bastards were stealing their lichen.

"Uncle Shelldrake," she began, "there's some bad stuff that you need to know. I've been having these really bad dreams the last two nights that I must tell you about. I don't know if I'm awake or asleep when they come. There's real danger lurking here."

Cheryl sat down in the chair facing the Chief. Her body shook involuntarily, and she almost levitated from her chair.

The Chief was completely transfixed by Cheryl's undulations, her eyes closed, her body rising off the chair until she was actually floating in the air. For more than a minute, Shelldrake simply watched his niece suspended there, completely unaided, the beautiful contours of her body filling out her jeans and her Evergreen sweatshirt, her face a placid mask. As her body slowly floated back into her chair, she opened her eyes with a broad smile.

"Not bad, huh, Chief?"

The Chief waited for her to tell her story. He reached down and opened the second drawer on the left side of his desk. He pulled out another pint of Spudka, opened it, and took a big swig.

"I'll take it straight and true, the way they gave it to the one-eyed Riley," he muttered to himself. The warm Spudka drained through his gullet and down into his belly. He continued to drink while Cheryl sat waiting for him to finish, wondering what he was talking about, hearing the vodka guzzling like gas into an empty tank. He put down the bottle, but still gripped it in his left hand. He didn't recap it.

Cheryl looked up at the Chief, groping for words. "Remember, Uncle, how Edward Teller got so depressed when Star Wars was killed that he jumped into the cyclotron?"

"Right, Cheryl," said the Chief, "that idiot liquified himself. Ha!"

The Teller mishap had actually been one of the funnier things that happened at the end of the Reagan Administration, the Chief remembered fondly. Poor sonofabitch Teller grunting in his guttural fucking Deutschball accent that if we didn't support Star Wars, we didn't deserve to survive nuclear war. If we didn't support Star Wars, space marbles, and all that shit, we were done for. The stupid bastard, thought the Chief. We'd already been zapped by the shit that he and his buddies had laid on us from Livermore. We have tribes filled with still births and dead babies. The guy jumped into a cyclotron to protest. Big deal. Besides, the bastard was making a comeback, he and his fucking space marbles. Just ask Buzzozzi about Edward Teller and the cyclotron episode. You wouldn't hear any sympathy from him.

"He's not like the guys that immolated themselves in Vietnam," the Chief tried to explain to Cheryl. "Big Ed never had the class of those bonze monks. So he gets liquified? What an asshole. Hey, tell me something new."

"Uncle, I dreamed that Nixon and Teller sicked this bunch of Doberman pinschers on you when you were starting to speak at the United Nations. Waldheim tipped them off that you were going to talk to the General Assembly. Nixon was shaving with an electric razor with dead batteries. He shaved day and night. That was the funny part. The bad part was that he had a guy with him from Chicago, a gangster with a long nose."

"Really?" asked Shelldrake. "He must be using the Ken Doll miniature electric razor. The guy with the long nose, that's Needlenose Alderisio." The Chief looked at Cheryl for more, but she was wiping her eyes again. "What else, honey?"

"Here's what it is, Uncle, two nights in a row. Tonka's in it. Sunman, you, and Durka. Nixon wants you dead so bad that he says to this guy that he'll raise five million dollars or the chance to kill you."

"He can't do it, Cheryl," the Chief tried to reassure her. "It won't work. The only way they can get me is to bury me under a big pile of rocks. I have to admit, though, that I've been having similar dreams. Did Tonka tell you about the one he had about Nixon and Walter Washington where Nixon meets Walter, who's Mayor of D.C. before Marion, in the Mayflower men's room and they match swords?"

"Look, Uncle, don't tell that one again," Cheryl protested. "It's no joke, Uncle, these beasts are preying on me in my dreams. They're using me to send their thoughts to you. They say you'll never know how it's going to happen or exactly when. You'll all be killed."

Shelldrake could see that his niece had completely lost her composure, despite her clever levitation act. He drank the bottle steadily and offered it in Cheryl's direction. She shook her head sideways, went over to Shelldrake's office fridge, and pulled out a Dr. Pepper instead. She popped off the top on the drawer handle, sat back down, took a long swig herself, and looked back at her favorite uncle, Chief Shelldrake, one of the top men of the Wamadadamaw Council, the ruling governing board of all the tribes of North America. She opened a box of Wheat Thins. The Chief reached in and took a big handful, then leaned back in his oaken throne office chair, a contented grin on his wide, handsome face.

* * *

The telephone in the outer office sounded and Cheryl turned to catch the rings. She decided to let the answering machine get it. There had been so many calls today, people trying to get in the campaign, trying to promote special issues, trying to get the staff to listen, trying to be heard, maybe even trying to get inside her uncle's pants. She had fielded one long distance call from a Mrs. Oteros in Dallas. The poor woman's gas utility bill was overdue, her baby was sick, her older daughter had just run off, and the city was shutting off her telephone and electricity. Without it, she wouldn't be able to cook for her family. The air conditioner was broken, too, and the housing people wouldn't fix it. She and her kids were baking in the Dallas heat. She had one friend who had written a letter to the housing authority, but it wasn't enough. Could the Chief do something? Would he be coming through Dallas during the campaign? Couldn't he do something? Cheryl knew that a big part of politics was doing basic casework: delivering the goodies where they're needed, doing things for people.

The visit by Nighthorse and the two little dummies had been an unsettling experience for the office staff, Cheryl felt. People wanted to leave early and complained of a strange smell emanating from the Chief's office. "How can the Chief stand it?" Melanie had asked. Melanie was the self-proclaimed computer guru of the office. She was the only one who was able to write letters and receive them on email. There was still no email capability in the office, in spite of Melanie's entreaties. But she was fighting for the chance to prove its value. All of the more urgent correspondences travelled in and out by fax.

Melanie had come over to Cheryl's desk with another letter from the Reagan people. They wrote that the Chief was ruining their fun and that they weren't going to leave the White House, no matter what happened in the upcoming election. Cheryl knew that Melanie had read the incoming letter. Her face told the story. "Even if we win, we still won't be able to get the job done." Cheryl gave Melanie a sympathetic look. She had warned Melanie in the past, though, about feeling and acting depressed. It was that attitude that started the downhill slide for everyone, Cheryl had cautioned. "Bad morale is infectious."

For Melanie, however, it all came down to technology. "We would have had this two weeks ago," she protested, "if you had let me get the email started. I think I can even get a free service."

Thursday p.m.

"WHICH BALKANS, YOU SAY?"

Chuky the asshole pulled the telephone even closer to his face, making the receiver almost disappear into the purplish, fat shrouds hanging down over his cheeks and neck. I could hear him mumbling something else, but I couldn't quite make it out. He put the call on hold and picked up another call.

This had been going on for a while. Urbanchuk had a phone stuck to each ear. Storms were picking up outside the lab again. Through the windows behind Urbanchuk, the blackened clouds were gathering from the south and moving in on us.

"Urbanchuk here, boss," he spoke into one of the phones, pulling his chair around so that he could see out the wide glass window in front of his desk. He stared out across the deep brown tidal flats, across the brackish pools of water, past the marsh grasses to the south. A slow, steady flow of rain and mist had left scarred droplets on the glass. Urbanchuk bent forward with his handkerchief to wipe the fog and moisture from the glass.

"Yeah. Yeah," he barked into the receiver. "I can't talk long. I got him on the other phone. Yeah. Yeah. And blah, blah, blah." At times, he would mention Montenegro or Transylvania. That's where he must be from, I began to think, somewhere near Croatia and Serbia. He turned and looked at us sitting there at our desks, lined up like a bunch of scarecrows waiting for the ravens to come and pick our eyeballs out. He looked like a combination of Rizzo and Agnew, but he was neither Italian nor Greek. Definitely Eastern European, I thought.

Every time Urbanchuk answered the telephone, he smoothed back the oily strands of hair that hung beneath his cap with one hand, while he gripped the phone tightly to his ear with his other hand and then wiped off his greasy hand on his pant leg. Next, he would take his index and abstercize his potex, to put it delicately. After that, he'd either transfer the newly found nose gold to his tongue or hide it under the desk, where the accumulation of what the scientists out here called "detritus" had already reached at least an inch in thickness. Believe me, no one wanted to look under Urbanchuk's desk.

How much worse could a job get? Anything would be better than this. I had to get out of this shithole, and pronto. Even if it meant working at some toxic waste dump. And there were plenty of those around here. Jackbox and bigmacs and mcdonies and tacoplus and textaco and mextaco and tacojunior and emilies and the new onion and the fried onion and chickbox and bostonchick and colkenchick. This list just went on and on. Surely I could find something at one of those places. I'd better keep my plans to myself, though; I don't want Urbanchuk getting wind of things, not until after I'm gone, at least.

Urbanchuk looked up from his latest call and stared at us again. Behind him, the condensation was really coming down now, whipping in from the southeast in an incredible frenzy. And as if that weren't enough, it was beginning to pour inside as well. An old leak had resprung over in the corner near the john, and water was pouring out everywhere. The ancient fish lab was shaking on its pilings. Hail was pounding down to beat the band. It was such a clatter that you'd have thought fifty roofers were right there over your head hammering the tin. Urbanchuk loved the racket, though, laughing at the top of his lungs as the hail pounded away at the building.

I was getting worried that the roof of the lab might collapse at any time. Our building would probably hold up fine if some basic preventative maintenance was done on it once in a while. With the kind of weather we've got here you need to be painting constantly, fixing cracks in the ceilings and walls, tightening door knobs, you name it. Earlier today, a suicidal seagull crashed into the glass beside the director's desk, sending us into a fearful retreat under our work stations. Urbanchuk, who was sitting right beside the window, barely looked, laughing quietly to himself when he noticed the gullblood streaking down the window. After a while, the blood finally coagulated into a thin smear across the glass, some of it actually oozing through the crack and dripping onto his desk. You could tell that he really didn't give a shit. About the bird. About the blood. About anything.

Now rain was really pouring down. We were getting blasted, even worse than the last few weeks. We were in monsoons now. The heavens kept opening on us. Huge hailstorms were unleashed from above and pounded down on our tin roof.

The guy next to me, Larry, sat in awe looking up at the ceiling. "It sounds like ackack," he said. "We flew through that stuff in Korea."

Larry grew up around here. He was a pretty old guy, about forty-five or fifty, I'd guess, and he'd been here ever since he'd gotten back from Korea. A really bad thing happened when he blew up a mine over there. His guts were blasted out. He woke up two weeks later in an Alabama sanitarium, missing different parts. His job was to read and record the daily temperature gauges in a notebook that was kept locked in a safe to prevent unauthorized people from seeing the data. He shuffled from the safe to his desk with the notebook every hour. In between, he drank coffee and waited, listening to the pounding on the roof.

"Mother Nature's really getting pissed," he'd venture. But otherwise, he kept pretty quiet, short stubs of Camels studding the edges of his desk. Larry was really patient considering the goings-on, as long as he could get his java and smokes on schedule.

Urbanchuk made a few futile gestures, his neck bent into a brace for the phone. His hand strayed to his black, oily ducktails. Rumors were starting to circulate around the office that he had worn his hair that way all his life. He turned our way and looked down at us with his most gruesome, angry, twisted grimace. He put his hand over the telephone receiver and barked down to where we were sitting: "I'm on to you people. You pull any more of this and you're finished. Just remember, I'm not going to accept your fucking excuses any longer."

On to what? I thought. He looked at us in a boiling rage, slamming his precious baseball cap down on the desk in a fit of disgust. He quickly got himself back under control, however.

"Just wait," he threatened. "They tell me: Don't get mad, just get even."

"Pardon me," he then said in a much calmer voice. "I have calls to take."

Despite the mounting fury right outside the window, Urbanchuk had inexplicably grown suddenly calmer. He sat back at his desk and stared down at us again.

"Thank you very much. I'm very grateful."

He returned to Line No.2 and quickly assented to something, and then went back to Line No.1. I could hear him say, "Okay, I'll take eight, but not before Monday. I can only start with two. I'll take a couple on Monday. We need time to train them. We have a lot of projects. Yeah, Bill, give me until Friday, anyway. I need forty-eight hours. Hey, man, cut me some slack."

We sat there watching. Eight what? Cut me some slack? Whatever he was talking about, we'd know soon enough, I guessed. After some more haranguing, he finally hung up.

The rest of us were beginning to feel ashamed of ourselves. But we really were afraid. Urbanchuk was still wearing his Croatian ustashi hat with the cross axes and the blood dripping down onto the brim. I tell you, it was scary and horrible. We felt like we were in a barracks in a concentration camp. We were becoming Dr. Urbanchuk's slave labor. We couldn't get out, but we had to get out somehow, just to save our lives.

Millie and I had both decided that we really couldn't take it any more. It was just too dangerous and too disgusting. A little while ago, Urbanchuk stood up to give the interns their assignments and exposed himself. When he started to talk, I looked over at him, and his penis was hanging out of his pants. I could hear him drone on about the specific assignments and the resources and effort needed to complete them successfully. I could hear his words, alright, but all I could think about was his penis. It was gigantic, especially attached to the body of dwarflike Urbanchuk. It kind of flapped around as he ranted on and on. He must have let it hang there for at least ten minutes while he continued to bark out orders to the staff. Then, suddenly, he put it away, out of sight, just like that. It happened so fast it seemed like a magic trick.

I looked around the room in disbelief. Everyone was absolutely stunned by the sight of Urbanchuk's penis. I was at least thankful that Rupp and Leon Henderson weren't around to witness it. The interns were terrified; most of them had completely lost their spirits. I told them they were on their own, that I needed to leave. The place was turning into a total nuthouse, and I was going to get out before it was too late. Millie and I were leaving; that was for sure. We had to figure out how to get out of here, once and for all. I couldn't take it anymore. I knew that it was only a matter of time before the bastard got it into his head to rape me, the same way we had been raping nature at the lab.

* * *

On a very clear day we could see Mt. Rainier, maybe a hundred and fifty miles away to the northeast. If we closed our eyes, we could even feel it out there, towering above the clouds. I didn't know exactly where it was, because I'd never actually been there. I mean, I've only seen it with my eyes from a distance and felt it inside sometimes. At Evergreen, there were porches at my dorm where we could sit out and see Rainier on clear days, straight ahead. Sometimes I watched it with my buddies all day long. We drew sustenance from that mountain. I knew *it* existed, at least, even if nothing else did. Here, though, I couldn't see it most of the time, and it stopped existing for me, even though I knew it was there. I began to feel a deep longing to see Rainier again, to be where it was, to be anywhere but here. I felt a nagging pull toward something distant and immense and undeniably real, toward my one real hope of freedom. Rainier was calling me. We dreamed of each other. Someday, I was going to climb to her top and kiss her rosy red lips.

* * *

I first heard about the work at the lab from my friend Ida. She used to work there but quit last May, before all the recent craziness began. Recently, we were sitting at the bar at the Olympiad, and I was filling her in on all the latest gossip.

Ida was by my side and another friend of mine, Meredith, was down a few stools from us, drinking a nice Hood River beer and eating some fries with her boyfriend.

Naturally Ida became incensed after I told her about what had happened to Rupp.

"Whitey's lab is where nature's turned inside out," she said. "Rape is what it is. Rape, rape, rape. That's what's going on. They're raping Mother Nature. We have to cut off their gonads to stop them. That's what it's all about."

Ida went on and on in her twangy local dialect. "Gangabang, gangabang, gangabang," and then with emphasis, stretching out the "baaang." Her voice grew louder and louder. "That's what's going on. We're all getting gangbaaanged! Let's just chop their nuts off and deal with this thing. And Chuky can take the whole fucking fish lab and stick it up his ass."

"Do you mean that figuratively or literally?" asked Meredith, who was still sitting nearby and listening in.

Ida jumped up from the barstool and screamed to the rafters: "Literalleeee! Stick the fuckin' fish lab up his ass!"

The rest of the Olympiad Bar patrons cheered Ida on. She climbed up on a table, kicked off her boots, signalled the bar to give everyone a drink on her tab, and stood there waiting for the screaming to subside. She gave a couple of V signs as the adulation died down and the patrons reassumed their listen-ready positions.

I pushed my beer toward Meredith and moved over a couple of seats. She stared at me like a big sister.

"Rhoda, it sounds very dangerous; you ought to get out of there." Meredith paused for a moment and stared at me. "Rhoda, listen to me. Urbanchuk is one of them."

Meredith turned back to her beer. Her boyfriend had gone to the WC, and Ida had started speaking again from her table platform.

"Here's the news for today, folks."

The whole thing was pretty hard for me to take in. The vibrations weren't real positive. The science of death and the death of science. According to Ida, there didn't seem to be any difference. It was a large concept for me to understand. I was beginning to see things more clearly, though; I didn't want to be put on the altar as an intern sacrifice. The dead crabs and shrimp that I picked up in the flats: that was all about money, lots and lots of money. It was basically just payoffs upon payoffs from top down to bottom. All kinds of money was being made off death. I was on the bottom rung of a big death money tree. Killing was all that kept this place in business. That was really all we were doing, killing stuff. Millie called it a monoculture of death. But it did create jobs, she had to admit, mostly shit jobs, but jobs just the same. I could expect that from her; she was a union person. But I would hate to have this job all my life.

My mind wandered in and out of Ida's speech.

* * *

I couldn't get the terrible image of Urbanchuk out of my mind. I said his name under my breath and imagined his putrid breath against my neck. I'll never get over my hatred of this man. I mean, let me out of here.

I had to watch him every day as he searched the perimeters of the tidal flats for signs of "breached" security. He was ugly and awful. "Sooner or later," he would caution, "they're going to breach this place, and I'm going to be ready for those fuckers!" He would emphasize the word *fuckers* like he was speaking French: foockerz-uh. He studied the tides and thought that he had a pretty good idea each day about when and where the attack might come.

Each of the interns had to take turns in the hatchery. Somebody had to be there all the time. Things could get pretty dicey, pretty quickly, with all the fish dying right and left from contagious diseases. Most of the time, we just used the word *ich* to refer to whatever they were dying from on that particular day. "Well," a technician might say, "we lost fifty percent of the salmonids last week. I think they got *ich*. The rest were punctured by the new salmonid-branding machine."

We devised an interesting schedule on the office computer where we could cover all the work, night and day, in different rotations with everyone getting the exact same shifts and no overtime. It was one of Seph's brainstorms. Our computer genius Harold worked out a perfect schedule for the group, with each one of us getting in forty hours and no overtime while covering the lab twenty-four hours a day, every day. That way someone would always be there to pull out the dead fish and check on the others. One of our newest responsibilities was to cut off a fin from the salmon babies so that when they were caught, fishermen could tell the difference between the hatchery fish and the wild species. Our new schedule made it easier to stay on top of all our tasks and also made it harder for Urbanchuk to keep track of us, giving us a little more leverage in the office. Democracy at work, I liked to call it.

Even with the improvements, however, the schedules could still be a little rocky at times. For instance, you might work two nighttime shifts in a row, then two 7 a.m. to 3 p.m. shifts in a row, followed by a day off, and then a single shift at the end of the schedule. I was on the last day of my schedule for this week. I already had done the two all-nighters. I would soon be off the clock, but I didn't feel it would be right to leave my buddies now, not alone there with Urbanchuk. I knew, though, that I was powerless to help them if and when he really began to work us over. We just hadn't seen what was happening to us until it was too late.

* * *

Meanwhile, Urbanchuk was now holding his phone tightly to his ear, even though it was pretty obvious there was no one on the other end of the line. He slammed down the phone, yelling, "Fuck it! Fuck it! Fuck it!" Then he turned to us and screamed, "And totally fuck you!"

His cap had somehow fallen off during his latest outburst. He put it back on top of his greasy pompadour and straightened out the bill. After a somewhat embarrassed silence, he finally turned away and back to his work, and we all returned to our own assignments for the day, or at least we tried to.

Up on the platform, Urbanchuk was whispering something into the telephone. He had cupped his hand over his mouth so that we couldn't make out what he was saying. He knew we were trying to read his lips. I could hardly decipher anything. Usually I heard almost all of every conversation he had, at least his end of it. But now, he was really hunched up with his hand over his mouth and mouthpiece, so that no one could hear what he said or read his lips. Something must really be up, I thought.

Urbanchuk looked like a giant, hideous fetus, curled up the way he was around the telephone. He was dressed today in a light, waterproof zoot suit, zipped up vertically at the front and crossways along his butt, for when he went to the can. Since his arrival, Urbanchuk had worn nothing but jump-style zoot suits, all the same special vertical and horizontal zippers, with their huge, grimacing teeth tracks.

I'll tell you, I was getting sick to death of hearing the bastard's name, either when he answered the phone himself—"Bill Urbanchuk here"—or when I had to get it for him. Most of the time, it was Cuzzukis on the other end. He'd recognize my voice and start right in on me, "Hey, Rhoda, it's you. Charley Cuzzukis here. Great hearing your voice. Tell Chuky it's an emergency." It was always an emergency.

Charlie Cuzzukis was Urbanchuk's supervisor. He called constantly, and, like I said, it was always an emergency. Cuzzukis had an assistant named Ray Fishman. Ray took over whenever Cuzzukis was out on a call in the field or just taking a day or two off. Ray was from New York City and was the top hit man in the fisheries department. He loved to bust people for fishing-license infractions. He'd become notorious, according to my friends here, for the severity of his penalties. Apparently, he had some kind of thing for the oysters. I'd only met him in person a few times, the first when he had just come in from the beach where he'd nabbed some poor bastard with a couple razor clams that he'd caught out of season. I remember that Ray was wearing a funny little hat at the time that everyone asked him about. He explained that it was the new style fishhawk, equipped with a visor that doubled as a nighttime sensor to catch illegal activities at the beaches after dark. Fishman had just stiffed his latest victim, the razor clam guy, with a $500 fine. He was gloating when he came into the office. "I tell these infractors that out here stealing a razor clam off the beach is like stealing a horse in the Wild West."

In some ways, Fishman reminded me a lot of the guys from the East that I met at Evergreen. But I had never met a fascist Jew like Fishhawk Fishman. I just didn't understand how a Jewish guy from New York could become a fish cop who loved to bust people for nothing. I didn't think that Fishman liked Urbanchuk any more than the rest of us, though. Actually, I think the two of them must have gotten off to a bad start. Urbanchuk was a vicious anti-Semite, in case I haven't already mentioned it, and would yell out stuff like, "Those kikes are getting everything. JesUS! That fuckin' Fishman!" for everyone in the office to hear, even when Fishman was around. I guess it would be safe to say that Urbanchuk really hated Ray. And I wouldn't be at all surprised if it was mutual.

It wasn't like that the first time they met, though. Cuzzukis had sent Ray down to check out the new station in the lab and introduce himself personally to the new director. When Urbanchuk saw Ray, he yelled out, "Here's my boy!" jerked his fat butt out of his chair, and stormed down off the platform to greet him. Urbanchuk made a big high sign to everyone in the staff section where I sat, then grabbed Ray in a hellish bear hug, crunching his arms affectionately around him and kissing him right on the mouth. After a minute or two, Urbanchuk finally released Ray from his grip, and the poor guy slumped down onto the floor. Urbanchuk then turned around and glared at the rest of us, saliva dripping down his chin, his eyes reddened with tears beneath his Croatian hatchet hat. He suddenly slapped his own face.

"See," he screamed at us, "I am a Christian white man!"

All I can say is, the whole thing, like pretty much everything else with Urbanchuk, was scary as shit. Fishman lay there on the floor for a while, almost unconscious from Urbanchuk's assault. Since no one was able to do any work anyway, we used the free time to collect a pot of change and one-dollar bills for the Balkan War Relief Fund. Eventually, Ray came to and got the hell out of there.

When Cuzzukis heard about what had happened between Urbanchuk and Fishman, he told my friend Bethany, whom he was dating at the time, that he thought Urbanchuk was a sadistic faggot. He said he had heard that Urbanchuk's Croatian father had actually run concentration camps in Yugoslavia in the early forties. Cuzzukis said that the elder Urbanchuk probably worked right alongside Waldheim. He also said it was rumored that Urbanchuk's father and uncles had murdered people all over Europe before finally sneaking into the United States in priests' clothing. Cuzzukis said that if he were Fishman, he would come down to the office and shoot Urbanchuk right between the eyes. After that, Cuzzukis wouldn't go anywhere near Urbanchuk, even though he was Urbanchuk's direct supervisor. Who could blame him?

Fishman didn't have the guts to confront Urbanchuk, though, and that was the reason, Cuzzukis told Beth, that the Jews ended up in the gas chambers. Beth and I both agreed that we were lucky that our families were spared all that suffering and loss. Whenever the three of us were out drinking beer, Cuzzukis would go on and on about the Nazis. I guess he had a point. Cuzzukis suggested that Fishman and I should really put an end to Urbanchuk, once and for all.

"Come on, you Jews, wake up," he said to us at one of our more recent after-work drinking sessions. "Unless you people start taking more responsibility, people like Bill Urbanchuk will always be in charge.

"And you know, kids," Cuzzukis always addressed the interns as kids, even the older ones, "I'm a minor political hack who's only doing this until I can get out of debt and get my truck out of the shop. And I'm going in the campaign next week. So listen and listen good. I'm going in, and I'm going to fight those goddamn carbuncles."

"Does that mean that you're joining the Chief?" I asked, sipping at my beer.

Cuzzukis pondered my question, and the table quieted down. Suddenly the other tables around us became silent, too. He nodded, chugged down his beer, and then ordered another round for the table.

"I've got to do it," he said, "or everyone is going to be brain-dead. We'll be too brain-dead to find out why they want us this way."

* * *

I had just returned to the lab from the Cage with my daily specimens. I was thinking about what Urbanchuk had recently said to us about work and honor and pride and quality. This time I had to count dead ghost shrimp that had been killed by an exotic new aquacide. We were always testing the effects of the new sprays, and my job as the chief summer intern was to do the mortality counts. Bill would lay out a map of the Cage and then go through an elaborate series of instructions, pinpointing the exact location I was to search. The day they hired Buzzozzi, I received a double assignment. In addition to the dead shrimp, I was also supposed to count the dead Dungeness crabs. I was surprised at the numbers of dead crabs scattered all over the flats. As I trudged through the deeper-than-usual mud, I glanced up and saw Bill looking through his telescope right at me. I knew that he was probably playing with himself while he watched me. I definitely didn't want to go back in there any time soon. It would be, "Hey, doll," and then that greasy asshole would look me up and down like I was just a piece of meat. I suppose that's all I was, as far as Urbanchuk was concerned.

Sometimes it seemed that all Urbanchuk did was look at me and eat Pringles. He ate Pringles endlessly; there were always new cans lining the window ledge above his desk. He just sat there crunching away, looking out the window and doing idle calculations on his calculator. He must have finished four or five tennis-ball-sized Pringles cans in a single afternoon, sometimes more than that. He offered them around the office, but only Stacy fell for that. Urbanchuk teased and tempted Stacy every chance he got. She was a little spastic from some kind of childhood illness or something and could be a little slow at times. Urbanchuk started on the

Pringles pretty fast in the morning and then slowed down after lunch. I usually scheduled Stacy early and intensely in the mornings to keep her away from him as much as possible.

Still, every once in a while he'd catch her off guard. "Okay, piggies, come and get it!" he'd shout. "Come get your P&G special." Most of us would just bury our faces in our paperwork, but Stacy would get snagged by the offer and start in on them. It was no wonder that she was farting all the time and blowing a loud chorus of grunts and squirts out in the john.

Stacy's time in the crapper also created some problems with Urbanchuk. One day, she was in the can when Urbanchuk suddenly decided that he needed to use it. It was a one-seater, and she had locked the door. Urbanchuk knocked politely at first, expecting her to surrender her place right away. But Stacy had eaten a lot of Pringles that day and was apparently having a pretty rough time in there. When she didn't come out immediately, Urbanchuk began pounding furiously on the door. Still, she didn't come out, and you could hear and smell the reason all the way over where I sat. Urbanchuk wouldn't give up, however. Finally, he pulled a fire axe from the wall and just smashed the toilet door to pieces. After he had shattered the door to shreds, he bounded inside, shoving Stacy out on the floor, her skirt and panties still down around her ankles.

"Hire the handicapped!" he yelled for everyone to hear.

You could still hear him shouting after he'd plopped his fat ass down on the porcelain.

"Yeah, that's the way we do it back home. If that doesn't work, we throw a firebomb on the assholes."

Millie and I stared at each other in disbelief. This was too much, even for Urbanchuk. Several of the staff gathered around Stacy and helped her up and into her chair. She was dazed and glossy-eyed. This time Urbanchuk had really gone too far.

A woman named Nancy, who did part-time office filing, personnel work, and some home nursing for shut-ins on the side, cradled Stacy's sad face and murmured to her, just loud enough for the rest of us to hear: "Stacy, you'll be okay. You'll be okay. But look, whatever you do, don't eat any more of those Pringles he's giving you. It's all a big setup; can't you see that?"

Even after he had returned from the toilet, Urbanchuk might blow a big one, just to get our attention. His soft farts could really be deceptive. It was an extremely effective way to end a conversation or a meeting. He would kind of lean back slightly and let go of a softy, staring you straight in the eye all during fartage. Urbanchuk would pitch it right at you, but you knew you couldn't possibly hit back what he was serving up. And there was nothing you could do to deflect it. It hit you right in the face. His expression when he did this was cold and merciless, completely unyielding. His refusal even to acknowledge the soft farts told me more about his warped, repressed nature than the devastating impact of his hard farts ever could. The hard ones, he couldn't cover up, after all. Millie said that it was all part of his Croatian heritage.

Urbanchuk's hard farts were a stark, naked warning that something bad was about to happen. When Urbanchuk let one of those go, people started fearing for their jobs, if not a lot worse.

Urbanchuk blew a fierce one like that yesterday on Millie. He had asked her to come up to his desk and take some dictation. Midway through, she started crying. All she wanted was to open an office window to let in some fresh Pacific air. Urbanchuk simply refused. Millie insisted that it was her right, but we all knew that there weren't any rights anymore, since Urbanchuk and his bosses had clamped down on everything. Many of the simple benefits were gone, even fresh, ocean air. Anyhow, Millie's request must have really gotten Urbanchuk worked up good. His ensuing fart was so harsh that it sounded like a tractor-trailer backfire. The overhanging light trembled as he browned us down. I really couldn't stand it anymore.

Meanwhile, Urbanchuk was still trying to molest me every chance he got, pushing me against the wall, pulling at my clothes, groping me, trying to put a handle on me. I was basically in indentured sexual servitude to the most disgusting creep in the universe. I hated him. At first, Millie said that he probably behaved this way because he had a tiny penis. I liked that explanation well enough for as long as it lasted. But, believe me, Millie's hunch was totally shot all to hell when Urbanchuk hung his enormous thing out at the last staff meeting.

Still, Millie, even in the face of this horrifying new evidence, wouldn't change her tune.

"That humongous piece of meat is one thing," she argued. "But what about his figurative penis, the one he thinks with? I bet that one's no bigger than my pinkie."

I wasn't exactly buying that theory, either. What if Urbanchuk's figurative penis was a gigantic one, too. Sometimes, Urbanchuk actually looked kind of like a giant penis. Maybe he was trying to look like that. Who knows?

But enough about Urbanchuk's literal and figurative penises and his putrid, Pringles-induced farts. That had nothing to do with me and my job here at the lab. Or at least it shouldn't have.

Don't fuck with me, Chuky. I'm warning you.

* * *

Cheryl only heard the thump. Shelldrake's head was down on the desk. He was starting to snore hard. He was gone for the day. The piles of land claims surrounded him like the walls of a dungeon. He continued to snore. Cheryl capped the Spudka and returned it to the drawer. She walked over to the fireplace and picked out a few roaches, and then moved to the window and closed the Venetian blinds. Cheryl checked her uncle's heartbeat and then left the office. A few moments later, though, she returned to the office, closing the door quietly behind her. She sat softly across from Shelldrake, careful not to wake him, and watched him sleep for a while. He was an utterly gorgeous man. Cheryl loved him, but she knew that she couldn't and shouldn't have him. She also knew that the booze was really starting to get to him. The curse of our race, she thought. The Chief definitely had some real straightening up to do. Cheryl lit up one of her roaches and took in a deep one. She'd have to remember to tell Durka that the Chief seemed really out of it lately. The stresses of the campaign and all the work on the land claims were really beginning to take their toll. It was easy to understand. After all, the Chief was currently masterminding the submission of nearly ninety thousand claims, covering more than four hundred and fifty million acres of Western land. The office walls were plastered with detailed maps of the land covered by the claims. Almost every county in the West was being forced to turn over land to the tribes. The Feds were slowly beginning to lose their grip on things. The states were in trouble, too. The Chief had been right all along that the only way out was total land reform. And now was the right time to take it all back.

Shelldrake snored on, gripping a fax from Greenland and the Afranexies Tribal Council in his fist. Cheryl looked at the clock over the door. It was 4:45 p.m. The secretarial pool had left at 4:30. Barb had departed in disgust over the incident with the garbage bins in the parking lot. Cheryl couldn't blame her. Lois had gone to pick up her husband at the fireworks stand. The other interns were gone, too. There was scheduled to be a -0.5 tide at 6:30 p.m., and Cheryl had to hustle over to the bay and meet her friends for some oystering. She would bring some oysters back in from the tribal beds for dinner. The Chief could gobble down dozens of oysters at a time, she knew, but he probably wouldn't be eating any tonight. She watched over Chief Shelldrake for a few more moments, his great frame silhouetted there against the map-papered wall.

Before she left the office, Cheryl called Durka but only got the answering machine.

"Cheryl here," she had said. "The Chief won't leave his desk. He seems walled in by all this work with the land claims. You'll have to come get him. I think he wants to rest a while. Anyway, he's dozed off for now, and I can't wait around until he wakes up. I'm going to the flats. See you tomorrow."

"Dream on," she murmured to the Chief, as she grabbed her bag and headed out the door. "Chances are," she continued to speak out loud to herself, "he'll make one more outburst before passing out cold. I've got to get out of here. How did this great guy get stuck in this pile of horseshit, anyway?"

As though to answer, Shelldrake began to raise his head from the big oak desk, still hidden by the piles of documents. He sat up solidly in his chair. While Cheryl watched, Shelldrake took an imaginary glass, opened an invisible bottle, pushed the glass away, and then tilted the imaginary bottle into his mouth, just far enough to ease the invisible Spudka pint into his yawning mawl. He gargled a couple of virtual mouthfuls and then wiped his forearm across his mouth, capping the bottle and putting it away in his imaginary drawer. He suddenly opened his eyes and looked at her. He was wide awake now, and he was hooked on her, alright.

"Go on, Cheryl, I'm listening," the Chief said. "As they say, I'm all ears. I hear all. That's why I'm Chief Shelldrake; but as you can see, that's still a poor excuse for a human being. Right now, I'm just really, really tired."

The Chief suddenly remembered some organizational matters that he'd meant to discuss with Cheryl earlier.

"We've got to get this work delegated," he insisted, "contract it out, get someone in like Price Waterhaus to figure this shit out. I can't stand it anymore. Call off the dogs."

Cheryl watched the contortions in his marvelous face, his sleek black hair hanging nearly to his shoulders.

"Uncle, I need to go," she said. "I've got to get to the flats. We're stringing lines. I'm sorry that I talked so much about the Nixon dream. It scared me. I'm frightened for you, for all of us, for Durka, for everyone."

"Nixon, huh?" The Chief suddenly remembered their earlier conversation. "Well, Heil Hitler! And Teller? Like Henry said, 'Let's tear another asshole in that fuck!'"

The Chief tried to rise to his feet to parody the Nazi salute. He fell back into his seat. Cheryl helped him over to the wooden couch, where he sat down for a moment and then rolled over on his back. She pulled off his boots. She had always admired how clean and fresh-smelling the Chief kept his feet, not like whitey's smelly, rotten ones. He was still stinking drunk, though. She hadn't seen him this bad since he started the project.

She covered him with a light blanket, turned on a small lamp near the couch, and then went out quietly toward the front office.

* * *

Shelldrake was sprawled out in the gloom on an old wooden slave couch that he'd found in the office when he moved in years earlier. From the looks of the thing, it must have been a hand-me-down from the Japanese interns who'd occupied the place before he arrived. Probably from Ohio. It reminded him of one of his favorite periods from the Shinto Dynasty, basic country carpentry with an empire flair in the hand-whittled legs.

The Chief thought he saw some lights go on and off, and then he felt some very friendly and very familiar hands removing his boots. Cheryl's hands. He could feel her withdraw, the softness of her presence vanish from his space. The quiet, padding feet, the opening and closing of the office door, the click of the light switch—it all amounted to the same thing. She was gone, and he was alone. He pushed the blanket off and stretched back on the couch. From the feel of the couch's buckled, warped center, he figured that maybe a hundred thousand souls had rested there before him. Hell, he must have crashed there four or five hundred times himself in the last ten years since the land claims work had begun. He wondered how long it would take before Durka showed up to take him home.

"Shit," he suddenly remembered, "I've got to get ready for Skankerville."

With Cheryl gone, the only noise that the Chief could hear was the murmur of the fax machine from the other room. Suddenly, the Chief could hear helicopters overhead. It sounded like there were three of them. The usual Coast Guard routine training flights, he figured. Those damned contraptions scare the total shit out of folks. That was what they were for, he figured, to scare the total shit out of folks. He'd have to check his messages in the morning. The lichen ripoff worried him. The only new industries the natives had been able to pull together recently had been agricultural, and almost all of them had been economically marginal, at best. He'd call them about it in the morning. He could worry about it then. More than likely, there would be nobody there to talk to. He knew that he was supposed to talk to some guy with an Eastern European name. Bresnooski? Bresnouski? Breshnuwitz? What the fuck was his name? He was sure they had it in the files somewhere. Anyway, he was certain that it was the same guy who did national security when they played the Communism card.

"Jesus, I've been working my ass off today." He shifted his body slightly, mumbling out loud to himself, "It's time for my shift drink. What a day. Some accomplishments and some setbacks. I really am worried about the situation with the elk. How can we get its head back on?"

The Chief dozed off after that. He had finished yet another hard day at work.

Oyster Bay Cove

IT WAS STILL LIGHT OUTSIDE when Cheryl got to her bike. The parking lot in front of the tribal headquarters was almost empty. Several vans and trucks were bunched together near the dumpster, and some guys were trying to jump-start a pickup that was sitting up on concrete blocks. The front wheels were missing and and the driver's door was leaning against the stump of a withered old tree where the staff took smoke breaks. A couple of the guys waved to her. Ronnie and Bill. She could tell from their buoyancy and the wisps of smoke in the corner of the lot that they were getting serious about fixing up the car and getting it out of the lot. She waved back and threw a couple of kisses.

To meet her companions on the flats, Cheryl had to ride over one set of hills to the bay, about six miles from the office.

The four women had their oyster shucking knives. They had brought with them lemons, Tabasco sauce, a six-pack of beer, and a bottle of champagne. They wore hip boots and miner's lamps, the batteries belted around their waists, and nothing else, having removed all their garments after they had safely rounded the bend from the fish lab. They always made sure that they were out of sight before stripping down to their boots. They figured they were spied on occasionally, but what could they do about it? Deborah had her stash bag on a thin leather thong tied with a bow around her waist. The four women called themselves the Eight-Nipple Gang. They took turns carrying a two-hundred-foot-long coil of rope which they would use to string the oyster shells. Faint streaks of night sky rose above the flats as they filed silently through the mud. A three-quarter moon floated above them, with a zillion stars hiding behind the evening hues.

Cheryl had led the way. No one saw the four as they passed the local fisheries lab. At least Cheryl hoped not. She knew that she could never count out Urbanchuk, who was probably at the window with his telescope, just waiting for her and her friends to wander into his field of vision.

"That sick fucker," she groaned just to think about him.

There were no vehicles in the lab's parking lot as they passed. They were strictly bureaucrats in that lab, with hours eight to four and then home to somewhere else in the county. Urbanchuk sometimes stayed late if something was going on. Cheryl knew the schedules of everyone there, both in and out of the office. After all, she had grown up with most of them. Gooch Street. Fiddler Slough School. Jones Jr. High. Eastern Star High. Rhoda, she knew from Evergreen.

A barbed-wire fence enclosed the lab and several acres of tidal grounds. The women worked their way along the outside of the fence before crossing a corner of Mud Bay onto the tribal tidelands. Cheryl was the first one to see the glow, a kind of hazy flash against the fading sky. A light was still burning in the lab. The women all knew the lab, and they knew Bill Urbanchuk. Jerebone, who was carrying the rope, had worked there for three years, before the Native Americans were screwed out of all the state jobs. She had worked inside the fence on many occasions. Right now, though, she was happy to be with her three friends as they headed through the muddy flats toward the tribal oyster beds. Jerebone followed Rebeccah, who followed Deborah, who followed about ten feet behind Cheryl.

Jerebone stared at the flickering light in the lab. "I'll bet Chuky is right in there now looking out at us."

Jerebone had worked these same beds since she was five years old when her grandpa's friend Charley John used to take his whole family out oyster farming. Charley was nearly ninety-five and still hustling the native Olympia oyster when he died, right there in the mud. He had been one of the first oyster farmers when the pioneers arrived at Mud Bay. It was all downhill after that. In 1890, the state legislature passed the Callow Act, which sold off the native people's oyster and hunting grounds. Jerebone's grandpa was a member of the original Indian Shaker Church.

She winced to think of some of the crap the white man taught: *"Olympia, the home of the gods; Olympia oysters, food of the gods."* Finally, through his total exploitation, the white man had exhausted the native oysters. Things had eventually gotten so bad that Chief Seattle wandered around Seattle trying to sell oysters for a living, oysters that he and his people had lost the right to harvest.

"And our bay," Charley John used to say at the tribal meetings, "has become like a big sewer."

Cheryl watched the pale flesh moving in front of her, the vertical slashes splitting her friends' fresh, beautiful buttocks as they trailed out toward an inlet half a mile beyond the barbed-wire fences leading off from the lab. Naked now, they were soon passing through a foot-deep stream running out of Deadman's Slough, weaving in and out of a nearby upper tidal marsh. They moved soundlessly, except for the continuous slurping as their boots were sucked into the mud.

When they crossed the slough into the far corner of Oyster Bay, they were finally on native land. They could look freely across the flats at acres and acres of oyster ground, much of it covered with stakes and line cultures that the tribe had built up over the last two hundred years. It was early twilight. The horizon was deepening into purple and red. The sun was going, going, and gone. The orange ball blasted Cheryl's mind as it dropped over the edge of the horizon.

With the sun now set, they stopped to turn on their headlamps. They each broke open a beer, setting the remaining beer, champagne, Tabasco sauce, and the huge coil of rope on the remains of an ancient dike built by the white pioneers to farm the oysters commercially. Deborah opened her stash bag and pulled out a big dubie. Jerebone laughed, "Hey, Deb, you're really rolling a big one." Deborah took a deep draw and handed the dubie over to Cheryl. The damned thing looked like a cigar, Cheryl thought. She took two deep draws and passed it on to Jerebone.

The girls were pretty stoned by the time they began to uncoil the rope. The work in the flats had been ritualized in minute detail over a period of two hundred years. They trudged over to nearby baskets of shells, from which they began to take individual shells and feed them into the line's numerous strands. The lights from their headlamps made fluorescent patterns over the mud and their naked skin. They giggled in unison whenever one of them accidentally slid into the slimy silt. They worked quickly, becoming easily adjusted to the pace of planting the rods. Their naked bodies glowed in the moonlight. Jerebone opened more cans of Pabst Draft beer and carried them through the mud to her companions. When Jerebone reached her partners, she shook her cans vigorously, and fountains of foamy beer exploded on their bodies. The girls' laughter shook the early July night air.

"Let's drink to the Tribe and the Eight-Nipple Gang!" the four screamed together.

The moon was now high as they returned to their work. Though hardly a word passed among them, they knew exactly what they had to do. As they prepared to install each line, they pushed plastic plumbing stakes into the tidal flats. At the top of each rod was a notch to hold the rope. Every two feet or so, the rope held an oyster shell between its strands. A pair of girls would set each line so that the rope and shell would be about a foot and a half above the mud.

A sea otter suddenly ripped out from where it had been hidden on the shore and ran past them at top speed, just a few feet from where Cheryl was standing installing the rope line. From the tall trees above the shore, the screams and cackling of herons ruptured the night air. In the distance somewhere, crows were cawing one last time before they went to bed.

Cheryl stood at the end of a row of rope strung across some plastic pipe driven in the ground. She held the mallet and was preparing to bang a pipe into the mud to start the next row. Deborah was holding the end of the line and setting it into a notch in the top of the pipe. The two women moved down the row together and unwound the rope containing the old shell and last year's natural set. The spots from the headlamps danced along the surface of the flats. There was just enough light to see one's hands and a few feet beyond as they bent to set the poles and lines.

Cheryl was startled to see a boot lying in the mud about five feet behind where she was standing.

"Deb, look at this."

Deborah set the line and then worked her way across several dozen stakes to where Cheryl was standing. They both moved up close to the boot and suddenly realized that it wasn't a lone boot. A second one was lying in the mud a couple of feet away. They were large boots, probably size twelves or thirteens, Cheryl guessed. The two women worked together, emitting in unison a giant "aaaarrgg" sound as they pulled furiously at the boots. Finally, the suction blew, and they both fell backward into the mud, the boots still in their hands. From where they had fallen, they could see the feet, two little feet, no bigger than Ken-doll feet, sticking a few inches out of the mud.

"Weird as shit," said Deb. "How did those little feet get so stuck in those big boots?"

They bent down over the tiny feet, looking for clues.

* * *

Later that night, after they had taken the White House and locked up the Secret Service in the basement, Chief Shelldrake stood on the roof with his bear rugs and buffalo robes and peered out at the Washington, D.C. skyline and the deep darkness beyond. He was in new territory, and he knew it. He stood looking at his conquest. He'd mostly taken the country over by the book, through the electoral process, though there had admittedly been a few rough edges along the way. Illuminated by their scattered campfires, the dark, shadowy figures of his followers paraded in silent fantasy among the teepees and makeshift lodges that they had erected on the lawn that afternoon after the mansion had been liberated from its previous occupants.

The Chief already felt terribly confined by the demands of paraphernalia of his new high office. The Secret Service was everywhere. He realized that his new throne was essentially an electronic national-insecurity machine, a kind of super-attenuated electric chair, worse in some ways than the real thing. How could he ever be sure that he himself wasn't strapped down right in Old Reliable, just waiting for the switch to be pulled? Only to Durka could he confess his doubts about the strange paradox of being the President of America and yet somehow being just as chained as his ancestral chiefs had once been in the prisons of the blue-coat soldiers and Sheridan, their chief.

Shelldrake had released the captured Secret Service men from their basement confines. He thought they had suffered enough. The odd thing was, they already seemed to have forgotten about the mansion's previous occupants and were eager to protect the new ones. They were hell-bent, in fact, on guarding him day and night. Brandishing their pistols, grenades, machine guns, and rocket launchers, they formed continuous phalanxes around him, dressed in their black suits and camouflaged fatigue hats. There were weapons galore. He felt as confined by their fanatical protection as he once had among the torrents of deeds and claims that had covered his office desk. It had definitely been a mistake to let them out of the White House basement right away, without any planning. He should have known better, should have known that whitey would do anything to satisfy his thirst for money.

The Chief looked over toward the Pentagon, dark and forbidding and silent. It was closed for the night; the parking lot was empty. Definitely no lights on over at the collossus. The brass must be lying low, he thought, waiting for the new administration to come in. Wait and see. Well, a little doubt never hurt anyone. The Chief knew that he still had a lot to learn and a lot to think about. At just that moment, he was thinking about his gonads. They were always there in the convex man. The convex man definitely had gonads, alright. When the Chief had jumped the White House fence, he had snagged one, and they had been hurting like hell for the past few hours.

"In another eight hours," the Chief continued to stare toward the

Pentagon, "I'm meeting with those assholes. We have a lot to discuss about the affairs of state, not to mention the lichen matter. And we have to find out where all these designer dwarfs are coming from. And we have to find and deactivate the main tarbaby switches. Remus is in danger."

He spoke the words loudly and distinctly, so that he could hear himself above the cheerful bedlam down below in the South Lawn Village.

The Chief pulled out a pint of vodka and started to polish it off, but he didn't like to drink alone, especially not now, since he had become President. He made blanket signals to the newly pitched village below, and Durka soon made her appearance at the edge of the White House roof. To reach him so quickly, she had climbed up a crude ladder nailed to the south wall. The Chief and Durka took a couple of swigs of vodka, crawled under the blankets, and made love to the joyous singing below.

"What do you think?" he asked her, as they cuddled together on the White House roof and watched the sun rise above the Capitol and the rest of the New World. The new dawn's cacophony was beginning to take hold.

Durka looked at the Chief in the early morning light. She loved him, even if his ugly puss was on every poster on every telephone pole in the country. She hated that he had snagged his balls on the White House fence, though she had actually been amazed to see how high he could leap.

"Listen," she whispered, but loud enough for him to hear above the sounds of the morning rush, "I think all that Hepplewhite is for shit. And you're not going to get me to move around the furniture, if that's what you think."

Durka's words trailed off into the morning. On the South Lawn, the first fires of dawn glowed near the teepees, and the dogs were barking up a storm. The campers were cooking up the catfish from the Potomac. Even on the roof of the White House, the Chief could smell it. "Man, that cat!" he said to Durka. The two of them lay together, breathing as one. Durka really likes cat, too, he thought. He felt her hands touching him, tenderly. He drifted away. As he passed through the interstices of sleep, he saw Nixon holding a small electric razor, trying to bushhog some particularly heavy growth around his upper lip.

Chief Shelldrake, he could hear Nixon boast, *we've got you this time, you bastard.*

Nixon gagged and giant rats the size of Dobermans started popping out of his mouth. Nixon's tongue gangplanked out of his mouth, and the rats scrambled toward the Chief. It was the worst dream the Chief had had recently. Durka held him tight, and he felt an enormous erection coming on. A shame to waste, he thought. He used it on her for a while and then fell back again into darkness.

* * *

Chief Shelldrake woke an hour later feeling like a solid citizen. He polished off his wife in a grand finale. She really seemed to enjoy herself at the time, staring him in the eye and kissing his nose. As soon as he had finished, however, she immediately disengaged herself and pushed him away. "I've only one thing to say, my darling Shelldrake. You better get them before they get you."

The Chief knew that he was no match for his enemies, if it came to that. Wasn't it obvious that these were his enemies, too, these snide, cynical American agents who were pretending to guard him now, who would be your friends one minute and then kill you the next? It was just the way the other chiefs were murdered long ago, along with their wives and children.

The Chief realized that he was at war with whitey, and that peace could not come easily. Real peace would never come until the logic of all war, everywhere, unwound to its final conclusion. Whitey had to learn. And for that to happen, the Chief would have to rip whitey's nuts right off. Do the Lewinsky Special. Smash whitey's balls into two flat pancakes. Taking whitey's nuts off was the only way.

It was a new ballgame. With his first executive order that afternoon, he knew that he was dealing a mortal blow to the arms makers, their salons of politicians and generals, the whole striped-pants crowd. They would all come screaming; he knew that. But for now at least, it was definitely lights out at the Pentagon.

The Chief's hands groped down toward the pain in his gonads. He couldn't get his mind or his hands off his gonads. He was becoming excessive about it. He knew that the press would have a field day writing about his accident. He imagined the headlines:

New Prez Meets Fate on White House Fence

Did Reagan & Co. Have Last Laugh?
Chief Rips Balls Off on White House Fence

Chief Shelldrake Sings Soprano for Supper

The Chief knew that he could count on the *Washington Post* for some particularly stinging headlines and commentary. He chuckled a little to himself, knowing the press would think up anything to sell their papers. It would be amusing to see what they came up with, just the same.

Taking the White House was only the beginning. The junior chiefs were already calling it the Battle of Rancho la Muerte. It staggered him to think of everything that had happened in the past twenty-four hours alone. Jumping the south fence. Snagging his balls. The rush of helicopters into the air, like startled vultures leaving their carrion behind. The young chiefs staking out their villages on the South Lawn. Not a bad day's work for a ragged bunch of injuns.

Reba Dickerman

SKANKERVILLE WAS ABOUT THREE HOURS from headquarters, if we didn't stop to pass Go, that is. This was always a joke with the Chief. He loved to pass Go, to stop for a few minutes there, at least, every time we passed.

Go was about a day's hike from the old Monte Cristo silver mines. The Chief said that for a long time it was called God by the white folks who had arrived there in the 1800s. For some reason, people in the town started sawing the "d" off all the town signs, unofficially changing the name to Go.

The town was about twenty miles north of Salmonville on Star Route 3. We had to take it slow because of the huge numbers of logging trucks and campers on the road. The trucks were coming up from California carrying giant redwood trees, one tree to a truck. It seemed like an endless procession, both ways. Chief and I got a kick out of watching a line of vehicles coming up the mountain and a line going down ahead of us at the same time. Where were they all going? And who did the scheduling? Who got the money? It was really only the tip of the iceberg, the Chief said.

I didn't really like to drive this route east because it always seemed as though we were on the outside, near the cliff, and that one lurch of a log truck could send everyone over the side. I couldn't stand the thought that the whole campaign would suddenly end right now because I went over the cliff.

We'd received a report from the field that they were lining up the biggest tanks they had on the super interstate highways. Everyone knew that the highways were made for these tanks. And everyone knew that the tanks were made for these highways. All I could think of was running head-on into one of the tankers. Or swerving to miss one and toppling off the cliff and onto the rocks below. At various points, we passed the usual wooden crosses and plastic corsages marking all the fatal crashes that had already happened here among these hills.

Hills? Hell, that was a euphemism. These were actually old logging roads, built along the rims of steep, jagged cliffs. You really took your life in hand every time you pulled onto the road out here. If the Chief was feeling any fear or anxiety, though, he didn't show it. He continued to look calmly out the window. He seemed to be counting the cattle grazing in the fields, trying to scan which ones were singing the Creutzerfeldt Sonatas. Thinking about their food value. Big steaks, dead meat. Brain death. Which was it, boss? Violent death to him was like farting a lot. Only certain kinds of farts could make him cry.

Everyone around here seemed to have been affected by the logging accidents at one time or another. It was just a fact of life. There were a lot of maimed families over in Diehard. It was sickening to have to go over there. So pathetic. Most everyone knew at least someone who'd been run over by a logging truck. I personally knew of one incident where a woman was driving her kids home from school and a fucking log rolled off on a curve and sandwiched her van. It was somewhere near Astoria, I think. The whole thing was such a piece of shit, any way you looked at it. And what if it were to happen right now? I'd totally fuck up the whole thing, the Chief's campaign, the land claims, the carbuncle, everything. I mean, I wouldn't do it on purpose, but someone could send eight of these trucks off the cliff this very instant. Just turn the wheel a fraction of an inch and *Pow!* Right over the cliff. Eight giant redwoods. One person. Come to think of it, that really wasn't such a bad trade-off. But not today, not with the Chief in the car and the whole campaign and the future of the world riding on his shoulders. We'd have to worry later about the fate of the redwoods.

At any rate, I wasn't so sure that I was ready to knock heads with the guys driving the trucks unless I could be absolutely sure to take out the ones who cut the trees, and the ones who made them cut them, and the ones who convinced us that paper should come from trees in the first place. All of them at once. That would really be something.

Meanwhile, the big trucks chugged up the slopes and filled the hairpin turns as we passed from one clear cut to another. Shelldrake sat there impassively most of the time, looking out the window, except when he'd occasionally recognize and wave to one of the other drivers, who'd then begin honking his horn in recognition. He also liked to spot trash and old tires along the road. Every time we made this trip, we'd inevitably stop at least once for him to pick up a big piece of torn rubber tire from some truck blowout and flip it into the back of the van.

I shouldn't be here now, I thought to myself. I could be several other places. All critical in my agendas for the campaign.

I had only decided to drive Shelldrake after hearing that he conked out a couple of the dwarf MTs on radiator—and then conked out himself after that. And it didn't hurt to see the Chief and to keep track of the developments. With the campaign tightening up, I wasn't able to see him nearly as much. We did much of our business by phone, which could also be really entertaining. Talking on the telephone with the Chief, that is. He always had a lot to say, that's for sure.

Anyhow, since Skankerville was coming up, and I hadn't been home for months since my Uncle Harry died, it made sense to drive to Diehard and stop off and see my Aunt Elena. She had become somewhat of a recluse since the night Harry croaked. I'd been feeling strong vibes from her the last few weeks, but I'd been so busy that I hadn't been able to go to her. And I wasn't really sure that she wanted to see me or anyone else. With everything that had happened, I could hardly blame her. When Durka asked me to drive the Chief to the Diehard meeting, it occurred to me that maybe I could stretch the trip. I also thought about how the Chief might actually cheer Elena up, if I could get him close to her. I hadn't suggested a visit yet, though. I knew how much the Chief would suffer just to be reminded one more time of his losses.

I hadn't seen the Chief since Wednesday when we went over to Scarposi's in Largo. Big Bill is an old buddy of mine, and the Chief and he go even further back. They both worked in the silver mines. Their grandparents' parents were in the livestock and slaughterhouse business at the turn of the century up in Seattle. They're both beautiful men. At least they are to me. You know, one good gang bang deserves another.

When we sharpened our teeth, so to speak, on the Saudi arms deals, Scarposi ended up with nearly a billion dollars in construction contracts. I was his intern, the watergirl. He was building airports, mess halls, race tracks, you name it. Once, at the bar on top of the Sorrento, he told me about his times in the Mideast, but not until after he had proposed to me and tried to feel me up. Anyhow, he was attempting to stick his thumb inside me, if you can imagine it—and at the Sorrento of all places—and we were on about our fourth martini and our third fois gras. He went on and on about the Saudi royal family and what a bunch of shits they were. Really mean assholes, he said. He told me that he had tried to keep track of the beheadings, but they occurred so frequently that he wasn't sure he got them all. Besides that, he said that all these guys were walking around with missing right hands or lopped-off fingers. Digits, he called them. Innumerable digits. That's what the Saudi royalty called their people, too. They'd yell at the foremen at a job site, "We got three too many digits; send some home!" Apparently, it was pretty easy to find as many digits as you needed over there. You could always find plenty of them lying around at the edge of the Riyadh marketplace. Whenever he needed some extra hands, Scarposi would just send a jeep over to pick a few of them up.

It was hell on one's social life, Bill had told me, his own fingers probing my interior walls, since there wasn't any toilet paper in Saudi Arabia. One minute people would be wiping their butts with maybe one lone index finger, and the next minute they'd be trying to shake hands with you. A really sweet image, I thought, with Scarposi's own index finger already a couple of inches inside me.

While Scarposi was regaling me with his Saudi adventures, Shelldrake was usually busy getting his shoes vulcanized. He stopped a couple of times a year in Wheeler where they melt the rubber down from these old tires and mend people's shoes. It was a regular routine whenever we were over on the coast. I'd gone off for lunch at the only bar in Wheeler with Scarposi and we were waiting for the Chief to get his new "wheels" made up.

A few local residents hung out at the bar in the semidarkness, their drab lives draped around their shooters and beer. We were sitting over in a bankette in the gloom near the pool table. Big Bill was fooling around with me again. He had wandered off to the john and eventually came back with his fly wide open. I finally got his fly closed, which wasn't easy, and we were just about to order another round when the Chief came in wearing his newly vulcanized sneakers. He slid into the booth next to me, sandwiching me in tightly between Scarposi and himself. The Chief flashed a big smile, and I felt uncomfortably like a piece of meat in a hot sandwich.

Bill and I had been drinking martinis for a while, so the Chief ordered four quick rounds to catch up. He ordered his favorite brand, Spudka, and also grabbed some hors d'oeuvres going by. Between noshing on the free bar food and guzzling down the drinks, he gave us a rundown of where he'd been and what he'd been doing on the campaign.

It appeared, at least according to the Chief, that the native people on the coast had decided to vote this time. The election was beginning to mean something with him running, and he couldn't let them down. A little old Italian guy, Papa Marco, the guy who worked on his sneakers, had told him—assuming the Chief wasn't embroidering the facts a little—that he could expect a big turnout if he could keep his posters up and the public focused. It seemed like the Chief was really in the race.

I thought about how much his attitude and personality had changed lately. He was definitely getting a little cockier than he had been a few weeks earlier when we had travelled down the coast to a reservation just outside of Wheeler. Goddamn Wheeler, the only place on the coast where the Chief could get his sneakers vulcanized. He also liked going over there, he explained, because the people looked so much like him. Everywhere we went, there were Indians. Jesus, what a mess. But today, we were heading to see the white man. And what a fucking mess that is, too.

* * *

But that was then, back at the bar, and this was now, on the fucking road to Skankerville and Diehard. And, shit, what a poorly executed move it was to bring him over here now, something that I, for one, definitely wasn't looking forward to. Sometimes Durka and the Chief acted as if I were their slave, their own personal valet and driver. I tried to remember my own reasons for wanting to come. I knew I needed to calm down and focus on helping the Chief, no matter how angry I felt. Durka had explained that he was just learning his speeches, and someone dependable and in-the-know needed to be with him the entire time to be certain that he was telling the truth.

It was true that with me he could probably be more himself. He could unwind a little. We had this history going back. We've definitely done our share together for the Triple Revolution. Like the bust at Mt. Pony and the lichen. Even Durka agreed that we'd made a contribution. But now she wanted more. That was fine. That cohesiveness there between Durka, him, and me—even if they did piss me off sometimes—how long could it last before it crumbled? I would follow the Chief straight to hell, but what if this campaign didn't work? If we blew this thing and the Chief didn't make it, we would literally be scratching for lichen.

While I loved my boss and I needed to be with him today because there was so much shit going down, it was still very unsettling diving into a hornet's nest like the Diehards. I looked down toward the Chief's cock, which was bulging out in its usual location. It could have been my imagination, but I thought I saw it moving. He was wearing his vulcanized tennis shoes. I guessed he meant business.

"Dickerman," the Chief laughed, "you're right. It is moving."

Oh, shit, there he was scanning me again. I hoped he hadn't been scanning the other thoughts I'd been having.

He began talking as soon we headed out of the reservation, "I tried to get you when Nighthorse was here so you could see the little soldiers."

"Yeah, boss, I heard all about it, and how they drank the radiator. Barb said Nighthorse smashed their heads together and threw them in the dumpster. She was really pissed. That was a bad mistake. Anyway, sanitation must've picked them up because I was over there yesterday and the dwarfs were gone. But there was an elk's head in the dumpster, and it was so big we couldn't get the lid on. It was the only thing in the dumpster. And I'll tell you what, that was really pissing everyone off. It was just so evil. The elk was the worst."

"Listen, Reba."

I glanced over and saw that his eyes were a little watery in the edges. I could see that he was deeply troubled. I told him what I thought: "How's that head ever going to get back with its body? We're going to have a very disturbed spirit really bugging us if the head and body can't get back together. The spirit will be hurt and sad that it can't get back together. And the spirit will think it can be free sometime, but it will really be locked up someplace, and it won't be able to get out."

"Well, what a mouthful, Reba, and as usual you put your finger on the matter. Barb's exaggerating a little. We'll see Horse at Skankerville. He's going to take us to the lab where we're doing these little guys over. But now that you raise it, when I left the office, the elk head was gone. I thought Horse took it with him."

"Bullshit, Chief, very big bullshit!" I practically screamed at him. "You saw the elk head in the back of Horse's truck from the office. Everyone knows that already. And it's back there again. I saw it this morning. No one knows how it got there but everyone knows that Horse had the two droppas with him when he came in."

The conversation was getting very heavy. I peered in the mirror and saw a car coming up *rapido*. I could see right away that it was Buzzozzi.

"And anyway," I said, "I've been to the droppa lab."

Shelldrake suddenly looked back and saw Buzzozzi speeding behind us.

"Hey," he said, "it's Buzzozzi coming up fast."

The Chief waved out the window and signalled for Buzzozzi to stop. I brought the van over to the side near a sign that read: *Old Nisqually Trail, 126 miles*. Buzzozzi pulled in behind us. He climbed into the backseat and sat there until the Chief had finished with the spiel he was still giving me about the lab and our search for the scientists. The Chief finally concluded with, "Reba, it's getting more confused; Nighthorse said that the two little guys that he brought in cut off the elk's head. The elk had been hit by a pickup and was lying injured by the road. The two guys jumped out of the truck and ran over, and then one of them pulled out a machete and hacked the head off the elk. Hi, Bill."

"Listen, I don't have much time," Buzzozzi announced. "Something's happening over at the bay. Some kind of hanky-panky over at the fish lab."

"Well?" said the Chief.

"Chief, it's not good. It looks like some of Krakens's men have taken over the lab."

"Well, look, Bill, when you're over at the coast, if you run into Rupp, tell him I need to talk to him."

"Chief, I'm telling you, I think it's Krakens. Rupp's been fired and is in bad shape. He's got colon cancer."

Buzzozzi mopped his forehead, and I suddenly worried that something was wrong. It was a very cool afternoon, after all, and we were now up about three thousand feet. When we left the reservation, we were only at two feet above sea level, and we'd been climbing ever since trying to get across the coast range. But even with all that climbing, Buzzozzi still seemed hot and flushed. The Chief didn't appear to notice. He was staring at Buzzozzi's eyes. They looked wild and fanatical. Buzzozzi continued his narrative, looking straight back at the Chief.

"They found Nighthorse's truck over at False Claim Slough, but no Nighthorse. We're pretty sure they've got Nighthorse."

I tried to get the Chief's attention, but he wouldn't return my gaze. It looked like Nighthorse wasn't going to be at Diehard after all. The Chief seemed to be staring straight at Mt. Adams. I could barely see the mountain, though it was a pretty clear day. For a moment, there was nothing but silence.

"What else?" asked the Chief.

"Those aberrations appear to be from a gene line passed down from the droppas, you know, the large heads on small bodies, the pretty sizable sexual organs . . ."

The Chief interrupted, "Are you telling me those dwarfs got Nighthorse?"

"The three scientists at the Mercetemp Laboratory are old Nazi scientists from the Third Reich, actually from Pennemunde," Buzzozzi continued. "They were trying stuff on the Russian prisoners there. They were smuggled in by Braun, Rudolph, and the OSS guys, slipped into the U.S. under Operation Paper Clip to get as many Nazi scientists as possible into the U.S. postwar industries. These guys are getting on in years."

Jesus, I thought, Buzzozzi's research never ended. He eventually got down to the bottom of everything. Buzzozzi paused and looked over at me. He was a short, powerful guy, about five-foot-eight and two hundred ten pounds. We loved each other. He was one of the ballsiest guys I'd ever met.

And now he was really giving us the load all at once. The Nazi mutations, he told us, were pets for Rudolph and Himmler.

I started to say something, but the Chief spoke first. "When," he asked, "did they start putting rat growth genes into humans?"

Buzzozzi stared at the Chief, sat back, and noticed the Spudka under the backseat. He pulled the bottle out of a paper bag, opened the screwtop, and started chuggling down the vodka. Buzzozzi lowered the bottle for a moment.

"They were doing the double blind studies on putting rat genes into human pituitaries. That was Germany, Poland, Russia, Switzerland. Now they're trying to do the same thing here. They're making some breakthroughs, as you can see.

"Here's a list of them," Buzzozzi continued, "the crimes, their political setup in this country." As he spoke, he pulled out a wad of papers from his inside coat pocket. He unfolded one page and handed it to me. The others he gave to the Chief, who scanned them while Buzzozzi resumed his monologue about the people involved in the droppa reproductions. "You know," he said, "in the last three days, I got about ten calls from Teller about his goddamn space marbles deal."

"Yeah," said the Chief, "that bastard is back and at it again. I told Barb to send his calls over to you. He's getting to be a real pain in the ass."

"Thanks, Chief, just what I needed. You know I'm really busy right now. I just got back from Bhopal on Monday."

While I listened to their conversation, I scanned the folder that Buzzozzi had just handed me. On the front of the folder, I read the title, *"Bhopal,"* in great big letters. I was staring at a picture of Bhopal the day after Carbide blew. Christ, bodies all over the place. Dead people and animals as far as you could see. I looked over at Buzzozzi and tried to catch the drift of where he and the Chief were going. Nowhere yet. He continued talking to the Chief, trying to translate into lay terms what he was talking about. But I was staring so hard at the pictures of Bhopal that I missed much of what he said.

Buzzozzi looked my direction and announced: "I've got to move fast. That happened last week. This is my first draft report. Chief, if you have any trouble with this, think of a giant can of Raid going off."

Buzzozzi was wearing his herringbone jacket and a matching beige golf hat, apparently made from the same material. He pulled off his hat, paused for a moment, and then looked at me, his bald scalp beaming in the July sunlight. His coat and hat were sort of a shit-brown color, like you used to see on those old two-toned Chevys. He was wearing a faded

Hawaiian bowling shirt, creased and yellowish around some purple pineapples. I looked down to his feet and noticed that his socks were different colors.

"Dickerman, that's the answer to your question about Pennemunde and Waldorf and his friends. But remember, this political stuff is not my department. I'm a medical man and a scientist. I'm sorry, but I can't help it."

He unscrewed the Spudka top and took another big gulp, almost too much, I thought, and handed it back to the Chief. Shelldrake looked briefly at the bottle and then tipped it up, finishing it off with two good gurgles. He handed the empty bottle back to Buzzozzi.

"Listen, Doc," the Chief asked, "who do you think's behind this, the fake dwarfs and all?"

Buzzozzi gave me a side glance, like I wasn't up-to-date with the Chief.

"If you really want to know," he said, "I think its Krakens, Bill Krakens."

"Krakens, huh?" the Chief replied pensively. "He's the one known as the Leviathan, isn't he?" The Chief turned to me with a worried look on his face.

"Reba, if it's Krakens, we've got our work cut out for us."

"But, Chief," Buzzozzi was growing increasingly impatient, "that's not why I'm here today, though I have wanted to see Dickerman for some time to discuss an important aspect of our lab work."

Buzzozzi was drinking from a water bottle that he'd brought with him, labelled *"Crystal Caverns."* He handed the bottle to the Chief, who took a swig and passed it to me.

"What's that about, Bill?" asked the Chief, looking at me as if I hadn't told him the whole story and as if my name were Bill. "How far gone are we, anyway?"

"Well," Buzzozzi resumed, "on the scale of things, I suppose it's no worse than the Gotterdamerung. We don't have those beautiful maidens, you know, those beautiful women and those bodies. What we do have is the droppa dwarfs. And it's worse in another way. I realize to my shame that national science has prevented information from getting out about it, and I think we got the stuff in spades.

"We don't know as much as we should, but we're getting some early confirmation that it's all over the place and totally out of control. That's what makes the droppas basically indestructible."

I watched Buzzozzi closely. He was getting agitated. His eyes were bulging from his fat head; he obviously hadn't shaved in at least a week. I hadn't really seen him since early July, a few weeks ago. He seemed to have put on some weight, maybe another ten pounds. He'd definitely changed some, and for the worse, since his wife split a few months earlier. I could go for Buzzozzi myself, I thought. I loved the guy. But things were just too complicated right now.

"Well, spit it out, Buzzozzi," said the Chief. "You're the expert. You're a man of science. What the shit's going on here?"

Buzzozzi frowned, reached into his breast pocket, and pulled out a giant dubbie. The Chief's eyes lit up, and I knew this was new stuff, not from the reservation. This was the shit affectionately known in Montana as Courthouse Dynamite. Buzzozzi lit up and took a big draw.

"I don't want to bum you out," Buzzozzi said, "but it's about the Nazis. And forgive me, I don't want you to think I'm a wise guy, because I know the Nazis are kind of obsolete right now, with worse people coming in, like, say, the Swiss and the Somalis. The Nazis are getting kinda passé, as if a few Nazis can't hurt because it's all so Nazified to start with. And then there's that fucking Thatcher."

Buzzozzi was getting it on. Finally, after a long diversion about Thatcher's pussy and her very strange clitoris, he started to find his way to the point. I'd heard it before, the Thatcher story. I swear to God, if I had to hear another person describe Margaret Thatcher's clitoris one more time, I was going to scream. Mercifully, though, Buzzozzi was finally getting down to business.

"It's dynacoccus," he explained, "these superbacteria that even radiation can't kill. They live in bomb plants and nuclear plants, and they're impervious to everything. And now I think they're part of the immune system of the droppas."

Buzzozzi took another long draw and passed the dubbie over to the Chief.

"But that's not what this is about either, or its possible relationship to Jack in the Box, you know, maybe the dynacoccus angle in the burgers. Right now, I can't say for sure exactly where it leads. The scary part, frankly, is the E. coli insulated by the dynacoccus. We just heard that the government is planning to spray herbicides on the lichen fields. Here's the fax I got. This was in my machine when I woke up this morning."

He opened his briefcase and handed over a sheet of paper. Shelldrake glanced through it and then passed it to me. More Indians massacred trying to harvest lichen. Same shit. Royal Mounties. A typically asswipe White House comment. Prime Minister McDuggery tells Quebec to remain calm. More of the same. They all knew exactly what it meant. No lichen, no food this winter. We were totally fucked.

Buzzozzi opened the door and started to get out.

"Got to get moving, Chief. I'm on a very tight schedule. I've also got to check out a mortality.

"I forgot to tell you," he continued. "The girls found a body in the mud over at Oyster Bay. It may be one of the droppas. Cheryl says it was a little guy wearing huge boots. They don't know what to make of it. I'm just going to check it out, find the cause of death, see who it was. When Cheryl called she said she was sure the boots belong to Nighthorse."

Buzzozzi hopped in his car and turned on the motor. The Chief and I had followed him out to his car.

"It might be tied to the fish lab shit Barb called me about last night," said Buzzozzi. "I have a hunch that Dr. Urbanchuk isn't who he says he is. Don't know much more about it."

Buzzozzi revved his motor, then let it idle.

"Chief, there's one other thing," he said. "What's this stuff I'm hearing about Genesis?"

"Genesis what?" I asked, looking to the Chief for some response. The Chief seemed to be nodding, thinking to himself.

"You mean the Garden of Eden?" the Chief said, still nodding.

"Yeah, Chief, the Garden of Eden, Adam and Eve, blah blah blah," answered Buzzozzi. "Cut the shit, Chief, everyone has heard of the Garden of Eden."

The Chief stood there, still nodding his head thoughtfully, waiting for Buzzozzi to say more.

"A guy calls me yesterday," Buzzozzi finally continued, "some reverend from the interpentecostal grange over in Montana, or something like that. He told me he slapped his face when he got up from bed in the morning, looked in the mirror, and—he's a white man, by the way—blushed right through his skin from the slap, blood on his face. He says his name is the Reverend Joseph John or something like that. He calls up and says, 'I want to speak with Dr. William Buzzozzi please.' He asks me if it's true that in fact I am Dr. William Buzzozzi and that I'm the top scientist for the tribes. And I answer that some people do think that I am a man of science. He interrupts me to ask, 'Do you study the scriptures?' And I answer, 'Not recently.' Then he asks, 'Do you teach the scriptures to the native people?' And he asks about Genesis, Adam and Eve, and all that, and he says, 'You know, we've been studying Genesis, and we've made a very interesting discovery.' 'And what's that?' I say, and he says, 'Well, we found out that Satan went into the Garden of Eden and fucked Eve and begat all you Jews and niggers and fuckin' wops.'"

"Yeah," said the Chief, "I heard about that."

"And he says that the Garden of Eden was really in Tanzania," continued Buzzozzi. "It's really pretty ridiculous."

The Chief spat on the ground near Buzzozzi's front tire.

"Well, Bill, what's the point?"

"Well," says Buzzozzi, scrunching up his face from the glare of the sun, "where *is* the Garden of Eden?"

"It's between your ears, Bill."

With that, the Chief gave Buzzozzi a wink and a wave. Buzzozzi gunned his motor, peeled out onto the highway, did a tight U-turn, screeching over the median line, and headed west toward the coast, a blaze of dust floating up against the sun.

I loved Bill Buzzozzi. *Buzzozzi's gone. My Buzzozzi. Stay safe and well, Buzzozzi. Come back to me soon.* I sang the words inside myself. The Chief was right, I thought, the Garden of Eden was really between your ears, where it belonged. At least I really hoped it was between *his* ears rather than where I imagined it might be, knowing the Chief. We leaned against the van and watched Buzzozzi disappear into the distance over the hills, a gray, smoky cloud of dust you could follow all the way west to the ocean.

Chief and I stood there a moment digesting what Buzzozzi had told us. We talked a while about what Buzzozzi might have meant about the neurons he was losing from his brain. There was something else in the encounter that was driving me crazy trying to remember it, but I couldn't quite recall.

Then suddenly the Chief remembered for me.

"Reba, the boots. The boots. Do you think they got Nighthorse?"

I couldn't imagine anything worse. I watched the Chief for some reaction, but his face was blank. He just said that when we got to the next stop I should call Nighthorse and see. He would probably still be there.

"Knowing Horse," said the Chief, "there's no way they can get him."

I began to wonder about my own brain and how many neurons I had left. I switched on the motor and pulled the van back onto the road. We continued to drive toward the hills and the mountainous coastal barriers. We still had to pass through the barren forests and do some serious hill climbing before we reached the plateaus leading up to Skankerville Heights.

Shelldrake was mumbling in some strange dialect that I couldn't understand. He hand-signalled me to slow down because a herd of sheep was just ahead, as if I hadn't seen it myself. I decided just to ignore his incoherent mumblings and keep my eyes focused on the road. It wasn't easy, though, with this huge hulk of a man sitting next to me, staring out at the universe one minute and down at my breasts the next. I always felt the guy could see right through my shirt. Right now, though, he was peering out the window at some cows. After I swerved to miss a tractor that was pulling out of a farm gate, the Chief switched back to English.

"Well," he said, "we're lucky we know Buzzozzi, Reba. The way he tells it, the whole thing sounds completely logical. I can see the dynacoccus angle with Jack in the Box, but I always thought the E. coli was the house speciality."

Around the bend, we hit Stumpville, a community of four houses and about eight hundred thousand stumps. A total clear cut as far as you could see. When I say houses, I mean the most modest of dwellings, with just one cabin and three spent trailers. One trailer was occupied. The other two were totally trashed. A guy named Reuben lived in the salvaged double-wide, which must have been the office around here back when the forests were cut down.

I knew the head count for Stumpville from our vote canvassing. Some insurance company in England owned the land here. When it went, it went all the way. I noticed Doc Spade sitting on the porch of his cabin. Doc waved as we passed. He pointed to a telephone pole across the road, and I saw the Chief's picture grinning out from his campaign poster. We began moving faster after we got past the outskirts. Some chickens bolted, trying to cross the road. I barely missed crushing one of the reds and the Chief gave me a precautionary look.

"Reba," he started up again. "Bad, bad karma to hit those chickens. It worries me about this campaign."

"You mean," I said, "if chickens could speak, maybe they could vote. I know you need votes."

We hit the next burg, Smegville, three miles later down the hill. There was just no way around Smegville, and I was sure the Chief would want to stop. He knew the mayor, Herbie Mone. Herbie looked like he was ready to make a commitment. I told the Chief that we hadn't called in advance to let Herbie know that we were coming, though I knew—even if the Chief didn't—that Bill Spoogie must have already done some advancing. I had forgotten to ask Durka about it, but she had sort of hinted yesterday that Bill was thinking about doing some advance work for the campaign. I wasn't sure where he was now, but I knew that there had been some campaign meetings. Maybe Bill had already contacted Herbie, but I couldn't be sure. I explained the situation to the Chief, who reluctantly agreed to forget about trying to find Herbie, who could, after all, have been anywhere. I guessed that he might have been over at Smegville Hospital, where he often worked nights, sanitizing the operating room. But I wasn't sure of his schedule, and frankly, we really didn't have the time to stop.

"The votes from Smegville will be a bellwether," the Chief insisted, visibly disappointed about missing Herbie this time around. We were on a course between the mountains, between beautiful fields and barren hillsides. Signs warning against slides were scattered along the roadside.

"I've got to talk to the Diehards," he continued, his eyes scanning a field full of cows, maybe two hundred of them, staggering around like they had the heebie-jeebies.

"Look at these cows," the Chief said. "I can't stand it. These cows have more character than all the burgerchefs and mcdoobies and Jack in the Boxes in the world—all of them, all those assholes—and they're all dead on their feet. Corporate schmucks, trying to sell us this dead, rotten meat. You can't even go in one of those places without your brain turning to mush."

With that, he began to hum the Kreutzer Sonata. He signalled for me to stop. We got out and looked down in the field. I left the motor running so we wouldn't be tempted to stay too long. You never knew with the Chief. I had to keep an eye on the clock to get the Chief there on time and in one piece for his keynote address to the Diehards. He got through one of the first passages of the Kreutzer, hoping, I suspect, that the cows would hear and recover from their fate. We passed along the field, and the cows were still staggering around all over the place, groaning to beat the band, many of them falling over convulsively near the fence off the highway. I took a couple of pictures. At the very least, I thought, I wanted Durka to know we had actually been heading toward Skankerville, in the event that we were diverted from getting there and I later found myself needing proof of the Chief's and my intentions. I took a snapshot of the Chief serenading a herd of dying cows.

The Chief eventually turned to me, his eyes filled with tears. "Look down there, closely, Reba, you can see them, the prions, all over the place."

I didn't know much about prions, I had to admit, but I could see the bits and pieces of protein floating in clouds around the cows. These were the prions, I was sure, which were driving the cows mad, destroying their brains and the brains of the people who ate them. From the look of things, I knew that we should probably get out of there as quickly as possible, but the Chief was crying, sobbing uncontrollably. We stood by the road, watching the cows collapsing one by one with loud groans, their intestines and udders exploding.

When the Chief was more composed, we climbed back into the van and he turned to me, his puffy face streaked with tears. "It's perfectly reasonable, Reba, to imagine that, if science can do this, they can invent a microbe that will wipe us all out. Except themselves, of course. At least that's what they think. Personally, I'd like to smash all the test tubes; that would certainly put a dent in things."

BUZZOZZI DROVE WEST, listening to an NPR tape about some goings-on in Toronto. Several women camping in the woods had recently been shot at by a man who had followed them for miles and watched them as they set up camp. Apparently, the women had drawn near to each other, or were hugging or showing some type of affection for one another, and the guy just freaked and shot at them, killing one of them instantly.

The remaining women ran for it, but the gunman cornered the two survivors near the highway, where they had fled for help, and shot a second one. The last woman raced across the highway and took cover in a gas station. The shooter began shooting at the pumps, eventually hitting one and blowing up the gas station. In the conflagration that followed, several cars exploded, along with their occupants, and the fires carried over to several nearby stores and an elementary school that fortunately was empty.

The second woman to be shot stumbled across the highway, still trying to escape. She never made it, though, collapsing in front of a double-trailer gasoline tanker that had slowed down for a stop light. The trucker swerved, hit the gas station, and ricocheted through a CVS drugstore. More explosions followed, including several chemical-laden tanks near the freight station. A bridge near Lake Ontario melted down. The shooter escaped on foot, heading to a forest preserve near London where hundreds of soldiers and police were trying to find him.

Buzzozzi listened to police officials and a prime minister lament the crimes and accidents. Nothing like this had ever happened in Toronto. Dozens were missing as one car after another exploded. Eight thousand people were evacuated.

The final resting place of the tanker corpse was in the playground of Greenleaf Gardens public housing off the suburban highway behind the gas station. Charred children's bodies littered the gym sets and sandboxes. Gasoline jettisoned into a day care center in the unit block and burned out the ground floor of the ten-story public-housing apartment building. No one could determine exactly how many lives were lost. The Ministry of Health announced that they would be sending rescue teams as soon as the flames died out, including special teams of Mounties. The woman who hid in the gas station got out the back just before everything blew. She was in custody, hospitalized, in shock, with burns over seventy percent of her body. Authorities denied rumors that they were investigating a failed drug deal in the forest, and refused to give the surviving woman's name until a police investigation could be completed.

The NPR accounts continued, but Buzzozzi couldn't stand the miserable bad news any longer, the vivid eyewitness accounts blasting on ad infinitum, like little atom bombs of heartbreak and despair going off across the airwaves. He switched off the radio, but not before being subjected to a nauseating bit of nonsense about a new "supermarket to the world." What a disgrace, Buzzozzi mused. The silence of the road, all blotted out by radiopathy. And even public radio was so dominated by transnational corporate giants that it was ridiculous. He had to shut it all out for his own sanity.

With the radio switched off, Buzzozzi grew more composed, watching for cops, staying carefully in the 50-mph range as he passed through savage clear cuts and crossed small bridges over bustling streams. Buzzozzi absorbed the time and space and sound around him, swallowed deeply, took two very deep breaths, rolled down the window, and with one hand holding the wheel steady, poked his face out the window, coughed it all up, and spit it out the window. He wouldn't have done it if a car was coming, out of courtesy, but with no one on the road east or west, he let it all go at once. He was getting good at this; he could expel a large volume of stress in one major vomit. Looking back at the road in his rearview mirror, he saw the big gob that he'd left on the pavement disappearing behind him, a real steamer.

Buzzozzi also wouldn't have discharged his stress in that way if anyone else had been in the car with him. It was simple decency. He wouldn't have done it even if only the Chief had been there, shot out a big one himself, and then ordered Buzzozzi to match what he had already done. He just wouldn't. He had his self-respect, after all. Vomiting out the window of your car going 50 mph over hill and dale could be provocative, even offensive to some people. He didn't want to take any unnecessary risks right now. He was glad he had been alone this time, though. Getting rid of that stress-filled gob had really done the trick. He felt immediate relief, as if he had just upchucked Bhopal. Lately, this was the only real kind of relief he could get from the minions of brain death. Get it all out.

Now he was finally free to think about his encounter with the Chief just a few minutes earlier. The Chief was definitely himself, totally in control, leading the dialogues, digging into Buzzozzi's craft of scientific investigation. His explanation of the Garden of Eden seemed to be right on. Between your ears did lie paradise, if you could find it; and maybe that was the only place that you could ever actually know paradise.

The Chief was right on top of the issues. He seemed to be well-informed about the human growth genes put in rats, even though that business was old stuff. They had been doing it for years. And now they were putting rat pituitary genes in humans, a real challenge to see what came up in the genetic lotteries.

Buzzozzi believed in the Chief. It was starting to look like the Chief could really pull it off. Reba had told him that the Chief was beginning to make some good moves. It was definitely a positive sign that the Chief's picture was hanging on every telephone and power pole in the country. Buzzozzi had been right there when Durka made her plan. A pint of mescal stood on the table between them, waiting for takers. They took it, and then she wanted the worm. She took the worm, and now she was going for the golden grail.

Durka had expected to run a winning campaign, concentrating on exposure of her husband to the whole political body. She had photographed the Chief from different vantage points and hung the photos in the campaign offices. She included the entire staff in the selection of the most candid shots for the telephone pole campaign, an approach she espoused as economically and politically sound. Buzzozzi thought it was a shrewd move. It saved money, after all, inspired commitment from the population at large, and was ubiquitous and repetitive enough that people wouldn't forget overnight what was happening.

Buzzozzi thought the encounter with the Chief and Reba was fortuitous. He had welcomed the chance to chat with them, even if he had acted impatiently at times. He felt a little bad, though, that he wasn't meeting Reba at Skankerville. He wanted a little time with her. The truth was, he wanted to plank her, but he knew he couldn't. She had a mind of her own, for one thing, and she might be big trouble later, if things didn't straighten out with her Aunt Elena. But if something didn't happen in Minneapolis real soon to bring his yoni home to him, he might have to take some action. He had written her several times in the last two months, begging her to return, but he'd only received a single postcard for all his troubles. He'd found its message to be a bit cryptic. *"Listen schmucko,"* she'd written, *"why don't you just suck yourself off?"*

Buzzozzi felt that he had to turn down the Chief's invitation to have some lunch at the S&B. It was very generous of the Chief. Buzzozzi knew he was a very busy man. But Buzzozzi, while feeling honored, knew he couldn't handle it. The Chief probably would have started in on Waco, and here he was, just wrapping up the Bhopal investigation. And, besides, Buzzozzi didn't crave the S&B menu right now. It did pain him a little that he couldn't see more of Reba. He felt for his cock, and it was way out there just from thinking about her.

Buzzozzi had actually just eaten at the S&B the night before last on his way back from Dayton, where he had summarized the Carbide report to some media and showed them a few of the pictures. He had found the lines at S&B to be a little too long and the customers a little too raucous. He preferred to dine in unpretentious surroundings where the nice gossip levels were a friendly backdrop for good eating. The bean thing at Slurp & Burp was alright, considering the place's business goals. It wasn't a brain killer to figure out the menu. The food was okay. There was an intimation of Basque.

On his last visit, he had sat at a table packed full of families with lots of kids. Between mouthfuls of beanball pates, the children snickered and made farting noises to gross out their parents. Buzzozzi didn't know any of them, and they apparently didn't recognize him either. That was alright. He thought it a little ironic that in Bhopal people were literally farting their eyes out, while here at the S&B, the cute little brats were farting just to gross their parents out. It had only been 6 p.m., and it was jammed. Buzzozzi couldn't help but be impressed with the pull of the place and its atmosphere. The S&B management had apparently hit a public funny bone with the Paul Bunyon belch, fart, and burp machine. And in addition to its popular experimentations in family entertainment, the S&B touted almost two hundred and fifty varieties of beans that the chef could quickly combine in quantum-leap variations, according to the taste of each patron.

Buzzozzi had ordered a Botero sandwich, but the Boteroes were cut off at 5:30 p.m. to keep the customers from noshing when they should be enjoying the full-dinner menu.

Maybe Buzzozzi had misjudged the S&B. After all, he had been kind of tired from his meetings over at Dayton. And he had been right in the middle of rewriting a chapter of his Bhopal report. Maybe he hadn't paid enough attention to the food. He had ordered a Flatulettuce Swarmy Bean Broth, not realizing that it was a two-person portion. That was always a basic problem of eating alone, Buzzozzi mused. There was no one with whom to share the interesting specials and entrees. Buzzozzi had tried to offer some of his meal to the others at his table, but they only shrugged and continued shagging the beans off their plates.

He managed to consume only about a third of the broth and had the rest packaged to take home. He tried a couple of other appetizers—tuna braised in pure silkworm oil and Crushed Fava Encrusted Mashed Grouper Wrapped in a Whole Head of Iceberg Lettuce. The latter was billed as a new menu entry and had cost $19. The farting noises in the dining room had intensified, and the hubbub of the flatulence and the children's pooping noises made him forget the menu. He sat back and faced the fact that he had failed in his quest for a quiet corner to review his Bhopal narrative.

Two little kids next to Buzzozzi were jumping up and down in their seats, impressively sipping their Shirley Temples, giggling and bouncing all at once. Buzzozzi had taken Bhopal out of his folder and was checking out his introduction and first chapter on the global implications of the chemical industry when Kathy the waitress, who was a real looker, appeared at his table. Kathy seemed to have a shining for the grouper and pressed him to order it. She said that she only had two orders left and that he'd be lucky to get one of them, and Buzzozzi succumbed to her charms. He watched her move around the table, her ample backside protruding in different directions as she went from family to family to take the orders.

The children at the table were ganging up on Kathy and their parents demanding this and that. A blond woman at the other end of the table tried to calm the children, obviously aware of Buzzozzi's discomfort. She kept poking the man sitting next to her, but he ignored her and ordered another round of binibombers, one of the house specialties. Finally, after a particularly severe poke in the ribs from the woman, the binibomber man responded, waving his arms and yelling, "Hey, kids, shut your traps, or I'm going to get separate checks!"

Kathy must have been impressed by the line. She looked back at Buzzozzi and lifted her eyebrow slightly. The kids quieted down a bit and began looking at the menus. Buzzozzi noticed that, at least for the moment, he was actually sitting at the quietest table in the entire S&B.

Buzzozzi tried the grouper. He found it to be a little bland but decided not to send it back. He ate slowly. The iceberg lettuce wasn't that fresh, but the favas seemed to give the recipe the push it needed. He guessed it worked. The silkworm oil was pretty innovative, he thought, since it gave the tuna some room to work in. Another creative touch was the double-thick, scallopped purple bean pie on which the tuna rested. The chef was obviously concerned that the tuna stay as moist as possible in the transit from kitchen to customer.

The children swirled around the table, making beaner blowguns from straws and blowing beanwads at each other across the dining room. Buzzozzi did his best to ignore them but he couldn't help comparing the frivolous current scene with the image in his mind of the dead and rotting babies of Bhopal. The kids were also terrorizing the other diners with the fart pillows that the management had conveniently placed under each seat. The methane explosions that the pillows produced fortunately did not smell as bad as the real thing.

When Buzzozzi had finished the grouper, Kathy brought him the dessert list, but he decided to skip the polysacharides and head straight for the Tabernacle Room, S&B's backroom bar behind the Botero Room. It was getting a little late and he needed to get home to pack for Skankerville, but not before a small libation. He felt moody, depressed, like he was stuck in the wrong place at the wrong time. He wished he were in his yoni's arms. The Tabernacle Room, where he went to get his drink, lived up to its name. With its large tablets beneath tall stained-glass windows, it reminded Buzzozzi a little of the Sistine Chapel. Naturally, the bartender and waitrons were dressed in black frocks, and votive candles graced each table. Little tin Planter's Peanut dishes were filled with Neco wafers. The place was pretty packed, but Buzzozzi was not really in a celebratory mood. There was no one—no yoni—with whom to celebrate.

Buzzozzi wandered over to the can and then the pay phone, where he picked up his messages. There was an urgent one from Barb Willis at the Chief's office, begging him to call immediately. Big trouble at the fish lab. There were also several crank calls—one a breather and another an outright hostile but unrecognizable voice. The voice was muted and cottony, an effect that had obviously been achieved with some cheesecloth.

"You little fat wop," the voice had said, *"if you think you're so great, why don't you go fuck the Pope in the ass?"*

There were also two messages from Teller, beseeching Buzzozzi to call him back. Buzzozzi didn't like these tactics, which seemed to be coming more frequently now that the the Chief's campaign was heating up.

After he finished listening, Buzzozzi called Barb at her home. When she finally answered, he knew there was trouble. Her voice changed dramatically the instant she recognized his voice. Barb could be a nervous Nelly, Buzzozzi knew, but this time it really did sound like something was up. She asked how the Bhopal report was coming along, but Buzzozzi could tell right away that there was more to her concerns than that.

Barb was quickly getting worked up.

"Dr. Bill," she wailed, "it's the fish lab! You have to do something. Ruppert Emerson's been fired. Millie and the girls are in fear for their lives. The new director is trying to rape them right and left. They say that the science at the fish lab is totally corrupted. Dr. Bill, help them! Help them!"

Buzzozzi questioned Barb further. He knew her well enough to be suspicious. She could get pretty worked up at times with fear and anger. Sometimes it got so bad that she said it made her teeth ache. Barb had arranged his tickets to India and all his train and bus transportation while he was there. She had never been to India, much less to Bhopal, but she acted like she knew everything about everywhere. Buzzozzi knew that she was just parroting what the Chief had told her. She finally admitted that she had been trying to scare him with her tales about India, but she now realized that was impossible. Barb had also told Buzzozzi some interesting things about her past. She had started at the fish lab twenty-five years ago when it was put on Emergency Accelerated Research (EAR). It had been her first job. The great listening post in nature, the EAR. She must have started when she was fifteen, he figured, meaning that she would be about forty now. A really nice forty, Buzzozzi thought. Dr. Teitel was her first employer, and then, as Buzzozzi had learned from someone else, her lover. Not to be believed, Buzzozzi thought. Harry Teitel? Harry should be close to retirement now.

As part of EAR, the lab was called upon by the legislature to take major initiatives to protect the state's seafood reserves. Barb knew the fish lab by heart, though she hadn't been at the lab in several months. The last time she was there was when she stopped by to pick up Millie on her way to Portland for a few days of hard-earned vacation. She had seen Ruppert there at the time and had learned that he was very ill. Millie had told her everything that was going on there. Harry Teitel seemed happy to see Barb, but things weren't looking that good for him otherwise. He was very depressed at the pace of the new lab construction, with Dr. Urbanchuk having arrived before he was expected. The new lab was months, if not longer, behind schedule. It looked to Barb as if Dr. Teitel might well be on his way out. Barb also described to Buzzozzi the stories that Millie had told her about the disturbing behavior of Dr. Urbanchuk after he had arrived at the lab. Apparently, the new director had been exposing himself to the interns and had actually attempted to rape Millie and a young intern from Evergreen.

Buzzozzi immediately interrupted her.

"Was that Rhoda, Cheryl's roommate at Evergreen?" Buzzozzi asked.

Barb just kept talking. She was all over the place and not getting anywhere. He had to cut her off. She finally acknowledged that it was Rhoda whom Dr. Urbanchuk had tried to rape along with Millie.

"I'm really worried for her," she told Buzzozzi. "She says Dr. Urbanchuk is wearing her down. He already did Irene."

"Tell the Chief I'll go to the fish lab. I'm leaving at first light." He hung up the phone and went back into the Tabernacle Room.

Back in the bar, Stu Mills was playing a little Dexter Gordon on the box Steinway in the corner. People that Buzzozzi had noticed at dinner were standing around swilling down different libations. He decided against a cognac, picking a grappa sampler with eight different vintages. The place was really humming. Buzzozzi still had quite a drive home; and with Barb's urgency about the fish lab he would have to get up early, maybe 6 a.m., to make the coast trip. Stu heated up the pipe organs and began doing a jazzy rendition of the "Ninth Symphony." Buzzozzi tried to catch Stu's eye, but Stu was really moving up the scales. He went back to his table and gathered his papers, checked out his eight samplers to see if there were a few drops left, and then plopped a ten-dollar bill on the table for a waiter wearing a St. Augustine frock, with chains on his wrists and around his neck. St. Augustine Jr. had been walking around the bar the whole time like he had a corncob up his butt. Buzzozzi continued to be fascinated by the shifting patterns and subtleties of the S&B experience. The only place he could compare it to, he thought, would be a sanitarium like St. E's. From one day to the next, the place looked like a total loony bin.

* * *

Buzzozzi still wasn't quite finished with the report. He wasn't sure about some of the wording here and there. Basically, however, it was a valid document, detailing the event, supplying the evidence, and drawing the only conclusions you could draw from Bhopal. Bad corporate management; the endless quest for the almighty buck; the injury and endangerment of the public; the attempted cover-up and the stonewalling. The latter, he knew all too well, would probably be successful, at least at first. And there were more Bhopals lurking around. Buzzozzi still had to give the Union Carbide nerve-toxin explosion report a name before he could release it. He was wrestling around with several different ideas and was veering toward a formal title, though he also wanted something that would be down-to-earth. He considered "Burnt in Bhopal" and "Eyeless in Eurasia." Probably, though, the subtitle would need to mention Union Carbide explicitly. Something like: "Carbide Asleep at the Switch. Indian City Totally Fucked."

A light rain had started up by the time he got to his car. Buzzozzi turned on the wipers and saw from the compass on the dash that he was heading northwest. He saw a sign for Forks—435 miles—and became almost comically overjoyed that he wasn't heading for Forks. The only thing in Forks worth a shit was a Chinese restaurant in the middle of town. The rest of Forks was deadly; the folks there were angrier than a nest of hornets. Thoroughly disemboweled owls had become the town mascots. Dead, mutilated owls hung from telephone and electric lines and all along the length of the City Hall flagpole. Where do all those owls come from, Buzzozzi wondered, if they're really so scarce? But Buzzozzi knew all about human corruption and ingenuity, and he figured that the Forkereans were probably just victims like everyone else, bamboozled by a corporate campaign designed to get everyone in the region pissed off at animal lovers and their New York buddies so that the company could push up the price of timber and screw the workers.

Even so, Buzzozzi thought, Forks must just be the meanest town in the West. When you drove into the place, even the skyline scowled at you. He remembered the big billboard that had greeted him as he entered Forks the first time:

The mills are closed. There are no jobs.
There's no toilet paper left.
When you take your dump, you'll have to
wipe your ass with the very rare spotted owl.
And we got plenty of those to spare.

Fortunately, Buzzozzi's only other trip to Forks was safely in the distant past. He thanked his stars that the fish lab wasn't there. He hadn't been there since around 1984 or 1985. He had been lucky enough at the time not to be tarred and feathered naked and thrown into the Wallicum River. They didn't like Italians there. He wasn't in a hurry to try his chances again.

Buzzozzi attempted to console himself that the Bhopal report, even in its unfinished state, was enough to go on for now. He still felt uncomfortable about giving it to Reba and the Chief, though. He knew how the Chief could react if everything wasn't just right. Buzzozzi was worried about the overall texture of the writing; he couldn't quite get it right for some reason. And some of the text still needed to be edited. He knew that there were probably too many split infinitives, a throwback to his Italian heritage. But it was all there: the photos, his collection of data, the interviews. It would have to do.

Buzzozzi looked at the speedometer and saw that he was again doing about 50 mph. The cloud formations up ahead were troubling, their cavernous black faces ready to spout iceballs. These must be the clouds, he thought, that were giving everyone hickeys. They appeared to be staying west of the barrier Cascadian Mountain chain. It was definitely hailstorm weather. Scientific to a T, Buzzozzi reminded himself that hailstorms were normally surprises. These forbidding clouds were different. They just didn't look normal, climatically speaking.

Pausing again to look at the speedometer and out the back for *carbiniari,* Buzzozzi began to plan his ascent into Garibaldi and then the two-hour trek over forest roads and through massive clear-cut country to the fish lab.

* * *

The Chief had gone back to sleep, and I kept driving, past desolate empty farms, silos caving in, barns falling down, overgrown orchards, and fields spotted with yellow gorse. When it wasn't the farms, it was clear cuts. What a mess. I kept driving east. What a total fucked-up mess. If it wasn't the campaign, it would be everything else. Maybe ten minutes went by as I tried to reconstruct what had already happened this morning, and we had hardly gotten started on our big adventure.

Waking up abruptly, the Chief started in on me immediately.

"Reba, this is like an opening campaign speech," he said. "I'm just writing it now in my head, and I can't listen to you go on about the elk and the lichen and these midgets. And these fucking sick cows and the Nazis are making me sick. Did you see that thing Buzzozzi did on Bhopal? A bunch of Eichburgers. I gotta puke."

And being the Chief, he did just that. He rolled down the window, stuck his head way out, did a gigantic barf, and then reemerged. You could hear it hit the road. I tried not to look out the back but couldn't resist; the Chief had left a pile on the gravel the size of a large cow flop.

I knew more about the dwarfs and lichen than he did, something that would become more apparent to him as time went on. Maybe he just didn't have the time, with his heavy schedule. Maybe he'd finally begun to understand what we were up against. It was that way with everything else we'd done. But if they had Nighthorse, all hell was going to break loose. The Diehards would totally explode. I knew everything Horse told him and even more than that. If we could catch these little guys, we could do speed training. I didn't like the idea of killing them off. There was the question of the elk head in the back of his pickup. Then the elk head disappeared, along with the dwarfs in the dumpster. Then their carcasses had disappeared and been replaced with the elk head. I didn't get it. And I was saddened by it and I knew that many other people would be upset about it until the head and body were safely back together.

Events had definitely been puzzling the last couple of weeks as the campaign had revved up. Horse and I believed that Krakens's people were behind it all. The bodies might be down in the third triple subbasement of the Pentagon, for all I knew, down in Admiral Frankel's basement office. Nighthorse? Buzzozzi? I suddenly feared for Buzzozzi. Maybe it was just a setup. Maybe it was some kind of diversion to separate the Chief and his top advisors. But the Chief, for all his bullshit, couldn't see it yet.

"Alright, Jack, have it your way." I stepped on the gas and raced over a hill. A sign appeared that read: *"Caution, Sunken Grade. Elderberry, 105 miles."*

I came out of the curve, around the hill, and into the forests. I eased off the gas and slowed to about forty-five because of the road conditions. I was pissed as hell by the Chief's fucking ignorance.

"Hey!! That's okay with me," I yelled at him. "I have a full agenda, and you're right. We'll save the gremlins and our vanishing food supply for the trip back, if there is one. You never know with the Diehards. They might decide to invite us to stay a few days and put us on the full agenda permanently."

I was soon out of breath and out of things to say. Shelldrake had gotten the message, however. I was about to start up on the crummies again, but he beat me to the punch. "I see, Reba, that you're right back into the policy on crummies again."

I plunged ahead down the road toward the top of S22, where we would start our trek across the great divide. When I reached the peak, I pulled the car over and turned off the motor.

"Look, boss," I was speaking more calmly now, "I've been thinking about what you said. You want us to take all the crummies from the big corporations and use them in a get-out-the-vote campaign. And then when we're finished, the big corporate assholes will be begging to live in our crummies. That's the plan, right?"

"Yeah," the Chief replied, "that's the general outline. It's part of what I'm taking to the Diehards."

"Now that you're really opening the campaign, they may get totally charged up, make you into their slave-chief, and lock you in one of their crummies."

I guess that telling him this was just my way of saying that I loved him and that I was worried about him.

"Dickerman," the Chief said reassuringly, "before I start I want you to know that I'm in this for the duration. I had a call this morning just before you came by. It was from Bella. You know, she's just come back from China and the UN Women's Conference. She said being with all the Chinks was really crazy after a while, but she wants me to know that our cause here is shared by many of the women she met over there. You know, she went to the China Wall and screamed 'Fuck the Pentagon' off the side as loud as she could. She did it twenty-one times in succession and said it was a twenty-one gun salute for all the boys sent to die in U.S. wars like Korea and Vietnam. Guys blasting their nuts off stepping on mines, and then looking up just as a cloud of Agent Orange dumped down on their heads.

"Well, anyway, not to get off the subject, technology is destroying not only old ways and customs, it's destroying womanhood. Bella told me that more than a hundred thousand women in China have applied for breast implants this year alone, according to the UN Population Crisis Committee. She says to me, 'Shell, you've got to make this run. I'd prefer a woman in the top spot, but, Chief, you can do the job.' Anyway, Dickerman, in case you're wondering, we may be able to win the women's votes if we pull off this campaign plan. She believes that I'm a credible candidate, seriously charismatic and attractive to women her age."

"So what's new, Chief?" I responded impatiently. "Bella said two years ago that you should be running and never looking back. She told me that you have enough charisma for five men, that you should go straight to the people, and that if you can't take it to the people, then you're just another fucking male asshole. That's what she told me. So, Chief, don't be an asshole. You're not looking to the Chinese breast implant victims for votes. We don't even have shit for a campaign yet, and you're already talking foreign policy.

"Anyway," I continued, catching my breath and trying to change the subject, "give me the speech you're going to make today. When we get to Diehard, I probably won't have any time to listen to the real thing. I wouldn't want to have to hear it twice, anyway, no matter how good it is."

"Who are you going to see over there?" the Chief queried.

"I was scheduled to see Buzzozzi, but that's not necessary now. I guess I'll go see my aunt. She isn't well."

* * *

The Chief turned his face to Dickerman and gazed at her profile. She looked up, and her eyes met his, even as she still watched the road. This wasn't easy for either of them. She knew he yearned for her but couldn't make the move. Everything had to go into the campaign, she knew that. It was terrible, when you thought about it. Really the pits.

"Which aunt, Reba?" The Chief knew exactly which aunt she was talking about. "You mean Harry's wife, your aunt? The late great Harry Teitel, I guess. Elena. Ellleena."

The Chief stretched out her name empathetically as though he was calling her from a great distance. "Elllllleeeeena." He yelled it even louder out the window toward a small forest preserve near a clear cut, a nothing patch of nature. A stand of cottonwood on a diked farm plot absorbed the Chief's mournful cries. "Elllleeeeeennaaa!" His huge scream penetrated the nearby forests. Flocks of crows flew out of the trees by the thousands screaming their heads off.

* * *

I knew the Chief still loved Elena, in spite of some weirdness that had happened between them. Elena was my aunt. The woman could scream. When Harry dropped dead—so to speak—in his sleep, it took a while for her to realize she was breathing alone, though her arms were still wrapped tightly around him. Several hours they stayed there like that. He was still inside her, hard as a rock, according to what Elena told me.

It sounded oddly appropriate, I thought when she told me, though I didn't saying anything. Elena was always such an appendage to Harry. She was always stuck on the end of his dreams or his plans or his prick. It was usually the end of his prick that Elena was stuck on.

Elena sometimes felt as if she hung by a tenuous thread of foreskin from his big prick, her reality a tiny toenail's worth of attention beside Harry's huge physical presence and his big important work. When Harry died, the Chief and I went together to pay our respects. Elena threw herself into the Chief's arms, slumped down to the floor, and screamed, "I'll never let you go!" Then she grabbed his leg and held on for dear life. The Chief was very patient; he slowly drew Elena to her feet and held her tightly. I stood in the corner, watching both of them sob convulsively over Harry. They held each other for hours, Shelldrake's great arms encircling my aunt Elena. It was like the end of the world, with all of us doomed but hanging on by a thread.

I dozed off for a while behind the wheel. I was really worn out. In his way, the Chief had me against the ropes.

* * *

The Chief had called me into his office. He was a little slow, though, and I had to wait in the outer office until he finished some cockamamie interview with some Joel something at the *Chicago Tribune*. I had a chance to talk to Barb while I waited; she filled me in on some of the campaign strategies and how the staffing was going. I liked Barb, the way she would always open up with me. There were bad vibes from Nighthorse's visit, Barb related. The elk's severed head was knocking office atmospherics apart. It had affected office morale at a particularly bad moment. And then there had also been the larger than usual number of crank calls. Barb thought it was mostly Edward Teller, because of the heavily scented German accent. "You know," Barb said, "Teller should be worried. It's the end of his star wars and space marbles. The Chief says he's personally going to stuff star wars and space marbles up Teller's ass. I can tell, he's really getting pissed now."

I was impressed at how the office was running. Cheryl was keeping the land claims paperwork humming, and Barb was like a second backbone for the Chief.

Finally, the Chief finished his interview with Joel at the *Chicago Tribune* and signalled for me to come in.

We sat in the usual configuration. I could hear the cacophony of the machines in the outer office. The Chief had recently added a fax machine. Barb finally convinced him that he couldn't keep doing everything by hand like some ninth-century monkish scribe. We had to modernize the office if we were going to take on the colossus. The Chief also authorized a box of pencils and pads of yellow-lined legal paper for each worker to take notes. Every desk had a wastepaper basket and enough stationery and envelopes to keep the correspondence running. There were plenty of telephones. The fax machine was working overtime. Durka seemed satisfied with the improvements.

The Chief didn't look happy. I waited for him to speak.

"Harry's death has left me disconsolate and depressed. I'm almost ready to throw in the towel. These losses are becoming too much. Harry's death was no accident."

I watched him closely, the old man who was going to pull us through. It would take a lot of pressure to keep him focused. I thought about suggesting that it had been some type of gonadal mix-up, that maybe what he really wanted was to be Harry, stuck for hours inside Elena. I held back, though. The Chief was no dummy. He understood the commitments that had been made, that we were already so deep in the campaign that there was no way out except at the other end of the clogged large intestine called America.

"You know, Reba, I was counting last night. I've outlasted a dozen of these creeps, just like Fidel."

"Listen Chief, keep your sense of humor; in the end, that's what's going to get us through. Neither of us like some of the things we're going through. I think you should get some rest tonight. We're really beginning to move fast. We've got to make it to Skankerville by Saturday afternoon. Durka wants me to be with you for the opening ball. Try to leave your binges at home this trip. I'm doing the driving."

When I left, he was still working over the land claims.

* * *

On the road to Skankerville, the Chief's thoughts were still stuck somewhere inside Elena. He turned toward me, and I noticed that his eyes were welling up.

"Reba, I hear your aunt Elena is really having some problems."

"Not the word for it, Chief; she's persona non grata," I replied. "Even with herself. She seems to have gone so far inside of herself that she doesn't have any use for herself anymore. And then to think of her sticking her precious poodle into the microwave—it's just too much, Chief."

I couldn't continue. Merely thinking about Elena gave me awful chills.

I tried to focus on the road; the sheets of heat rippling off the pavement created mirages that made me feel like I was back in the middle of the Sahara Desert. I could hardly even see the road anymore, but I knew we were getting near to an S&B stopoff. I wasn't sure I could make it. I began to slow the van.

"Chief, I just can't talk about it right now. I need to take a break."

"Well," the Chief finally responded to my earlier comments about Elena, "what happened to her poodle could happen to anyone. Of course, not everyone can fit in a microwave. Maybe some refreshments will ease the pain. While we're eating, I can work on my text for Skankerville. We're nearly at the S&B."

More of the same fried-poodle shit from the Chief. What a heartless bastard he was being; his officious pandering made me want to barf, right on his goddamn vulcanized sneakers.

From the distance, I could hear the sound of the totem. It was right around the bend. *Hurry, car, get there,* I thought, *before I blow a really big one right on the Chief.* He was still missing the point about Elena. He thought it was the poodle. He was so far off I couldn't stand it. How many times had we been over this? The poodle had become an expedient symbol for a lot of people, not just the Chief. But he, more than anyone, should have understood. His suffering over her silence, however, meant he'd probably never find out what really happened to her the night Uncle Harry croaked.

Up ahead, I could see the grinning face of the seventy-five-foot Paul Bunyan figure towering above the tree line. Paul rose impressively out of the adolescent forest that had been planted by Georgia Pacific twenty years earlier, after the entire old growth forest was wiped clean. The new plantings had risen to only about twenty-five feet high, so Paul was really up there, a massive statue carved, it was said, from the trunk of a single cedar tree that was rumored to have been more than six hundred years old. The rest of those enormous old trees were long gone. Paul was well-bearded, dressed in a red-and-black checkered shirt and bright red suspenders. The wood carver had made sure to fashion an impressively large pouch in his pants. His Goliath boots must have been seventeen feet tall, with carved-out leather thong laces. All in all, it was a really beautiful and masterly piece of work.

A sign across the road promised: *"Good Forest Management—More Pulp for Paper in 2000."* I checked my watch—five minutes of. Paul's eyes were beaming. If my watch was right, we would hit the Slurp & Burp Diner just as Paul let out his hourly call, a gigantic belch, followed five minutes later by a horrendously vociferous fart, welcoming calls that could be heard nearly five miles away by travellers who were lost or in need of food and spirit. I knew the place by heart. Most of the time, the food at the S&B was pretty good. Like any restaurant, though, it had its ups and downs. We'd been here when it was really great. Sometimes the specials would be really interesting. It was pretty rare not to have a good meal there.

It was a relief to stop anywhere at all. We reached the Slurp & Burp and turned into the crowded parking lot as Paul erupted with an enormous moose noise. Just as it was dying away, he slammed off a powerful gargantuan belch, loud enough to wake the catatonics. The parking lot was nearly full with cars and tour busses. Whole families stood gawking at the massive statue, countdowning the five remaining minutes to the big one. Call me a spoilsport, if you feel you must, but I wanted to get inside before Paul encored his belch with his notoriously bilious farts.

The Chief and I managed to push through the crowd toward the front door. I saw Wally Amis, the owner, waiting there to greet us. He gave us big high signs and hellos all around. Wally knew the Chief well from his frequent stops over the years. He sat us down near an enormous window where we could see a waterfall crashing down into the headlands of the Rogue River. As the guests around us took their places, the hydraulics of the air-filled cushions beneath the seats gave way; loud moist farts ripped across the room. We sat down with several other people at a window table.

One of our fellow customers, an old guy across the way, seemed, from the look on his face, to recognize the Chief. He picked up his mug of beer and toasted us. "Chief Shelldrake, here's to the big one." The Chief picked up an imaginary glass from the table and offered a toast in return. I'd never seen the old guy before. Satisfied with the Chief's attention, he sat back against the window. He and the rest of his dinnermates—I assumed they were his family—were all look-alikes. Around these parts, folks could be as incestuous as a bunch of jellyfish.

A younger man who was sitting at the table across from the old man was the next one to speak.

"I'd like you to meet my dad, Bill Spoogie Sr. This is my wife Delores, not to mention our daughter, Lillian Spoogie. We're celebrating Lil's graduation from fourth grade. It was a real fight; wasn't it honey?"

"Listen, everyone," Lil answered appreciatively, "if it hadn't been for Dad's encouragement I'd probably still be in second or third grade."

"I would like to salute you, Bill Spoogie, my old buddy."

The Chief raised another imaginary glass. It wouldn't be long, I hoped, until the crumbs were brushed off the table, the places were set, and the drink orders taken. I wonder if the Chief could hold out.

"Reba, shake hands with one of my great old friends. We were in elementary school together. Bill and I caddied together at the Mt. Olympus links. Bill's dad, Spoogie Senior, commanded a lot of respect. He was just a teenager when he and a few buddies turned the tide at the Ardennes. Got out somehow without a scratch, though everyone else he knew was slaughtered or totally maimed."

The elder Spoogie nodded furiously.

Reminiscing about the Great War—the Chief definitely knew what he was doing. It was an excellent way to get the campaign rolling.

"Bill's one of the great ones. Huh, Bill?"

I looked over at Bill and the rest of his family, his missus and big daughter. And I mean *big*. She was about ten years old, and she must have weighed in at at least two hundred and fifty. And Mrs. Spoogie had to have been twice as large as her girl. The fourth at the table, old Spoogie himself, was a really ancient old fart, maybe in his nineties. The Ardennes Spoogie. You could tell that he was definitely the grandpa of little Lil, who I noticed was now chewing on a giant burger of some sort. Generous portions of the day's bean specials were piled on salad plates within her reach.

As for grandpa, I liked him immediately. He looked like he could have been my own dad a few years down the line. He was solid, if you know what I mean. He sat in a kind of trance with a fork in one hand and a spoon in the other, and he kept nodding at the Chief's salutations. His white cropped hair was neatly cut and his loving blue eyes followed each of his family as they scarfed down their lunch platters.

I couldn't help but notice that he was also eyeballing me. Some of the lima beans in front of him had fallen off the plate, but he just kept staring in my direction. The lima beans were making little shadowy stains on the bleached white tablecloth. But Spoogie Sr. didn't seem to notice or to care. He was also watching the waitress, the erotic movements of her ample body as she plunked down dishes and menus on all the tables. Finally, Mrs. Spoogie started spearing the fallen beans with her fork and filling her face from grandpa's plate. He ignored her, though.

The Spoogie family's plates were crammed full, just like everyone else's, but what seemed to distinguish their selections were the piles, hills, mounds, mountains of lima beans and baby fava beans. It suddenly occurred to me that they didn't care at all what they were eating. That no one in the place cared. I began to feel sick and depressed by what I was seeing, like I was losing my already-tenuous grip on reality.

But what I was seeing was real, alright. In fact, the dining room was packed full of happy, satisfied diners. I was apparently just letting my own biases and depression get in the way. What did my feelings matter, after all? Why was I so selfish? So I could see through the shit? Why not just slice through the shit and make myself a sandwich, just like slicing through bologna? Through the awful din, I began to make out the mooshing and chomping sounds of people who were really enjoying their meals. At the next table, a young couple were toying with a giant pile of either lima or fava beans on a huge, hideous bed of lettuce. All around the room, customers just kept snorting away in their food.

I noticed across the table that Old Man Spoogie was staring at me again. The Chief interrupted my musings, however. He needed a temporary audience of one before he was ready to unleash his wisdom and charm on the public, and it looked like that audience was going to be me. Spoogie just kept watching, and Wally wandered up to take our drink orders, just as the Chief began to get going.

"We're home, Reba," said the Chief. "I'm really going to miss this once we get to Washington."

I did my best to ignore him. He knew better than to be talking about Washington around here, the campaign still not having been officially announced.

"Want the usual, Chief?" asked Wally.

"Yeah, two binibombers," the Chief replied. "Say, Wally, do you think you'll ever open another place, like in D.C.?"

"Right in downtown D.C.?" Wally laughed. "Pigville? Huh, Chief? I might, if you'll be my first customer."

I was really hoping that the Chief would go for something beside the binibombers this time. It was going to be a long ride to Skankerville.

"Well, there's hope for the world then," said the Chief. "I'll let you know if I get there."

I gave the Chief a funny look, as if to say, *"Shut your big mouth. Whatever you're doing hasn't been announced yet."* I think he got the point.

"Two binibombers coming right up," said Wally. "Reba, what can I do for you? And can we get something else for the rest of you folks?"

The noise level was pretty high, and the Spoogies seemed to miss the offer of another round. I motioned to Wally to go ahead and take our drink orders. Maybe the Spoogies would order again in a few minutes when Wally came back around.

"Coming right up, Chief," Wally said as he prepared to leave. "I guess you're going to Skankerville. I hear there's going to be ten thousand there. Well, Reba, have you decided?"

I looked at the Chief. "I don't think I want a binibomber today, Wally. I'm driving. Just bring me a draft Blatz."

The giant fart went off outside again. I could hear the cheers in the parking lot. The building seemed to shake approvingly. Suzy, a waitress with long legs and a short skirt right up to her panties, came by with menus.

The Chief scanned the menu. "Suzy," he said, "give me two long legs, panties, and some mustard on the side. Bring my friend Reba here Mr. Hoagie's thick, juicy tube steak, the ten-inch one."

The Chief laughed. I thought I saw old Spoogie smile. Suzy grimaced and mumbled something that sounded like, "Those aren't the specials today, sir. I'll be back in a few minutes to take your order."

He was pissing me off again. "Hey Chief," I said, "you promised you were going to stop scanning me. And then you squicked Suzy. You've got to stop this. It isn't fair."

The Chief laughed some more and looked out at the waterfall. "Remember the last time we were here, Reba?"

"That was the time before last, Chief. The last time we were here they took you in on a stretcher and gave you the last rites."

"OK, Dickerman," the Chief completely ignored me. "Here it goes . . ."

He plowed right into the opening lines of his stump speech as I unfolded my checkercloth napkin and placed it my lap. His open mouth displayed rows of clean, white teeth, beautiful teeth, the kind of teeth you see in dental posters to show what's possible if you have the whole works. But with the Chief, they were real teeth. I don't think he ever had a filling, much less a cavity—except for all the cavities of the women he loved, all of which I know he wanted to fill. He said it was the dentist in him.

"When in the course of human events . . ." he paused. "How do you like that to start with?"

"Boss, I don't have time for this shit!"

The man made we want to scream. First, he had tormented me in the car, bringing up Elena as I tried to watch the road, logging trucks careening all over the place, cliffs coming up like the succulent lips of giant vaporous holes of death. And now he was hitting me with all this sexist shit. IT WAS BAD ENOUGH BEING HIS FUCKING SERVANT AND DRIVER! I was sick of this bullshit. We didn't need Lincoln. We needed action.

The Spoogies, meanwhile, ignored the Chief's ridiculous posturing. They just forked their platefuls down. Old man Spoogie kept staring at me, his eyes prying somewhere between my neck and my nipples, trying to get attention, rattling his fork, trying every once in a while to mouth something in my direction. I figured we still had time to order, but the Chief's crappy speechmaking was annoying the shit out of me.

The truth was, this stop at S&B was beginning to feel like some kind of fix. I smelled Durka's maneuvering. What if Spoogie was the one advancing the trip to Diehard? I stared at him for a moment and suddenly realized that it was true. For a second, our eyes met, and he gave me a secret signal to let me know that he knew that I knew, moving his left hand slightly across the table, leaving his forefinger resting on his butter pad and aiming it in my direction. That must be the code, I thought

Spoogie, however, apparently wasn't sure that I got the message. Just so there wouldn't be any doubt, he stuck his thumb into the butter pad and raised it up in front of his face, a square pad of butter impaled on his finger. He stared at the pad, his eyes crossing comically as he moved the butter pad closer to his face. After a moment, he returned the pad to the butter dish and disimpaled his finger. Then he sucked the fat off his index while continuing the cross-eyed act. He was the one, alright. He was doing the advancing this trip. I avoided his unrelenting stare and tried to regain my composure. The cushion farts were starting up again, and we still had to get our orders in. There'd be hell to pay if we didn't get to Skankerville on time. I signalled Spoogie to quit the code shit, but it took him a few minutes to get the message. That Durka really pissed me off sometimes.

Why Spoogie? I wondered.

What the hell; it was time to order.

"Listen, Chief," I suggested, "let's rest for a few minutes and look at the menus. Then you can tell me what your keynote is going to be today."

Suzy returned with the double binibomber and my draft Blatz. The Chief eyed her some more. He just wouldn't let up.

"If you weren't here, Reba," he glanced over in my direction for a second, "I'd say to Suzy, 'Hey, what's your special today, Suzy? Double pussy on Russian Rye? Give me two and one to go for my friend, over easy on the pussy. And give me a side of panties, au jus.'"

I did my best to admonish him, but I knew it was hopeless. "You know, Chief, you always wanted your own restaurant. Maybe now's the time, before you get too deep into politics. You're really disgusting. You know, you can really be a fucker."

The Chief's sexist shit. Durka's manipulations. It all made me sick.

My comments seemed to slow him down, but only for a moment. I looked at the guy, probably the most handsome and beautiful man in the country, probably, smart, articulate, courageous, a real leader. And now all he could think about was Suzy's cleve—and probably mine too. He started to laugh again, and I knew he was up to something. He downed half his double binibomber in a single bite. He shifted a little in his seat, grinding his ass on the cushion and blowing a huge fart. Across the room, a guy started laughing and blew one right back at us. Now old guy Spoogie started bobbing up and down in his seat, blowing several farts off sideways at the booth next to us, with a great big smile on his face.

The Chief looked over at the farting man across the room. "Hey, it's Jerry Grogan. Hey, Grogan, try this one." The Chief partially stood and then free-fell onto the cushion, giving off a really loud report. *"PfPFarrrt!"* Grogan replied with a *"PfPFarrt!"* of his own. Before you knew it, most of the customers in the restaurant were blowing cushion farts at each other. I had figured that sooner or later it would start, just like it always did, even before we could get our hands on the menus and hear the daily specials.

The room quieted down for a moment, as though everyone were waiting for someone to raise the ante. After a brief interlude, however, the sound of scarfing resumed, as everyone returned to their food. Suzy returned with the menus, and the Chief was ready for another binibomber.

Sur Le Table

SHELLDRAKE DECIDED TO GIVE Reba both barrels. She was really being a bitch today. He had been thinking about his speech on the way over in the van. His thoughts were beginning to take form, so he decided to blow out a big celebratory one, extemporaneously, just for the hell of it. He'd try to save most of his intestinal prowess for Diehard, where he'd have a bigger audience, but he knew that a lot of it would pour out of him involuntarily on the way to the S&B. Just for the edification of Reba. He couldn't stop it, once it started. It was his fatal flaw.

At any rate, he had to get on top of that speech. He did his best to contain his thoughts and to speak slowly and carefully. He knew deep down inside that it was about Elena that he was obsessing. Elena and all the events around Harry's death. Harry's demise had been conspicuously purposeful. The Chief had been careful not to say so publicly, but he suspected that Harry was murdered. He was certain of it, in fact. Elena believed that Harry's despondency over the burnt-up poodle might have produced a silent thrombosis, resulting in his death. She had done her best to convince him, to convince herself, but the Chief knew better. He had to remind himself again and again not to bring up the circumstances of Harry's murder in his new version of the kickoff address. It was bad enough bringing up Harry and Elena in the van now. Reba really had come pretty close to losing it. He decided to bide his time and wait for the right moment. He would let the evidence pile up on its own. But here at the S&B, the Chief decided to stick to the more immediate matters at hand.

"Here it goes, Reba. Listen carefully."

He didn't stand up until he'd finished his initial comments, but the room fell silent at once. All eyes and ears were focused on the Chief.

"Listen carefully." The only sounds in the room were the perestalsis, gurglings deep down inside of the more gluttonous of the diners, their chests and bowels arguing—and losing—a bitter case against nature.

Another giant erupted outside in the parking lot. Reba looked at her watch and noticed that nearly an hour had passed since they had arrived. They hadn't even gotten to place their orders yet. She noticed hungrily that some of the tables were piled high with Botero sandwiches and various bean dishes. A few groans could be heard, but most of the room erupted into applause as the Chief stood up and launched into the heart of his address. He raised and then drank from his binibomber to toast what appeared to be a new sculpture installation hanging down from the ceiling. Another artistic coup for Wally.

* * *

"Hey, Wally!" the Chief shouted, "is that some new art on the ceiling?"

Wally was busy bussing a table across the room, putting away a high chair for a family who'd just finished their meal. Everyone looked up in unison. About a dozen of the things were hanging down from the vaulted ceilings in the main dining room.

Wally finished his business and turned toward the Chief: "Chief, you're right. This is a new exhibit. It's made out of something called ripened olestra. It's sort of like Crisco, but different. I mold them up in my spare time."

I divided my attention between Wally's new art and this really cute baby a couple of tables away. I noticed that every time the cushion farts went off she would start giggling. She was watching the swaying art on the ceiling above her and kept giving me these delighted, knowing glances. Amidst the total chaos of the S&B, she kept smiling away at me. Suddenly, the ceiling installation began to sway more violently, and she became terrified. Her mother had to pick her up and hold her before she would quiet down. By the time she recovered, it was time for them to leave. The baby gave me a cheerful little wave as her dad carried her out of the room. She was so cute and happy and content. Seeing a happy baby like that made me feel hope, like I was growing a new heart. Seeing a sad baby was another matter entirely. And there were so many sad ones. Creating a world where all the babies could be happy and content was really what this campaign was all about. If the Chief couldn't lift the spirits of the people and blow out the corporate assholes, what else was there to hope for?

Wally piled some plates and glasses on another table near the windows. "Hey Reba," he whispered to me out of the corner of his mouth. He held an overflowing dishpan between the diners and me to keep them from hearing what he said. "It's not really straight olestra, not exactly. These are actually fecostalagtites. Be sure to tell the Chief. Don't worry about it, but just don't stand under one."

"Okay, Reba, here I go again," said the Chief, bending over to fork some of Spoogie Sr.'s fallen limas, gazing around the restaurant and back into the Botero Room. Behind that, hidden from the Chief's view, was a little church-style piano bar that Wally called the Tabernacle Room. Sometimes the Chief and I would stop by there for a beer and some refreshments. It offered more privacy than the other rooms in the S&B.

"Tribes and my friends and supporters," the Chief lifted his arms by his sides, "almost everyone will agree that we live in a deeply troubled society. We hate this society that breeds war and imperialism.

"The sexism, the ethnocentrism, the greed, the self-hatred have produced massive psychological problems and economic defeat for our peoples. It will be hopelessly difficult to reform the technology and industrial base of this country."

By now, the whole dining room had become silent again, with every face turning to listen to the Chief. I examined everyone closely, scanning the tables for signs of interest, distress, any kind of emotion that might give me a clue about what they felt and what they were thinking. Mainly, though, the faces were blank and sullen. Here and there was a set of bright eyes focused deeply on the Chief. Those faces, at least, were still alive.

Meanwhile, the Chief, probably one of the best extemporaneous speakers around, continued his speech, with a single note in front of him, his double binibomber in one hand and the other orchestrating the issues. The Chief could really be a spellbinder when he wanted to.

"We need to overwhelm the tide of technology and reverse the inhuman system that enslaves our people. We are in servitude. We hate what is in whitey, and what is now in us as well. We must raise the friction levels between the people and the machines until the machines die or we can kill them. If we can weaken the machine world and smash the remnants beyond repair, so that the system cannot be rebuilt, then we have a chance to have a full life again. Then we can regain our self-respect as people, as human beings."

The Chief paused to take a small bow, as the crowd cheered. Before he started again, he turned to me and whispered: "Well, Dickerman, how did you like the opening?" Suzy put some more menus on the table in front of us as the people in the crowd returned to their meals. The Chief, though, was ready to start up again.

"Chief, you can sit down now," I pointed out to him. "Everyone has started eating again." He sat down relunctantly, turning to gauge crowd reaction and then focusing his attention on the menu. He didn't really seem that interested in my reaction to his speech.

"Our specials today are . . ." Suzy began. "Oh, and Chief, the Botero is back. We're serving it on some nice N.Y. Jewish rye, or pumpernickel, if you like, with a side of capulet and a nice touch of bean-stuffed trout. These are Rogue River baby trout from the backyard."

Suzy pointed at the crashing waterfalls outside the window and waited for the Chief to respond, eyeing him with both longing and contempt. Finally growing impatient with him, she jutted out her chest in his direction, then started toward another table a few feet away.

The Chief turned and looked across the room to an alcove jammed with diners. "Hmm, the Botero, huh? I thought you only served it in the Botero Room. Last time . . ." The Chief's thoughts trailed off as his attention refocused on Suzy's breasts. She turned back toward us, but was clearly growing more and more impatient with the way he was treating her. The Chief could be a real asshole sometimes, especially with Suzy. For some reason, he loved to razz her about her panties and her panty hose. I still remember one time when he sang that song to her, "Don't Put Your Nose in My Panty Hose." It literally brought the house down. Suzy, however, wasn't amused. Not then. Not now.

"Well, Chief," she was doing her best to stick to business, "we used to serve the Botero only in the Botero Room. That's where you had yours, remember? When you crooned me with that stupid-ass panty hose song." I could tell that Suzy was getting pretty livid, but she held back and went on about the specials. The Chief didn't seem to notice, though. He was busy eyeballing her chest, which Suzy, in spite of her obvious irritation, kept pushing further and further toward his face.

"Since then, though, the Botero has become so popular that we had to bring it out to the main dining room." She glared at the Chief. "Our choice was either to rename the whole place the Botero Room or just to move it out here in the main dining area and keep the Botero Room as is.

"Frankly, Chief, we decided that the Botero might just be a passing fancy. We decided not to get caught up in big policy decisions about what to call the place where the people were eating it. Besides, it's just a sandwich special; why would you change everything around just for a special? We were of course wrong about Botero's popularity." Suzy dropped the issue and asked us what we wanted for dessert. The Chief didn't seem that interested, at the moment. Instead he helped himself to another forkful of the loose lima beans scattered around old Spoogie's plate. In fact, the whole Spoogie family was now sharing their lunch fare with the Chief. I noticed that Spoogie's daughter, Lil, was staring at the Chief.

Before the Chief could lift his third forkful of beans to his mouth, a voice reached him from across the room: "Chief Shelldrake, tell us about the carbuncle."

Suddenly, and in unison, the whole place was pleading with the Chief to get up and talk. "When are you going to blow the carbuncle, Chief? We want to know about the carbuncle. Or are you just another pusball yourself?"

I didn't recognize the woman who made the pusball comment. This was one of the first open challenges to the Chief's authority that I had heard since he gave his tarbaby speech a few weeks ago. I wondered if the woman might have been a plant.

The Chief looked around the room; the whole place was in turmoil, with people clapping and clamoring to hear him speak, to see how he would respond. He wasn't ready to respond to the pusball comment. Not yet, at least. While everyone yelled and applauded, he continued drinking his binibomber, all the while raising his left hand in gratitude for the display of support. People were standing up and yelling, "Chief! Chief! The carbuncle!" Wally came over to the table and whispered a word of encouragement to the Chief. The Chief nodded and then stood, but not before reaching over and groping another handful of beans from Lil's plate. As he walked away, Wally took a few beans for himself from the edge of Lil's generous helping, dropping them down his throat like gumdrops.

The Chief rose before the crowd, his long black hair down to his shoulders, his phenomenal countenance, his magnificent body. He was so handsome that I almost couldn't stand it. And, of course, there was the matter of that enormous lump bulging out from his jeans. The entire room was standing now, urging him on. "Carbuncle! Carbuncle! Tell us about the carbuncle!" The room began to shake from their stomping and clapping and cheering. I looked up and one of Wally's ceiling sculptures was sort of shivering precariously above the center of the room. It looked like it was about to detach from the ceiling and fall into the crowd. Wally's mounting job seemed to be coming apart. For all I knew, it could have been a deliberate plot to disrupt the Chief's speech. All at once, everyone in the room saw what I saw; all eyes were suddenly riveted on the dark, mushy, shivering fecostalagtite which was hanging by a thread above us, ready to drop, to plop right on top of us. It was a big long one, just the right consistency, the kind that the Africans said was a measure of good liver health.

Wally rushed across the room and pushed the dessert cart out of the way, just as the nasty thing crashed down onto the floor, smashing right between two tables. Huge cries erupted from every corner of the room, like cheers of vindication, like the cheers that erupt spontaneously in a cafeteria or a restaurant whenever a waitron accidentally drops a huge tray of dishes. The damned thing must have been eight feet long. The Chief stood there, an oasis of calm amidst the bedlam, totally nonchalant, sipping at his binibomber while the Spoogies beamed away in delight. Finally, the Chief signalled to the crowd that he was ready to speak again.

The Chief spoke slowly as he began, like he was still trying to decide whether the falling turd had been some type of omen from the blue or an ill-fated assassination attempt. "Reba," he would later confide to me, "the only way they can get me is to bury me under a pile of rocks. I don't think Wally could really be in on anything like that."

But now he was speaking to the crowd:

"It's not every day that Wally Amis can deliver on his promises." General laughter. "Good food and good entertainment for the people at affordable prices. And every mouthful is worth it. Let's give a big hand for Wally."

Wally was busy covering the stinky stalagtite with a blue tarp. He paused a moment from his task and raised his left hand in salute. The Chief waited until the moderate applause for Wally had died down. In the back of the room, someone started to sing a country dance tune, *"We're in the shithouse now. We're in the shithouse now . . ."* It looked like things were beginning to get out of control again. People were jumping up and down on their seats, blowing even bigger and nastier pillow farts than before. The Chief stood silently and waited until it all quieted down again. Finally, after the last errant fart had faded away, the Chief began to speak again.

"You want to hear about the carbuncles and the triple revolution, I know. And I want to talk about the 'pusball' matter. First, let's deal with the pusball matter."

He searched the faces in the dining room.

"I'll neither confirm nor deny that I'm a pusball."

Apparently that was the end of the matter, at least as far as the Chief was concerned.

"Before I begin about the carbuncles, though, I want to introduce those of you who don't know the Spoogies to Bill and his fine family. The Spoogies, the offspring of the great senior Spoogie. Over here is Mrs. Spoogie. Here's their daughter, Lil Spoogie. And, by the way, Spoogie Senior here held back those boche assholes at the Ardennes."

Mrs. Spoogie, a magnificently fat woman in a bulging, worn-out, sweat-stained Anne Taylor summer dress, a faint mustachio on her heavy upper lip, acknowledged the intro. I had heard about the Spoogies, but I had never met them before. Durka had mentioned that they were very distant relatives, probably by incest, and that they might be able to help in the campaign. Old Man Spoogie still had other things on his mind, though. He was flashing me a devilishly seductive smile and shining his deep blue eyes at me. I had to admit that he was pretty attractive, at least for a guy who had to be at least eighty-five. I felt like he was scanning right through my garments. All of a sudden, though, the Chief did something that grabbed the attention of both Spoogie Sr. and me.

In a burst of generosity, the Chief reached over, took little Lil's hand, and lifted her from her chair. She was right there next to him, right there in his shadow, but her shoes, I swear, were nearly three feet off the ground. All two hundred and fifty pounds of her were suspended in thin air. The Chief's left hand raised her effortlessly by her wrist; his right hand was still holding the binibomber. Lil was floating happily in the air. The Chief continued to hold her like that, with no apparent effort, and continued his speech.

"I know you have something to say, Lil. Folks, Lillian Spoogie graduated fourth grade today, and I think we should honor her with a toast. Let's hear it for Lil Spoogie."

The Chief raised the girl's arm in triumph, bent back his head in a forty-five-degree angle, and polished off the rest of the binibomber. Lil's chubby face beamed a thousand miles wide. Lil was clearly getting happier and happier by the minute. As the crowd quieted down to listen, Lil prepared to speak. That fucker Shelldrake had her wired, alright. He must have scanned her.

Lillian Spoogie

"EVERYONE HERE AT SLURP & BURP, and, hey, folks, can you hear me? Can you hear me over in the Botero Room? Am I loud enough?" Lil was enchanting the crowd. "I graduated fourth grade today from Tosterone Elementary. I wasn't first in my class. But in my writing class, we had to write poems. I wrote this one for my grandpa, and I read it at the graduation."

The Chief was gazing around the room at this point, watching the ceiling and keeping an eye on Wally. I knew the Chief wanted to give Wally the benefit of the doubt about the falling-turd incident, but the guy did have a reputation. He might try anything if you didn't keep an eye on him. I had heard through the grapevine that he was planning a test franchise in some big cities in the east called "Flatliners," filled with the real thing, if you know what I mean. I got sick to my stomach every time I heard about it. Wally was always playing the odds. He obviously figured that someday there would be more flatliners than assisted suicides and that he would be there to cash in on the surplus. He wasn't sure that he had the time, however, because the S&B and his other franchise plans were very time-consuming. There had also been rumors that he might team up with Mortons or the Palm group and do an upscale hospice steak house.

While I was thinking about Wally, Lil droned on and on to the crowd. Around the room, people began to gossip openly among themselves. I couldn't tell what was going to happen next. For a second, Lil turned away from the crowd and whispered something in the ear of elder Spoogie. The old guy listened intently, nodding and staring into her eyes, his face not six inches from her. Lil slowly withdrew from him and stood up again, her dutchy clothes supporting her imperious but obviously still preadolescent face. The girl was a little tub of lard, alright, a real carnival fatso with the headlights turned on. Ten years old and two hundred and fifty. I mean, forgive me, but *please.* I could see some tears starting to well up in those fat, puffy sockets; she was barely holding it together. I reached over for a loose napkin near a side of pestezolli topped with a large scoop of boiled latherbeans. Original, I thought when I saw it, but not for me. Not today, at least. I knew that I had better eat lightly or my driving would definitely suffer. So far, I had only ordered one beer. Anyway, I pushed the napkin as discretely as possible in Lillian's direction. She took it, wiped her bulbous nose, and gave me a really sweet smile. I could tell now that she was still on top of things, even through all the emotion.

"My poem is called 'The End,'" said Lil tentatively, "but before I start, I need to say that I don't have the poem with me. The teacher, Mrs. Grossman, wanted to keep it, and I let her have my only copy. I'll try to remember it for you, though. Grandpa says he knows I can do it."

Her somber face and puffy, swollen eyes left me worrying that she would never make it. A lone tear rolled down her left cheek and across her chubby lip. She wiped it away with her sleeve. She stood there for a minute or two before she was composed enough to begin. Shelldrake, who was once again holding her at his side, gripped her wrist tighter but in no way painfully. He was as tenderly attentive toward Lil as he would have been toward Mary's little lamb.

Lil recited the words slowly and deliberately, word by word, one following the next in magnificent procession. Slow, to the point. It seemed as if she were almost speaking in slow motion:

The End

The shadow cutting across the wall.
The knife cuts through the bread.
Life still had not a call
Of the ball that dropped them dead.

The scene of Hiroshima, to this,
Could have been a shower,
But the people will see the power,
Double in the hour.

And when you get your diarrhea,
You start to think about Korea.
And your gut goes green
With a broken spleen,
And your cunt falls off in smithereens.

We were all totally stunned by her subtle words and her magificent delivery. Lil wasn't just fat; she was deep, too. For a moment, the room was filled with the noise of all. Then, from the deepest corners of the room, the cheers and applause began to build and build until the whole S&B was filled with the roar of the appreciative crowd. Lil collapsed, exhausted and sobbing, into her grandpa's arms. The poor old guy was completely crushed beneath her. It took a good ten minutes to untangle the two, so his suffering went on for a while.

The Chief seized the moment, addressing the room in a voice loud and clear enough to pierce through the cheering and applause. His words even reached the drinkers and diners in the back of the cavernous Botero Room.

"You want to know how to blow the carbuncle?" he asked the crowd. "Well, what about the truth of Lillian Spoogie? That kind of truth can do the trick.

"I know there are folks who want me to blast the carbuncle, destroy it all at once, completely ignoring the dangers of a full carbuncle blowout. In my opinion, the blowout approach is very risky, much too great a risk, in fact, at this time. And I have said as much during this campaign. I know there are those among you who disagree, however. But I, for one, believe that we should exercise restraint so that we won't unnecessarily endanger ourselves and those around us. We must be cautious and prudent if we're to reap the real rewards from the blastoffs. Of course, you realize that there are many different kinds of blastoffs.

"I won't deny that for the last three weeks we have gotten a torrent of telephone calls from the late Dr. Edward Teller. Of course, you know who he is. He's called the father of the hydrogen bomb. And now he's directed his attention to space marbles."

The Chief looked around the room; he could tell that he had the place in the palm of his hand. Everyone in the crowd was staring intently at him, taking in his every word.

"And why is Eddie Teller calling so much?" The Chief paused for effect; every eye was fixed on him in rapt attention. "I'll tell you why. Because he's a schmucklevits. And that's only part of it. He's recently been diagnosed with cerebral proctosis. And I can assure you of one thing: There's no space marbles on Eddie's horizon. Take my word for it."

With that, the Chief suddenly sat down and dug into his entree, the Botero Special and the Flatulettuce Salad, the latter composed of huge piles of organically grown greens and beans. It had been a month since he'd eaten one, and he decided to order it again. It didn't taste as good as it usually did, though. That was the thing about the S&B; the food could be inconsistent from one visit to the next. For instance, the Chief noticed that today Wally was aggressively pushing the Almond Bean Ground and Grilled Salmon Compote to the customers at the next table. He heard Wally talking and he looked over. The Chief could tell something was up by the way Wally was taking orders and making recommendations.

"You want four Slurpy Noodle Bean Soups and three Junkyard Dogs. And, Bill, you want the Flats Domino Pudding on Baby Toast Points."

To Wally's credit, the Chief noticed that he tried to sell the ABGGSC with sides of kale, limas, and collards. It didn't seem to be working, though. Or was it? It was hard to tell by the blank faces of the diners. Wally failed, or did he? Interesting question. The Chief knew how effective Wally was with point-of-sale, face-to-face transactions. He also knew that Wally sometimes had a hidden agenda. Maybe he was pretending to push the Salmon Compote, but really wanted to move the L and O.

"I'm telling you, folks, you sure can have the salmon if you want, but I think you'll be a lot happier with the Junkyard Dogs. We also have platter-sized portions of liver and onions for two. Shorty's doing a nice job with liver and onions right now. If you go for that, we've got a wonderful companion dessert, you know, the Deep Pile Pie, which really goes with the L and O. And folks, that's the original, the real Original Deep Pile Pie."

The Chief smiled, admiringly. That Wally really did know how to make a sale. Wally bent down and took one of the Deep Pile Pies off the bottom shelf of the dessert cart. He put it in front of the Chief. "Chief Shelldrake, we love you. We love you for what you're about to do for the country, and we love you for who you are."

The Chief was visibly touched by Wally's generosity. There were few things better, after all, than a really nice dessert from Wally.

* * *

All around us, people were staring at Lil, many of them still cheering and asking for more. Wally had returned his attention to what remained of the dangling turd mobile, which was dancing and waving on the ceiling. By the worried look on his face, I was pretty sure that the one that fell earlier had been an accident.

From one corner of the room, I began to hear a group of people trying to imitate the sound of the broken carbuncle. I could hear that disturbingly familiar oozing sound. It was definitely time to get out of the S&B, and pronto, and I let the Chief know it. We divvied up the checks, with the Chief leaving some additional money on the table. Old Man Spoogie had been searching through his pockets but ended up a little short. He only had about twelve cents, which he threw ceremoniously on the table. "That oughta hold them bastards," he muttered and then sat back, looking over at all two hundred and eight-five ovirdubois of his granddaughter. She was a fine young poetess, and you could tell he was proud of her.

"But we haven't had dessert yet," protested Lil's mom, as the rest of us prepared to leave. A long, loud collective *"uuuuuhhh"* erupted around the table. But the woman wanted her dessert, and she wouldn't be intimidated. "We always look at the desserts, honey," she insisted, motioning to her husband Spoogie to call the waitress. Spoogie smirked in my direction, waved his arm behind and above Mrs. Spoogie, and pointed his index finger to the back of her head for all to see, pushing his finger up and down like he was drilling a hole. He never touched her, and she never noticed what he was doing or why everyone was laughing. Everyone except me, that is. It really pissed me off that he would do that; it showed a real lack of character and respect. Or had the signal meant something else entirely and been directed at someone else in the room? The whole campaign thing and all the intrigue around the Chief was really beginning to make me paranoid.

The Chief, however, showed no indication he had seen Spoogie's insulting gesture against Mrs. Spoogie. And Mrs. Spoogie, for her part, seemed absolutely unconcerned about anything except the dessert tray, which still hadn't arrived at our table for her inspection. Finally, she caught the eye of Suzy, who was just coming out of the kitchen and carrying several platters of entrees. The first chance she got, Suzy worked her way through the crowded tables with the desserts, sidestepping the tarp under which Wally had temporarily hidden the fallen turd, finally delivering the overloaded dessert cart right under Mrs. Spoogie's nose.

"What I've got for you today is inspired," Suzy began, searching the eyes of each of us for some reaction. "Ken, our pastry cook, is really a doll, and he came up with the Carmel Icicle Frozen Olean Pudding Bar that you see on the menu there. He says it really melts in your mouth, and when he says Olean, he doesn't mean Olean, New York. We also have our regular Botero, Jr. Creme Flume, sprinkled with powdered polysaccharides. And I still have several Deep Pile Pies left, just like the Chief's, splattered with some sexy chocolate you-name-its."

Old Man Spoogie noticed that his son, who had apparently been embarrassed by his father's earlier display, was trying to sneak some additional change onto the table.

"Dad, that was only eleven cents," the younger Spoogie explained when he realized that his action had been discovered. "Suzy deserves more than that."

"Well, you're right, son," said Old Man Spoogie, "she certainly does. If I was your age I'd be forking Suzy right here at the table. When your mom was here . . ." At this, Old Man Spoogie trailed off, reaching across the plate and pushing a few of the remaining lima beans that he had spilled earlier into the pile of tips in the middle of the table. "Well, that oughta hold them bastards. How much is that, Suzy?"

"Well, Grandpa, it looks like a bunch of lima beans to me."

"Suzy, I guess I just can't tell that foreign money anymore."

"Suzy," interrupted Mom Spoogie, "I'll take one of each for take-out. We'll eat them in the car. We have to make it to Belfair by evening; I know Dad wants to stop at a casino over there."

"Sure, Mom," answered Suzy, this time completely freaking me out. Mom? All the time that I had known Suzy, I had never realized she was a Spoogie. I guess I had never heard her last name. I certainly would never have connected her with this bunch.

"Take Dad to the casino where he can see all the girls naked like he does. Shit, Mom, the way he looks at me sometimes, I think he's going to do an incest on me."

Suzy turned to me, sensing my confusion. "This is my mom. Mom, this is my friend, Reba Dickerman. Remember when I worked at Paco Taco? Reba was my best friend then." Mom's huge countenance bounced like Jell-O. She shot me a big smile and said, "Pleased to meet you, Miss Dickerman; my son Bill speaks very highly of you." Well, that certainly confirmed my suspicions that Spoogie Jr. was the one advancing the Chief.

The Chief and I followed the Spoogies outside. Their RV was parked just a few spaces from our van. I wondered what would happen next and what fresh bit of news I would discover. There were certainly some weird vibes in the air. It was astonishingly quiet in the parking lot, given the cacophony that had greeted us when we first arrived. Big Paul just stood there silently, his huge handcrafted bag of a crotch towering at least twenty feet above our heads. I wondered what was up. Looking around, I noticed a bunch of workers fiddling with the fuses in an electrical box at the base of Paul's enormous feet. A blown fuse? That must have been why there were no sounds coming from his ass or his mouth. The poor guy was paralyzed, at least temporarily.

As I stood there watching, the Chief angled over to where the men were working, apparently unsuccessfully, with the switches and fuses. I knew that I had to get the Chief out of there as quickly as possible. We couldn't afford to waste any more time. Once he got lost in the crowd again, it would take forever to pull him out of there. But he was in his element now, clearly working the crowd, and there was nothing I could do but hope for the best. As the other men watched, he poked around in one of the electrical boxes behind Paul's right leg, pressed a couple of switches, and before I knew it, Paul's larynx and anus had fired right up again. What could I say? The elder Spoogie stood over to my left, cackling uncontrollably at the warm-up belches beginning to issue from Paul's giant lips. The Chief started back over my way, eyeing Old Man Spoogie as he did. The Chief approached, taking the old man's hand and holding it up in a victory pose for everyone to see. Both men's eyes were damp with tears as they waved to the parking lot crowd. "It's good to see Paul back on his feet," the Chief said privately to Old Man Spoogie.

Old Man Spoogie slipped his slender arm as far as he could around the massive waist of the Chief. "Look out for the long knives," he cautioned. "When you get to Washington, D.C., make sure you walk down the center of the hallways. Always stay in the middle. They'll be trying to stab you from the dark corners. I know it well. I seen it happen more than once."

Just then, the two men separated as Mom Spoogie pulled up to the curb in a bright red RV. Lil was sitting beside her in the passenger seat in front. As fat as she was, she was still so short that her face was level with the glove compartment instead of the front window. Old Man Spoogie crawled weakly into the back. Bill Spoogie was nowhere to be seen. Now was the time to make our getaway and lose the whole Spoogie clan once and for all. I decided that I didn't like the guy, after all. I'd have to tell Durka to keep these schlmozzles out of the campaign.

* * *

We shot down Rt. 589 right past Blotz Corners. Just past the Blotz Grocery and the Canteen there was an unpaved bypass around Salmonville. By going cross-country, I decided, it could take at least thirty minutes off the trip. We cut right on through. I also wanted to keep clear of our new advance man, Bill Spoogie. I sure as hell didn't want to get hung up in Spoogie's scheduling any further. Damn that Durka. She was determined to keep an eye on the Chief. Probably on me, too. But why did she have to get Spoogie mixed up with it all. Bill Spoogie and his whole family of Spoogies.

I had to hope that heading for Salmonville would shake Spoogie from the trail. The Chief didn't seem to notice the abrupt detour that I made, though he did wave back as an old couple trudging on the road cheered us on.

There were about ten cars in the Blotz parking lot, maybe eight beat-up pickups and two beaters. The regulars, I guessed. Two guys stood with cans of beer near a one-wheeled cycle. They both waved to us as we passed. Everything else we passed was empty—stores, gas stations, feed barns— all shut down and deserted.

Meanwhile, I couldn't believe all the ideological crap that the Chief was pushing at me. I knew that most of what he said was true, theoretically, but, buddy, if we don't act on our beliefs at some point, then we're all just dead. As dead as this abandoned town and this abandoned roadside we were passing through.

I was in this campaign all the way, though. Don't get me wrong. I just hoped that the Chief here had the stamina to steer his way through all the crap and stay the course. And even if *he* could, could the rest of us match his endurance? I'd followed him for ten years, ever since all these ideas started taking hold in his mind. Pull the industrial world apart, de-nut the military, pull the plug on these leeches running the corporations. If we couldn't at least get that far, we were goners. Believe me, the time had come to act. We'd wasted too much time and energy talking.

"Very cultured bullshit, Chief," I finally said. "That's what it sounds like, very, very *cultured* bullshit. But if you must talk so much—and I guess you must—I think that you at least need to talk in shorter sentences, so your supporters can figure out what in the hell you're talking about. It could play in Skankerville, I suppose, but if it doesn't, don't come crying in my lap." I paused, correcting myself before he could get the wrong idea. "I mean, on my shoulder.

"Why don't you just say it the way you mean it?" I asked. "Talk about the Triple Revolution and your platform and what you're actually going to do, not just talk in this Harvard-like phony intellectual crap. No one wants to hear that shit."

I decided to push the Chief to the wall. He deserved it after all the shenanigans he'd been putting me through. "I'm willing to listen to you prep your remarks, Chief, but I've got so much on my plate now that I'm seriously approaching overload. Complete burnout. Do you want me to crash this heap off the cliff down with those fucking cows? Don't you realize we have a major food crisis and this whole thing with the fucking Pablum Division? I've got Sunman on my ass. And Nighthorse and his cockamamie military plans. And now he's offed a couple of these little fucking mercenaries. We've got the campaign to worry about now, and we're heading for Skankerville and Diehard. And all you can worry about is this fucking intellectual bullshit. It's no time for joking around. Horse should have brought those guys back alive. And on top of everything else, there's the little matter of the elk's head."

I was as stern and serious as I could be, but the Chief didn't seem to be getting my message. He just sat there, staring blankly out the front window.

* * *

We were bulleting down the road now. It must have been about an hour since we'd left the S&B. The Chief had fallen asleep. It must be all those binibombers. God! Look at him! The campaign was on. This was it, and the Chief was taking a fucking nap. In my mind, I kept arguing with him about his priorities for the campaign, his endless focus on ideas, his lofty, over-intellectualized style of speech. He had a great delivery when it came right down to it; he just needed a lot less of the intellectual bullshit. A big vocabulary was okay, I suppose. But he should just tell it like it is. If all the other parts of the campaign came together and the Chief kept telling the people the truth, we just might make it.

The real burning question, however—and the thing that was driving me crazy—was trying to figure out why these driving trips with him made me so horny. Just thinking about that lump in his pants, I could feel the dampness spreading on the seat beneath me. All these thoughts and feelings were making me dizzy with desire. I needed to slow down. I couldn't handle it all at once. Things were getting much too complicated.

As I pressed my foot lightly on the brake, we passed a highway sign that read *"Stella, 87 miles."* At last, a familiar landmark to steady my nerves.

Slowing Down

THE CHIEF SAW THEM BEFORE I DID. I thought he was out cold and totally unconscious. He was way ahead of me, though, shouting for me to stop immediately. He pointed over to the right side of the road. A group of people were down in the gully, four women dressed in striped jail garb. It was totally incredible. We had come across a chain gang. Hovering above the women was one of the bigheaded Mongolian droppa dwarfs, dressed in military black and holding a large black gun. From his shoulders to his knees, he wore bandoliers.

I suddenly recognized the girls, and I was pretty sure I recognized the other one, too. I careened the van, skidding toward the empty space to the right and almost catapulting down a steep cliff. The first one I could see was Rosemary, who was standing in the front and holding a shovel. In my haste, I stopped the van just short of what looked like an endless drop. It was really a close one. What a shame it would have been, I thought, for the Chief to go like that right now without accomplishing his mission.

The van stopped right on a dime, though, its brakes screeching dramatically in the gravel on the roadside. The Chief jumped out of the car and walked quickly across the asphalt. He towered over the little soldier like he was a street-sweeper and the little guy was his broom. In a single, swift motion, the Chief jerked the gun right out of the little guy's hand and hurled it over the cliff. I could hear it crashing through the trees and bouncing off the rocks below.

The four striped prisoners, still holding their chains in their hands, seemed totally stupified to see the Chief appear suddenly like that, out of nowhere, and just lift the guy from the ground. The Chief held his captive at arm's length and scanned his face. The name tag read *"Ding."* The Chief, smiling now, pulled the guy over to my side of the van. His yellowed, leprous face, which was pocked deeply like Noriega's ugly mug, gave no clues to the Chief, other than that he wasn't one of ours. I knew who he was, though, even if the Chief didn't recognize him. I had definitely seen him before, at Buzzozzi's lab.

"Reba, let's get the girls." He was right; first things first. We could make a decision about what to do about Ding later. I made my way as fast as I could down the side of the road into the ditch where they were standing, huddled together and completely terrified.

The four were chained together at the wrists and ankles. They were Cheryl's buddies from Oyster Bay: Mallow, Dot, and Rosie. The fourth one I didn't know. I learned later that her name was Carey; she was a friend of Mallow's from Chicago. They were so scared. Shitless. Speechless. I hugged each one of them and did my best to comfort them. They were so scared that they weren't crying or making any noise. Their eyes, though, were filled with moist fear. Finally, one of them spoke up, "They've got Nighthorse. They took him. They took him. Cheryl got away."

I did my best to comprehend, but the whole scene completely overwhelmed me. The four of them were wailing now, and the shock of it all was starting to get to me. I held them, tried to stop their crying and screaming, but I really thought that I might scream myself. I just kept holding them, and they held onto me.

When I finally looked up, I could see the Chief up on the road about seventy-five yards away, still holding his monstrous little prisoner at arm's length and staring him straight in the eye. The Chief was trying to scan Ding, or whatever his name was. I could have told him that it wouldn't work, though. Even if you could scan one of those bastards, you wouldn't get anything worthwhile.

The girls cheered up when they saw the Chief manhandling their former captor up on the roadside. They yelled and whooped, and their chains clanked as we broke suddenly into a spirited freedom dance. On the road above us, Shelldrake was still trying futilely to scan the guard.

* * *

"We'll take them to Diehard, Reba," said the Chief. "What do you want to do with Ding?"

"Chief, I hate to say it, but I think we better take Ding along and turn him back in at the lab. I really wonder how he got out."

I looked closely at Ding. I tried to remember everything that I could about him from the lab. Buzzozzi's techmen had brought him in a few weeks ago and had retrained him. But here he was retrained again, but by someone else, and to guard their prisoners. But whose prisoners were they? And why on this road of all places? Maybe he had been given a message of some kind. We could question him, but, then, they didn't talk much. I didn't bring it up to the Chief. Ding definitely wouldn't be saying anything. His massive head was really disgusting on his tiny body. The little guy definitely belonged back at the lab. He was way over the age limit. He might actually have been a grandpa to those guys that Nighthorse had brought over to the office to meet the Chief. He was either from Bing, Bang, or Bong, one of those tribes in Montana where they rounded them up in the first place. I could tell from the way he looked at me that he knew I had seen him before, probably when they were testing the droppas for their multiple masturbation research. To test their prolificacy, the droppas were required to jerk off again and again, basically nonstop, with us there watching them. He had watched me as he masturbated. Not a pleasant thought.

I had to admit that I had been stunned at the time by the size of their gonads. I mean, they were really enormous compared to the size of their bodies. Ding, if he was the one I'm thinking about, kept staring at me throughout the testing, finally shooting a hot load through the bars at me that a technician managed to catch in a Ball jar. So much for that.

After I had finally gotten the women secured in the van, the Chief called me over, the droppa still at his side, and questioned me again.

"He's a pretty old one," said Shelldrake. "How long do these guys last, anyway?" He didn't wait for me to answer, but gave me an order instead: "Dickerman, Horse tells me you're training these guys in parade rest. Do your thing."

I commanded Ding to assume parade rest, and he complied immediately. The Chief and I secured him on top of the van, tying him down with bungee cords. Ding blinked a couple of times as we strapped him down, but he remained completely silent and in formation.

The women were crying and laughing at the same time, still completely stunned by our fortuitous arrival. Rosemary examined her swollen wrists and the dark bruises covering her arms. The girls began to remove their prison garb, and I noticed that they were completely naked underneath.

The Chief opened the back of the van and got out some blankets, which we gave to the girls to cover their nakedness. I thought the Chief handled the whole thing pretty well.

Diehard

WE GOT OUT OF THE CAR, and I told Dickerman to wait. I had to go behind a shed for a leak. I was really letting it out. I showered the wall for at least a couple of minutes. The last triple binibomber milkshake had left my bladder ready to blow at any moment. Reba's leftover Flatulettuce Salad and my binibombers produced an unbeatable combination, tastewise—but maybe an unwinable one, too, stomachwise. I could barely walk to the back of the shed and was about ready to blow it out in every direction. The girls had livened up a little by this time and were placing bets on whether or not I would make it to the shed before I blew sky high. I would never admit it to Wally; it would hurt his feelings. But I think I ate and drank a little too much this time.

I still felt a little shaky after I finished my business, and I practically crawled the whole way back to the van. I could barely get my fly zipped up. In the backseat, the girls were polishing off the leftovers from Reba's lunch that I hadn't already devoured. Someone lit up a dubie, and the smoke was so thick that I could hardly see out the front window. Smoking a dubie with Wally's delicious cuisine—a mixture of Joker and Destroyer, I thought to myself.

Somewhere between Oblivion and Diehard, we hit two huge potholes, one right after another. Seeing it coming, the girls screamed and then groaned at the inevitable. Dickerman must have been sound asleep at the wheel. We could hear the thuds against the roof, where Ding was bouncing. "Hey! Ding-a-Ling Ding!" I shouted out the window, and everyone laughed. "Hey, shit, Dickerman," I then said, "watch those potholes or we'll start aiming the chuckers in your direction."

Just up ahead, a sign read *"Diehard, 46 miles."* Reba seemed to have recovered her senses, but I thought we'd better stop and take a rest break, for my still insurgent stomach, if for no other reason. We pulled over alongside an empty, broken-down chicken franchise that had once been known as the Bold Onion. Some asshole from New York City had come planning to open stuff like that all around this part of the country, especially around the casinos. Those fucking Jack in the Boxes all over the place. I couldn't stand it. At least this one had failed. Give me the Slurp & Burp anytime.

To get Dickerman to slow down, everyone in the car had been forced to yell "Pull over!" at the same time. She was a complete wreck by the time we got her out of the car. We carried her to some soft grass and laid her out where she could rest for a while. She was a hell of a woman—and a hell of a driver—that Dickerman. Despite everything I've heard, I still think she was driving me around better than Burroughs did when he went down to Mexico. While Dickerman rested, I talked with the rest of the girls and saw just how badly they had been battered and bruised by the chains.

* * *

Desdemona: "I have to admit that I got a little concerned. The Chief just stood there, staring at us, scanning us, seeing right through us into our orgone. All I could think of was that our last three days had been anything but fun."

* * *

Reba: "We all got out to get some air. There wasn't much talking at first. We all stared up at Ding, now covered with dust.

"We just stood around looking at him. I knew from the beginning that there had to be a decisive conclusion to Ding, and I could think of several possibilities. He was in a small heap, harnessed to the roof of the van. He didn't make any noise, though, the whole time."

* * *

Chief Shelldrake: "It was really weird. This was the third one I'd seen in the last forty-eight hours: the two young ones that Horse brought in and left in the dumpster, and then this guy, who could be their grandpa. And they put a Ho Chi Minh face on him.

"What's this guy doing running a chain gang with the beautiful native women? Oh, shit, the thought of Desdemona naked.

"I opened the back of the van and got out the cooler. I gave water to the girls. 'Where's Cheryl?' I asked them right off.

"We moved further away from the van so we could talk, and I started in with the questions again. 'Des, tell me what's happening. Where's Cheryl? I don't think the guy can hear you.'

"'Well, we heard they lip read, but right now, he's looking the other direction.'

"I watched her. She was one of Cheryl's best friends. She lived in the forests south of here, near Testerone where the Spoogies are from. I was completely mystified about this chain gang. I hid my ignorance, which was pretty much total. I'd just have to play it dumb. Up until the time Nighthorse first brought them in, I had heard about the mercetemps but hadn't really had a chance to get acquainted. I hadn't thought anything more about it since then.

"I'm chained to my desk most of the time working on the land claims, and now that the campaign is beginning to open up, real time is short. It was last Thursday when he brought Ping and Pong over. Thursday, right? That would be the day before yesterday. You have to entertain people that come in the office or at least humor them. But I never really gave much of a shit about them. I had already received reports from my staff about sightings. There didn't seem to be any women, which did seem a little strange. But there's so much weird stuff going on with genes and shit that inventing a new kind of cop or foot soldier or people for Wackenhut just didn't seem that much out of the ordinary.

"Like I said, there were only a few of them at first, but now they seemed to be all over the place. This whole chain gang thing: could it have been staged? Were the MT midgets being thrown into the Northwest to stymie our campaign? That's probably a little politician's paranoia. But, you know, you have to consider every possibility.

"I kept watching Desdemona, her volatile breasts quivering as she spoke. I grew up with her parents. As the fear began to disappear from her eyes, I looked to the other women. Diedre had disappeared into the bushes to take a leak. And Rhonda was sitting on a rock, drinking from her water bottle. I looked up at the sky. It must have been nearly 3 p.m., I figured. We could probably still get to Skankerville in a couple of hours, if nothing else happened."

Durka Takes the Chief Home

DURKA MADE A ROUGH ESTIMATION of Shelldrake's office. She hadn't been there since Wednesday, when they were going over their campaign strategies. At that point, he had seemed alright. His binge personality was on hold, and he had raised his considerable and valid concerns about her plans to push the Triple Revolution. She was confident, though, that he accepted the Carbuncle Theory. The goddamn country was like a giant carbuncle. Spearing it would explode the pus from which rivers of white gunk would gush out. Look out that you don't get swept away in the stuff. Without taking the proper precautions, you could easily be washed and drowned.

The Chief thought it was a good strategy. But their respective staffs hadn't quite come together on tactics yet. The differences were causing some serious friction at times. Durka knew there had to be differences. She and the Chief were different people. The whole thing came down to timing, really. The Chief argued his case for methodical dismantling while Durka wanted to blast the fuckers into the stratosphere.

Durka wanted a tough campaign and expected a fight to the death. It was a long way to the White House. But if he made it to the top, they were going to turn this skankball country around. It was the only way. The campaign was also a chance for them to get the word out so that people everywhere could start making changes. The country needed a one-two punch to explode those pus bags. Durka had lived in mud all her life, and she knew how to throw it. The really pathetic thing, though, was the huge number of people who would rather have bingo and pachinko than justice. Those people bewildered and disgusted Durka. Well, look out, folks. It's coming whether you like it or not. And don't get swept away in the slime as it slides by.

Though the outer office was dark, a light shone through the glass door to his office. Once she turned on the lights out front, she noticed piles of faxes on the floor that had apparently come in since everyone went home. She'd have to check those out, but first, she had to see about the Chief. Once inside, she took a good look at Shelldrake, motionless, dead out of it, arms by his side, but Durka could hardly ignore the look of peace and serenity on her husband's face. When was the last time she had seen him like that? She left him alone for the time being and returned to Barb's office.

Knowing everything that poor Barb had been through with the Chief lately, Durka decided to straighten up a bit. She picked up a bunch of faxes and put them on Barb's desk. The top one drew her attention.

Eastern Canada Tribune
Special from Reuters

July 29—Canadian Mounties parachuted into the disputed lichen fields of northwest Greenland today to demonstrate Commonwealth solidarity with the U.S. White House, according to government sources. The air drop of nearly 500 Mounties apparently was a secret plan to forestall native Indian claims for the lichen harvests that were supposed to start nearly two weeks ago.

In a violent encounter, according to government spokesman Bob Peabaddy, six Indians were shot and killed, and one more was critically wounded, shot in the face and belly, after violating curfews and attempting to enter the lichen fields to scavenge for food.

According to Peabaddy, the parachutists' landing was arranged earlier this year as a contingency plan, if matters continued to deteriorate with the Indians over control of the lichen fields. "It's strictly a routine maneuver," Peabaddy explained, "since law and order must be kept and the Indians are way out of line saying that the lichen is theirs."

World Indian Councilman Bob Armstrong condemned the military maneuver as more "agitprop bullshit imperialism from Washington and their stooges in Ottawa." Asserting that the Indians have been harvesting the lichen fields for thousands of years, Armstrong called for tough tactics from the North American tribes to defend their ancient lichen fields. "Whitey kills us; we kill whitey!" Armstrong screamed, holding up what he claimed was an 1815 treaty guaranteeing permanent Indian possession of the lichen lands. "Estatas Unitas has never had a treaty it didn't break, and has had plenty it never signed," Armstrong lamented.

Peabaddy said that the governments of U.S. and Canada, while sympathetic to Indian claims for the lichen, called on the Indians to observe continental laws and regulations. He insisted that the 1815 treaty is a "sham." Meanwhile, according to U.S. military sources, a battalion of U.S. reservists will be flown into Greenland to provide security while the lichen is being harvested.

Durka laid the fax on Cheryl's desk and looked quickly at the others. The whole thing pissed her off, but she already knew long ago what the outcome was going to be. There could never be any trust, any settlement, any understanding with the colonialists. Even if they didn't need the lichen for themselves, they'd make sure the Indians wouldn't be allowed to touch it. There was already talk of either sending it to Somalia for the starving millions there or dousing it with herbicides to poison the food supply. Enraged by the white man's phony parliaments and toad-shit-ridden congresses, Durka knew that there was only one way to go. And that was just where she was headed. To overthrow, once and for all, the bastions of this sorry bunch of pigfucks calling themselves human beings. By the time we're finished, she thought to herself, the fuckers'll be mainlining their own crapola.

"They'll felch each other out the gazoo," Durka said out loud, laughing as she did, "until whitey is nothing but a majestic molehill of shit from some clogged toilets." Durka loved politics, even the worst of it. The ravaged, angry bitterness inside her somehow flowered into a dark but good-natured humor. If it wasn't fun anymore, then it was time to get out. That was the lesson she had learned from her old friend Morty Wasko during the Vietnam War. Morty led the Jewish Peace Faction of the national mobilization; he was always trying to shlup her in the back of the shul. Trying to impress her with his sense of responsibility, he'd shape his yarmulke into a condom and wrap it around his thing. Durka thought it was pretty pathetic.

"'If it isn't fun anymore,' Morty was always saying, 'it's time to hang it up. If we Jews and blacks can't mobilize together, we're goners.'" She tried to picture his scrunched-up face as he stroked his Vietnam Spring penis right there in front of her and then collapsed in patriotic delirium, spraying a generous load of jism across the face of Eugene McCarthy. The two of them were working together, designing posters for McCarthy's campaign. They smeared the sticky, warm fluid into the candidate's smiling mug, nailed the poster to a stick, and used it the next day in a death march around the White House. Morty loved politics, that was for sure.

Durka examined the rest of the faxes. There were several updates on the lichen crisis. From Paris, there came the claim that Waldheim had just met with the Pope. He was preparing to negotiate a final settlement of the war in Croatia, Serbia, and Bosnia, but was urging that the Transylvanian militia be used as a peacekeeping force. Waldheim apparently believed that it was doable with UN assistance, provided the Pope gave his full support to the peace plan. Totally out-of-ass, thought Durka.

The heading from another fax caught her eye, from UPI in Washington.

White House Wary of Indian Power Bid

The story was old stuff, written by UPI White House reporter Blaine Thompson, an undated filler talking about new filings of land claims that effectively returned most of the eastern U.S. to Indian control. The story had to be at least a month old, she reasoned, since those claims had been filed in May. Durka decided to check the claims register on Barb's desk, just to make sure, and she opened a notebook coded with the filing dates. She was right. The matter had been completed on May 12. Now late July, Thompson was apparently just catching up with the filings, or else the White House had just heard about them.

Durka finished reading the new faxes. There were at least a couple dozen, but nothing new or noteworthy. She took the messages and laid them on Cheryl's desk. The Waldheim news fax pepped her up a little. Who would be a better negotiator in Croatia, after all, than a Nazi war criminal? No time for Waldheim now, though. Durka suddenly remembered that she needed to get back to the Chief. She'd wasted too much time with the faxes already.

When Durka reentered his office, the Chief was still dead asleep on the couch, snoring up a storm. Seeing him like this reminded her of a recent trip they'd made to Salmonville for a political speech, when she'd found the Chief dead out of it in the backroom of the conference hall at the Salmonville Hotel, one of his famous giant erections rising up majestically out of his fly. His belt and pants were wide open, and he was sticking straight up, like a big, blind salute to anyone who happened to stumble in.

Luckily, it was she who had found him, rather than someone else. Durka had locked the door and made the most of the situation. After wasting about ten minutes futilely trying to get his pants refastened, she decide to try a more creative approach. She climbed up on the table and straddled the Chief, who was still sound asleep, or at least pretended to be. Opening her thighs, she slid down the length of him, swivelling her hips in a slow, steady rhythm, rocking in widening circles with Shelldrake's enormous penis throbbing and turning inside her like a slow-motion whirling dervish. Still securely impaled, Durka kozzotskied several times around the top of the conference table until the hotel loud-speaker announced that the meeting in the main hall would shortly reconvene. Durka knew that she had to move fast. She jumped off the Chief, pulled him together, at least as well as she could with such short notice, handed him the notes for his presentation, and led him toward the conference hall. Before they parted, the Chief tightly embraced Durka for a moment. He turned back toward her on his way out the door.

"Durka, I think this is the awards night for the best cheerleaders."

Shelldrake took his accustomed place at the front table. After the dinner break it was his turn to speak prior to the entertainment. Before he began his remarks, however, the Overdrive Rocketeers marched through the hall, twirling their batons in perfect unison, throwing them high up near the gym ceiling, and performing various stunts for the dinner crowd.

The girls chanted at the top of their lungs as they marched through the Skamania dining room:

> *Three cheers for the Jones Junior High.*
> *It's the best junior high in Toledo.*
> *For Jones Junior High, we would die,*
> *Die! Die! Die! Die! Die!*

> *Our colors are purple and white.*
> *Purple for chastity, white for fight.*
> *Fight! Fight! Fight! Fight! Fight!*

Durka watched and applauded as the girls jumped up and down. She had joined in with the dinner crowd as they sang the verses along with the girls:

Three cheers for the Jones Junior High.
It's the best junior high in Toledo . . .

They crowd must have sung Jones Junior High's fight song at least a dozen times before the girls stopped marching back and forth, their skirts flying high above their waists.

From the corner of the room, Durka had watched the Chief standing and applauding the girls, who were stunt-flying right in front of the honored guests. Breathless and exhausted, the girls had come together to create their annual showtime pyramid. Durka knew it was coming. The girls loved the Chief, and they made it for him every year. They always made a point of showing their best to the Chief. Finally, the pyramid collapsed under its own weight, the girls giggling and groaning and panting on the floor in front of the Chief, who made no attempt to hide his delight.

Millie, standing next to Durka, had openly voiced her disapproval. "It's disgusting, Durka!" she wailed above the roar of the crowd. "And it's not going to help the Chief's campaign."

"I know, Millie," Durka sighed. "You know these politicians. At least Shell is doing it out in the open." Anyway, Durka decided to advise the Chief to be careful, at least. But not now, though; she wouldn't spoil his fun this evening. She climbed the stairs to the front table and whispered a kind word into the Chief's ear. The Chief smiled, took Durka's hand, and held her out in front of the crowd. The immense cheering that greeted her made her forget her other concerns for the moment. She left the Chief with the rest of the VIPs sitting at the front table and returned to her place in the back of the hall with Millie and her niece Cheryl. Most of the people sitting around the Chief were a bunch of rotten shits on the chicken circuit; that was for sure.

"Durka," said Millie, "I have an important question. Can sixteen-year-olds be bimbos? If I'm supposed to be one of the bimbo-busters, we're going to have to rethink the whole thing. It's like busting my own teenage daughter, just because she likes to show the Chief her tonsils now and then."

"Millie," Durka explained, "it's the price we pay."

Finally, when the dinner crowd had returned their attention to their fried chicken and broccoli, two of the twirlers, Naomi and Jane, who incidentally had the best grades and most extracurricular activities at Jones Jr. High, came up to the front table to receive a special tribute from the Chief.

Millie blanched. "Durka, I really think the problem is that this is becoming an annual event. We should stop this before it becomes just another bad habit."

"Auntie," Cheryl chimed in, "when the Chief calls, are we supposed to come?"

* * *

Now, barely a week later, Durka was standing in this mess of an office, gazing worriedly at her work-spent husband, who was lying prostrate on the couch in front of her. Try as she might, she couldn't ignore it, simply couldn't ignore the implications of the Chief falling into this state at this time. What it could mean for the campaign. What it could mean for the country. She struggled to control the demons that the sight of his exhausted body had awakened in her, and her anxiety and disappointment began to subside. Shelldrake's the man, she reminded herself, chanting the phrase again and again, like a mantra, as she knelt beside him and checked his pulse. She was especially worried about the damage that his excessive drinking was doing to his liver. A lot of heat in that liver, she mused. Too much radiator.

She stepped back for a moment, scanning the length of the Chief's massive body, from his heaving chest to his always-swollen crotch to his enormous feet. She noticed that his boots were untied and on the floor. The blanket that had been covering him when she first looked in had also dropped off. She let her eyes wander back up toward his crotch. Jesus Christ, she thought, he's dead drunk and he's still sporting one of his big ones. He was at the same time both the most repulsive and the most beautiful man she'd ever known. She took the Polaroid from her bag and snapped several pictures, from different angles, that might look good up on the office bulletin board. For a moment, she thought he might have moved, but she couldn't be sure. She shook her head in dismay. How can anyone get any work done when Shelldrake is like this? The only way we're going to get this guy to the White House is on a gurney bed. "Right, Chief?" she said aloud.

Finally, Durka decided to leave him alone again, at least for a while. She turned off the light and gently spread the blanket across his seemingly expired form. He was moderately grizzled, she noticed, looking like he probably hadn't shaved in several days. He smiled in his sleep, looking as serene and content as if he had left for good to the happy hunting ground. Durka bent down close to his nose and lips. He smelled good, a hell of a lot better than most politicians. Impulsively, she reached down and gently fondled his crotch. "Package check, you bastard," she whispered.

For a moment, she considered changing her mind about leaving the office just yet, gazing lovingly and longingly at his strong countenance. She could feel his already-swollen penis stiffening even longer in her hand.

"Listen, dream lover," she whispered in his ear, "if you think you're going to be in Skankerville past Sunday, call me and I'll come over. And don't be surprised if I show up anyway. And no funny business."

He was awake now. She bent down and kissed his full lips a little more than briefly. She knew he needed his rest for the important trip ahead. But this was important, too.

After they'd finished and the Chief had fallen back to sleep, Durka turned the desk light down and took her travelling bag and left the office, that was, his office. Durka was amazed to see that the sleeping Chief was still just as hard and stiff as he was when she found him there. She had to remember to get someone else to drive. Maybe Reba. She couldn't let the Chief make the trip alone. He wasn't quite ready. Maybe Bill Spoogie could help do some advancing. She noticed some unopened salal cakes from the last couple of days. If he needed to snack tonight there would be enough to carry him through. She knew that he hated salal, but there was a price for everything, she thought; the Chief needs to make some sacrifices somewhere if he is going to keep his health.

On her way out, Durka picked up the remaining faxes that had littered the floor while she was tending to the Chief. She would have to decipher them later.

* * *

I knew Durka was in the room now. I couldn't open my eyes. My lids were too heavy. I needed the sleep. Tomorrow was the opening day, when I threw out the big ball.

If the campaign works, I thought, I'll be in Washington again. Durka and me. Dickerman will be Chief of Staff if she comes along. But she says she's not sure she wants to live in the White House, being cooped up in a glass bowl. She's worried that her work for the Triple Revolution will be strangled in the bureaucratic setup. I tried to convince her that we don't have to live in the White House and that there won't be any bureaucracy. Hell, we can live on top of the White House if that will make a difference. She's a Washington person—we spent some time there years ago—so it's hard to convince her of anything. She already knows the score too well. She reminds me that Haldeman and Erlichman weren't that bad before they got the power. That political power is scary. That it turns you into a kind of monster. She insists that, if I love myself, I won't do it. That I'll be much happier and much more effective here near the reservation. I probably won't have a choice about it, though, with the campaign building the way it has lately, with my picture on every telephone pole in the country.

Fate will take me there for the cleanout. I'm the Drano that America needs—the red devil—to clean out the corporate intestines of the country. Uncle Sam's going to drink the stuff I give him straight. And if that doesn't work, I'll forcefully administer a giant colonic irrigation to flood out the bastions of corporate bullshit. We'll twist the balls off the military and pop their boonies. As simple as ripping a chicken's head off. Then we'll pierce that putrid carbuncle on the ass of history known as the United States of America.

I really believe that Durka and I can work together in the Triple Revolution. But we don't have much time. There's so much to do. I've got to call Remus. They're trying to close in on us. But they're a bunch of ridiculous assholes. And real troublemakers. I wouldn't underestimate the tarbabies. They make lots of folks afraid, just like those helicopters that are now hovering over us again.

Sambo

THIS SAMBO WASN'T LITTLE, and he wasn't black. But he definitely was Sambo. Remus stood at the edge of the Cascadian foothills as Sambo headed out down the dirt road toward the central valley to check out the latest tarbaby. Sambo had a small green knapsack over the back of his coveralls and a small briefcase containing his measuring devices. In the knapsack were a number of items to assure his safety: a flashlight and backup batteries, a whistle, a compass, a barometer, copper tubing, a poncho for two, a miniature chess set, and an old Zeiss monocular inherited from his father. It was the dry season now, so Sambo wore a simple pair of lederhosen and sandals. On his teeshirt was an icon for the campaign:

Turn cannon balls into matzoh balls

Remus did everything in his power to persuade Sambo to wait until morning, when it would be safer and he could get a better look at things. But Sambo said he was on a tight schedule and would have to go at night to scope out this particular tarbaby.

"Look, Remus," Sambo had explained, "you're the one who told me the Chief asked we check this one out, that it might be the biggest one yet."

"I knowds dat, Sambo," Remus had countered, "an cuz dis'un . . . dis ah biggie, mo pepple get stuk in dere. It tretious out dere."

As urgent as the mission was, something told Sambo to listen to Remus. He knew the tarbabies could be really trecherous. They could pull people right in, get them really stuck. Those things were the eighteen-wheelers of brain death.

Next, Remus described to Sambo how he first saw the tarbaby. He had been in his garden, spreading some compost on his veggies. He carefully detailed for Sambo the strange feelings that he had experienced when he turned around to discover the coal-black shiny tarbaby poking its head over the hill, looking straight at him. He had gone straight into his house at the time and dialed the reservation. At first, Rose, the receptionist, told Remus that Chief Shelldrake was in a meeting. But as soon as she heard what he'd just seen, she got the Chief right on the line.

"'Mo ta'babies on da way, boss,' ist wat I tole im," Remus informed Sambo.

Remus had explained his sighting to the Chief in great detail. He had told the Chief that an even larger one was probably right behind the one he saw, though all he could make out was its shadow.

"An Chief, I'se amost done dat memo yo done axed me fo bout growin stuff."

Sensing the urgency of the situation, the Chief had immediatley called Barb into his office.

"Get Sambo over!" he exclaimed. "Remus just called and more tarbabies are on their way."

* * *

Barb flushed with anger when she heard about the tarbabies. The damned things were driving her crazy. First, there had been those fuckin' dwarfs that Nighthorse brought in to show the Chief. And now, the tarbabies were starting up again. What a bunch of bastards. Barb could hardly keep it all in. She tried her best to remain calm, but she was really pissed. She didn't want to misplace her teeth again, the way she had the other day when she was upset about the droppas in the dumpster. That had been so humiliating. She would never get over the embarrassment that she had experienced when the Chief saw her that day. She definitely didn't want a recurrence. Still fuming, she picked up the intercom and called for Sambo.

Barb kept her ear to the phone and stood in front of Shelldrake. The Chief, who was studying some land records from Michigan, looked up and saw her staring furiously into his eyes.

"I don't like this, Chief. I don't like this one bit. Something's going on; that's for sure. I just hung up with Millie. She's very depressed. They just canned Ruppert Emerson. How do you like that?

"Those fuckers!" she screamed, her ample teeth clenched as her lips twisted into an even greater rage. "Chief, this is why the campaign is so important; dontcha know?" She was a bit confused and slurring some of her words beyond recognition, but the Chief definitely got the message. If her teeth went south again, man, then there would be some serious problems.

The Chief carefully etched a note on the edge of the pad in front of him. He didn't look up right away but instead methodically analyzed all his concerns before he raised his head.

"You heard me, Chief," she continued. "They fired Rupp from the lab. I am totally pissed."

"Well, listen, Barb, calm down," the Chief did his best to be reassuring. "You don't want to do that tooth deal again, do you? It might get to be a bad habit. But keep talking. I'm listening."

Barb took the chair in front of the desk but didn't sit down. Instead, she jumped up on the seat and stood above the Chief.

"Let me tell you something, Chief." She could barely control her rage now. "Millie had to call me secretly because the new director won't let anyone use the telephone. The only way she was able to call was when he went in the bathroom. Millie and the others are trying to get out. They're afraid he's going to try to rape them. They're really scared. And Rupp, I feel so sorry for Rupp. Millie and Rhoda and the other interns are locked in the lab.

"They rape and steal and kill us every day," Barb continued. "They poison our food. They shit everywhere and they shit in the bay too. And just because Rupp drops one of his little turds out there on the flats every once in a while, they canned him. You know, Chief, Rupp's the best you've got."

"Barb, there's more here than meets the eye." The Chief still wasn't sure what to make of the situation. "Maybe Rupp is just an excuse. They got rid of Harry and put in a new guy. If Rupp was around, there wouldn't be any new guy; you can be sure of that.

"Anyway," the Chief asked, "where's Rupp now? I've got to see him."

Barb replied that Millie wasn't sure where Rupp was. She said that Harry Teitel had called a meeting to talk about Rupp. Harry had sent Rupp out to get pizza, to get him out of the way while he staged the fake meeting. It was very fast. The new guy took over. A kind of Ukrainian Croatian dwarf.

"But the thing is," Barb continued, "Mille says that he's really huge and really ugly. And Millie says that you'll appreciate this, Chief. He's got a giant set of balls. Millie says she's sure that the Kraken people are behind it.

"Well, Chief, you can't just sit there; we have to do something. Millie says that she and this other woman over there, Rhoda, are trying to escape. He's trying to rape Rhoda in broad daylight, right and left, and she wants out. So they're leaving. It's causing quite a bit of office talk."

Barb stopped talking but continued to look at Shelldrake, her face twisted and contorted with rage.

The Chief had heard murmurs and rumblings about the things going on over at the fish science lab. Cheryl's Evergreen roommate Rhoda had filled her in, and she had told him stuff. He knew the lab was in the midst of a deep administrative depression. Rupp had also tried to keep him up-to-date on things at the lab. The Chief had seen Rupp several times since Teitel had been booted, doing his best to stay in touch. It wasn't good, Rupp getting sick like that and getting replumbed. Rupp was as good as they came.

The Chief shifted back and forth in his mind, trying to guess what might have been the actual cause of Rupp's dismissal from the lab. The administrative judge had ruled that Ruppert Emerson required a permit to foul the baywater if he was to continue his job. That was the kiss of death. The Chief knew that Rupp's depression would increase if he was forced to leave the lab for good. He knew Rupp had been really sick, but he had no idea just how sick he was. Only Rupp would know that for sure. One thing was certain, the Chief thought, Rupp had been a great leader in our country's history. He'd seen it all.

The Chief's thoughts were broken when he noticed that Barb was leaving and heading back to her own desk.

"Barb, look, I think we better take some action."

She turned back to face him again; her eyes were red and brimming. "Tell me, Chief, what can we do? They're over there, and we're over here."

"Barb, call Buzzozzi. Tell him there's some hanky-panky at the fish lab, and he should go check it out."

"Chief, haven't you got anyone else? Dr. Bill is just finishing up the Bhopal report. I know he's really busy."

"Barb, please. Just call him. He'll understand. It's a scientific matter. Also, see if you can find Rupp. Tell him I need to see him at our regular meeting time on Thursday."

The Chief turned back to his land claims work, pulling out some stats, wondering how quickly the campaign could move into high gear. He was ready for it; he knew that.

Anyway, I won't overdo it, the Chief thought. I'm not ashamed to call upon my best friends for help. I need Rupp. I need his analysis, his basic analysis. Where are we anyway? I've got almost all the land back, and we're ready to go. Rupp's the man.

* * *

Last Thursday, he and Rupp had sat together at a little fast-food tavern in Portland, eating some burgers and fried oysters. The place was called Berchesgarten West; it had formerly been a little tavern in a burger chain. The new décor suggested a kind of Austrian gulag, with window boxes full of plastic geraniums and cuckoo clocks hanging here and there. It was very dark inside, so they had decided to sit out by the curb. To the west, the sky was threateningly dark as well. One hundred and fifty miles away, they could make out the approaching gray front, darkened by enormous black clouds descending on the coast. The Chief scanned the horizon and could see that the hailstorms were starting up again.

They were throwing back vodka oyster shooters. Bill, the bartender, wandered over every so often to fill their requests for more.

"I can't do too much of this, Chief, you know. I don't have a shitpipe any more." Rupp concentrated primarily on his burger, chewing for a minute or so and then looking up at the Chief. "I don't think I told you this, but the girls told me that the new guy took his cock out and let it hang there for about ten minutes while he harangued them about their work. They're trying to get out of there before he rapes them. I'm very concerned."

Rupp waited for a response, but the Chief didn't acknowledge his concern. After a few moments, Rupp continued his appeal to the Chief.

"Millie says this guy is trying to rape her and that gal Rhoda; they're planning to escape some time soon. Millie says it's too late for a strike. Since Leon and I aren't there, they've lost heart and aren't strong enough for any real job action."

"Well, you know, Rupp," the Chief finally replied, "Cheryl's keeping me informed on the lab. But I agree, it doesn't look good. Those intern jobs have lost their quality; that's for sure."

"Chief, I don't like being like this." Rupp felt that he wasn't getting through. "I'm sure you know what I mean. It was bad enough at the lab going through all that muck, even before I got sick. When I got sick, it was really bad. The kids took care of me, though. The interns are a good bunch; Millie's right in there. But Chief, I've had it. My physical capacities are very limited. I can't do the things I want to do. I really don't want to live anymore.

"Were I well," he continued, "I would go back to the lab to that fake scientist Dr. Bill Urbanchuk, expose him, and blow the whole fucking mess wide open.

"I want you to know that I've put in several calls to Jack, but I haven't heard back yet. The truth is, I love to work. But if I'm not working then I want to be off the hook. You know, dead, dead meat. I'm really not strong enough to deal with all of it: the colonization, the tarbabies, the hairballs, the hailstorms. It's all about stifling dissent, if you ask me, and I'm sick of it. Give me a Kevorkian any day."

Rupp fell abruptly silent. He had said it all. The Chief knew that he was witnessing, even if he couldn't fully accept it, the downward spiral of his good friend Rupp, the complete disintegration of one of the best minds on the planet.

The Chief continued eating his burgers, followed now and then by a couple of shooters and some french fries.

"Rupp," he said, "I figured you'd bring in Kervorkian when I heard what you were going through with your large intestine. I heard from Millie that you ate too much white bread. But I don't want to talk to you about that right now. There's something that I need to know first. You can't die on me. I need a lot of help. We really need your economic input for the campaign."

Rupp smiled involuntarily as the Chief spoke. It was just like the old days. The Chief noticed Rupp's eyes sparkling through his jaundiced complexion.

"Anyway, Chief, I won't bother you with this, but you know, I've worked a lot of places and seen a lot of things: chicken factories, rendering plants, government. You know, during the war, I ran the WPB. I saw it all back then, but it's not that way anymore." Rupp, who was growing gloomier by the second, stared down toward the pavement as he spoke. He burped a couple of times and said angrily: "I hate the fucking mess I'm in, Chief; I'm getting out of here."

The Chief finshed another burger and ordered some more vodka shooters, barbecued shrimp, and Olympia oysters. Rupp really had hit the bottom; the Chief could see that. He was burping quite a bit. Between burps, Rupp hung his head down between his knees and gave off a wretched groan, somewhere between a belch and a moan.

"You know, Rupp, I'm sorry you feel that way, because I really need you in the campaign."

They ate in silence for a few moments. Rupp was putting it down fairly slowly now, the Chief noticed, which probably meant that his insides were getting ready to explode. He just couldn't stuff any more in there. Hoping at least to mitigate Rupp's total digestive failure, the Chief decided to finish off Rupp's burger and fries. From a policy standpoint alone, it was critical, the Chief thought, not to let Rupp get too overloaded.

"Are you or aren't you available for work?" the Chief asked.

Rupp picked his teeth with a broken wooden match and gave off a big smile. "Hey, you know that work's my middle name."

That was more like it. The Chief got more serious for a minute. He needed Rupp's counsel.

"Rupp, a couple of weeks ago we talked some about economic planning to save the country. And you said, 'Chief, we got to go back to the nickel economy or we're goners. It's time to pull the plug. It's time to crash this fuckin' mess.' Do you remember telling me that?"

Rupp didn't respond immediately. The Chief munched on some more fries that Bill had brought out to the curb.

"How's you fellas doing?" Bill asked. He was a thin, wiry guy, pasty-looking from working in the dark way too long, but no one could fault his generosity. The old timers and out-of-work locals would line up with their Safeway carts in front of the bar each day to receive the fried calamari, smoked shrimp platters, and baby burgers that he'd dole out for free.

Rupp was a bit cautious about saying too much within earshot of Bill. Bill knew way too much already, he figured. If he somehow got wind of their economic strategy, it could seriously damage the Chief's campaign. With that in mind, Rupp waited until Bill left to retrieve yet another round of shooters and respond to the Chief's last question.

"Sorry about that," he finally said. "Chief, I did say that. I told you to get rid of those phony Federal Reserve creampuffs, and then lead the country through to the nickel economy. We could do some real belt-tightening on those rich assholes. Their sappy little bank dicks would sing for mercy; believe me!"

Well stated, thought the Chief. He had doubts, though, about Rupp's nickel economy. Would Rupp live long enough to see it happen? The Chief questioned Rupp closely for nearly half an hour more, discussing the timing of their strategy. Though he hadn't said anything about it, the Chief was worried about Bill, too. He had always been a little unsure about that guy. He'd heard that he had a moonlighting job working for some corpos. He could easily have a device on him, the Chief thought, and could be feeding our plans right up to the top people. Were the girls right that the Krakens were the ones behind all this? Anyway, Bill was an easy mark. The Chief could see him heading toward them again with a plateful of miniburgers, those one-biters that left a weird, gunky feeling in your mouth after you ate them. You could eat all you wanted, though.

The Chief popped a miniburger into his mouth, wondering if Bill might have been co-opted by some of the Minnesota and Iowa people who frequented his bar. Bill finally wandered out of listening range, and Rupp started talking again. The Chief noticed that a line of people had formed, waiting to grab the curbside space once he and Rupp were finished. But their meeting wasn't over yet. They would just sit tight for a while. They still had a big agenda to cover. The Chief looked at Rupp, who was sticking a toothpick through the wide crevices in his teeth. He still didn't understand exactly why Rupp had been fired from the lab in the first place. It couldn't have just been the matter of the colostomy bag. That was too trivial. Rupp could have always purchased one of those cockamamie permits that would have allowed him to leak as much as he wanted to all over the tideflats. It must have been something else, something bigger.

Bill brought out another round of oyster shooters and set them on the curb. "Chief," he interrupted them, "you got a call here. He said he doesn't want to interrupt your meeting, but he's got an emergency."

The Chief looked at Rupp, got up, and took Bill's portable phone. Remus was on the other end.

"Hey, Remus," said the Chief. "Whatcha got?"

Rupp could tell from the Chief's side of the conversation that Remus had spotted another tarbaby coming across the foothills. After a couple of minutes, the Chief turned to Rupp and nodded seriously; clearly, it was a bad one. By this time, Bill had returned to the curb with more shooters.

The Chief sat back, looking serious and dejected as he listened to Remus over the portable. Rupp listened to the news in bits and pieces as the Chief gave Remus instructions. Remus didn't seem to know exactly how many tarbabies there were.

"Just be on the lookout," the Chief advised. "Don't take any risks."

Finally, Rupp grew impatient and interrupted their conversation. "What kind of tarbaby is it? And ask Remus where it's going. Is Remus safe, Chief? You know we're counting on him for the new food and farm policies."

Rupp toyed with some loose cigarette butts in the gutter near his foot while the Chief did his best to get the rest of the information from Remus. A lot of them had lipstick marks, he noticed. Someone had dumped them from their ashtray. He noticed a couple of roaches as well, picked them up, and then looked up at the Chief.

"Hey, Remus," the Chief was saying, "I got your buddy Rupp here and he wants to know what kind of tarbabies you're seeing out there. Listen, he wants to talk to you."

The Chief handed the phone over to Rupp. After some initial buddy-buddy stuff, Remus went over the last couple of days' events. Rupp turned halfway to the Chief and whispered: "I'm very concerned, Chief; if they get Remus, we might as well kiss a big part of our constituency goodbye."

When Remus had finished filling him in on the details, Rupp handed the phone back to the Chief. He'd tried his best to get down another fry. He knew everything he had to know.

* * *

When he'd first seen the tarbaby, Remus had been out at his woodshed, cutting his annual winter firewood. A few trees had fallen down near Remus's hut in the summer storms, leaving him plenty of logs for cutting, including some nice cedar for kindling. Remus called the Chief and told him exactly what he'd seen. Another tarbaby was appearing on the horizon about a hundred and fifty miles east of Elma.

"Keep an eye on it," the Chief had said. "It sounds like it's a big sonofabitch. Sambo will scout it out for you. I'll see you at Diehard. I think we got you a couple of hours to explain the new agriculture policy."

That's the way it had started.

Remus was pleased to help the Chief's campaign any way he could. He owed the Chief. The Chief had saved Remus from being lynched several years earlier over in Kentucky, in Hanging Limb. He'd been picked up by the local authorities for trespassing the city limits. All he'd been looking for was a job.

* * *

"'Dat tru bout yo bein da nex bigman?' I axed im dat." Remus was still talking to Sambo about his conversation with the Chief. Sambo was just about to leave to scout for the latest tarbaby.

It was about 6 p.m. Sambo had arrived shortly before noon, and the two men had spent the afternoon together. Like just about everyone else who met him, Sambo had immediately hit it off with Remus. Phil Remus was a gentle man with white whiskers and shortly cropped white hair. His round, dark, hairy face was usually set in a smile. Small, kinky curls ringed his leathery features, as his fat lips and big white teeth broke into his famous grin. Always happy and full of life, the old man was liable to start tap dancing at any moment, singing some jigalig or other country tune.

But Phil Remus wasn't dancing today. Looming ominously, just above the horizon, was the horrible sight that he had called the Chief about. He had never seen one this big. When Sambo arrived, the tarbaby was weaving back and forth, maybe twenty-five or thirty miles away, near the eastern rim of the Cascadian foothills.

Remus loved to tell stories. He often told them when he was worried about something. During the course of the afternoon, as the two men waited there to see what would happen next, Remus entertained Sambo with some of his favorite stories. Remus spoke in a kind of Ebonics, Sambo thought, like old slave talk. Sambo kept an eye on the tarbaby throughout the afternoon, catching its undulations, while Remus told his stories.

* * *

Remus ended his last story on a bitter note. "How was I invented?" he asked Sambo. "I always have the feeling that I'm a product of racism."

Sambo got up and embraced Remus. "Don't take it that way, Phil; you're a true patriot, facing down these tarbabies the way you have. Just remember, you saved Jemima's ass. The way things are going, she could be sucking olestra over at the P&G."

Sambo shook Remus's hand goodbye, noticing that he was sweating with fear, and then went down the path out of sight. He was afraid, alright. He didn't want to admit it to Remus, but this was the worst. If things continued the way they were going, he was a total goner. If the Chief's worst fears were confirmed and the tarbabies were aimed at Skankerville, it would be a catastrophe. Darkness had begun to fall, and a bright, eerie moon hung above the trees, illuminating Sambo as he made his way up and along the hillside.

Remus watched Sambo disappear into the night. Sambo still had a long way to go, thought Remus, through the thickets and underbrush and stickers to reach and disarm the tarbaby. They had done this before and had been able to stop the tarbabies before it was too late—and without getting stuck themselves. But this one was much larger, and it kept moving around all over the place. It definitely had a mind of its own, compared to most of the others. By any definition, it was a monster tarbaby.

Out there somewhere, beyond where Sambo had disappeared into the night, the tarbaby was lurking, its monstrously voluminous and villainous black shape rocking back and forth until it lurched and heaved unexpectedly out of sight. The great bulk of the tarbaby was hidden from view on the valley floor. Remus estimated that it must have been at least seven hundred feet tall. Sambo had warned Remus to stay at least two miles away from the molten heap, or else he could be in grave danger. Remus calculated that the tarbaby was still twenty-five miles away over the hills toward the Cascades. But Sambo could easily mange forty-five miles by morning. That should give him enough time to get there and back, so that the two of them could figure out what to do next. Sambo would have to be careful, though. Remus and Sambo both knew that the tarbabies could really put up a big stink. And no one wanted to be caught near that stink of brain death.

Once Sambo got back and the two of them had a chance to assess the situation, they could head over to Diehard, make their report to the Chief, and then get over to the festivities. But all Remus could do now was wait. He sat down at his portable desk under an old growth cedar tree, lighting up a lantern that he had retrieved from the van. The light momentarily blinded him. When his eyes refocused, he could still see the giant coal-black, haystack-shaped tarbaby in the faraway night. He opened a small pouch and handrolled some dried gericurl that he'd grown in the back of his garden.

Lighting up, he opened the pages of his memorandum and began to write up his report about the new agriculture, the land reform that would come when the roof was finally blown off the rotten pile of shit of a cesspool called America. It was definitely time to let in some fresh air. Remus laughed as he mouthed the words that he was writing. He wished he had more time to work on his report. He paused for a moment to take another look at the tarbaby and then began to write again.

Remus lived in a remote, rural area. The people who lived around him mainly liked to talk about the weather. The weather led to the news. Remus chuckled. He took another deep draw from his gericurl. When the chemical industries finally cave in, after most everyone is poisoned by the pollution, the few people who remain will begin to grow the new gardens. Remus took another deep draw of gericurl and crossed out a few words. He stared into the night, still able to make out the monster in the distant valley. He thought about what the Chief had said in one of their recent conversations: "Remus, take a whack at the new agriculture plan. You know more about farming than anyone in the country. You know how to grow good, clean food. That's what people have to have, believe me, or it's just going to be a fucking dead zone, with rotten chicken and dead meat all over the place and the E. coli up to our eyeballs."

Remus continued to work on his report to the Chief, scribbling away furiously on the old stump he used as a desk.

"Ah knowds dis ta beh da trudt."

It was almost dawn when he finished. A full moon lit up his stump. His dog Spot lay next to him, her body pushing against the elderly man, as if she were trying to prop him up and transfer to him all her energy and warmth. Remus bent down and petted her, scratching her between the eyes. She eagerly accepted a medium-sized dog biscuit from her boss, chewing away mechanically. Remus hobbled over to get a beer from the cooler in the back of the van. He and Sambo needed at least a vanful of beer for the trip, he figured, since there's a lot of needy folk at Diehard. He looked up at the full moon and thought it was the most beautiful thing that he'd ever seen. The bright glow was suddenly disturbed, however, by the dark, ominous silhouette that jerked through the sky, golden rays of light splintering across the eastern sky.

Remus wondered how far Sambo had trekked by now. It must have been around 4 a.m., he estimated from the light. If everything went well, Sambo should be back by 8. That would give them plenty of time to pack and load their gear and still be at Skankerville by dark, if they didn't putter around too much on the way. Remus decided to go ahead and fire up the coffee for Sambo's return. Sambo always drank a wet double espresso el grande. Remus like it straight himself, but you could never be sure these days, with people's coffee tastes. It was just like how you couldn't tell who liked raw pussy anymore and who didn't. Remus'd take pussy any way he could get it, if the truth were told. Raw, well-done, medium-rare: he definitely wouldn't complain. Liquid pussy, though, was better than any kind of coffee, even Hannibal's or Starbucks. And it was much better for you.

Remus had been pretty clear with the Chief from the start. He wasn't going after this tarbaby himself, not for love or for money.

"I sure ain't goin make a trip like dat," he had told the Chief. "Too darn far. I got too much work to do. And besides, I got to get to Diehard by Sunday. I gotta gib ya de farn pollecy. An I sho hope dat missible tarbaby ain't going to Diehard wid me."

When they'd talked, Remus had tried to hammer home to the Chief just how seriously the food situation had become. The corporations were making food from rat shit ingredients, literally goddamned rat shit, and peddling it as nourishing health amenities. The Chief wanted to know how Remus had found out about the rat shit. Remus explained that he'd learned it all from a guy who'd come out here from MIT to do some genetic splicing. It seemed that some of the big burger people were trying to find out how to stop the deadly bacteria that consumed the meat even when it was super well-done.

But the bacteria were surviving the furnace. And the laboratory rats were eating the meat and liking it. No matter how the scientists charred and scorched the burgers, the bacteria still thrived.

* * *

Rupp was still sitting on the curb, belching now and then as his alimentary gasses sought to escape. A small, smokey cloud rose above his head like a halo.

"I can't even fart right anymore," he complained to the Chief.

Bill stood above them with a tray of oysters and some more shooters. The Chief noticed the line of men stringing its way down the street, waiting to get into the food kitchen next door to Bill's place. One of the guys near the front of the line wandered over, recognized Rupp, and yelled back to the line of men standing sullenly near the building housing the soup kitchen. "Hey, men, it's Rupp! Rupp's here. Jesus Christ, Rupp's here!"

The Chief noticed that the soup kitchen line was moving very slowly. The soup probably wasn't ready yet when the first of them arrived. He thought about what he'd said to Remus on the phone about his worries regarding the coming food shortages and the dependency of the tribes on lichen.

The men from the soup kitchen had already begun to surround Rupp and the Chief, their faces momentarily full of excitement. "Rupp! Rupp! Man, it's Rupp." After a few moments of enthusiasm, their faces returned to the vacuous holes that they had been, their dead eyes peering out at Rupp, with his foggy fart rising above his gnarled, tired face. The Chief was glad that those eyes weren't staring at him.

The original bedlam that had erupted around Rupp was subsiding, the guys now standing stiffly around their hero. The Chief noticed a familiar-looking guy over to the side, wearing a Boston Braves baseball cap. The Chief strained his memory to place him. The guy was pretty scrawny. His teeth looked rotted out, and his nose was a giant, red schnozz the size of a tennis ball. The Chief and the guy made eye contact and started scanning each other intently. They continued scanning, losing touch with the words with which Rupp was now doing his best to inspire the down-and-out men.

"Chief, my name is Bullets," the man finally said. "You may not recognize me right now, but I've served you a lot of burgers in my time. I was fired from my job a half hour ago. I am really pissed, not to mention depressed. What am I going to do? I can't wait for you guys to make policy. I got to live. I got a family. I got payments to make. No matter how great your program is, it's never going to help me in time."

* * *

The Chief was committed to Rupp's whole program, even as much as to his own grand plans. It was inspiring to listen to him now, working up the soup-line crowd with his cutting-edge economic agenda. Ripping the shit out of the military. Cutting the nuts off the corporate assholes. Giving everyone a homestead and a still, some seeds, a dog, a cat, a cow, a sheep, a couple of chickens, and a pig. Everyone was looking for the old forty acres and a mule, but it wasn't like that anymore. People needed something new. We're going to have to give them something new, whether they like it or not; that's why we're pulling the plug. But even with the massive land reform and population demands, there was very little left to divvy up. Still, the Chief and his followers would knock out the insurance companies and the banks and turn those little weenies out to look for work.

"We'll turn those bankers into shitballs," Rupp promised the crowd.

I could definitely go for that, the Chief thought. Then forty acres and a mule, or Rupp's new version, at least. We have to do everything we can to counter the impending threat of total brain death. But how can we alleviate the brain death of these guys right here? Look at this guy, Bullets. He says he's a full-employment man. He's trying to rouse these guys to do something, but they just stand there. I don't know how I can help Bullets and these other guys unless the whole thing is blown apart.

When he'd finished speaking to the crowd, Rupp stood up and shook hands all around. The Chief rose, too, the soup-line men standing back in awe to see Shelldrake tower above them. Bullets came up and stood between Rupp and the Chief, and all three men wrapped their arms around each other.

Realizing that this was his big moment, his chance to get his point across to the public, Bullets turned to the other two men and asked: "Chief? Rupp? You're such hot policy shits right now. I just lost my job at the Cantina. What are you gonna do about that? Frankly, I'm pretty sick of theory. I want action. What should I do?"

The soup-line men stood around, bleary-eyed and starving, waiting to hear what the Chief and Rupp would say in response. They formed a circle, leaving just enough room for bartender Bill to get through with some miniburgers for the men so they wouldn't get mean. Bill brought more plastic glasses and several bottles of the Chief's favorite, Spudka, which he offered to all the men. The Chief knew that the vodka wouldn't last that long at this rate. And the line was growing all the time. The Chief suddenly resented all the blank-faced men who were now competing for his beloved Spudka.

"Why don't you get your goddamn jobs back?" the Chief shouted as he stormed into the center of the crowd. Rupp noticed the tears on the Chief's massive cheekbones. The men remained silent. They held their dishtrays by their sides, each one waiting, Rupp thought, for something solid, something real, something that they could think about overnight in their hovels, something that might stir their bowels. To get a better view, Rupp stepped up on a small dumpster near the side of Bill's Place. Bullets climbed up beside him and glared out at the crowd of men.

Sensing that the Chief was about to lose it and alienate a crowd of potential supporters, Rupp yelled: "Men, I hear your silence out loud! But I say, the Chief's right; no matter how fucked up you think you are, you'd better start working on your self-interest. Your vowels and your bowels, that's what I say. Start moving those vowels and start moving those bowels. It's the only way out of your stagnation."

The Chief was openly crying now. He challenged the men: "Are you alive or in the eat-shit-and-die school? What do you want?"

An interminable silence followed. Rupp saw the tears running down the Chief's cheeks. But the men just stood there. What were they waiting for? Someone to speak for them? Someone to give them a job? Or just some more burgers and Spudka from Bill? Rupp couldn't tell. They had all disappeared so far into themselves that they couldn't even talk anymore. They're all pretty much brain-dead, as far as Rupp could tell.

Bullets guessed that there must have been about six hundred in the crowd as he began to speak: "Friends, fellow countrymen, I've lost my job, my stinking job. I was fired for nothing 'cause I wasn't doing nothing. Chief Shelldrake is over here sobbing away, but it's not his fault. It's my fault. It's my fault that I lost my job. And it's my fault if I don't get it back.

"And I'll tell you, we'll blow those assholes out of the water when the time has come. And the time has come now. No more of this corporate shit. I'm getting my job back."

No one stirred.

Bullets pulled off his baseball cap and pointed to a large red crease in his skull. Rupp figured that the injury was a couple of days old, a swollen red beginning to turn to purple. It looked like the whole side of his head was crushed in. On closer examination, it appeared that he had probably been hit with a three-fourth-inch crowbar. "See this, you silent sonsabitches?" Bullets shouted. "This is what they done to me. Then they kicked me out on my ass."

At the sight of Bullets's wounded head, the crowd perked up a little, rubbernecking to get a better look at the gash and to hear what the Chief would say about it all. Shelldrake wiped his eyes on a napkin. He was clearly shaken up by the whole thing. Bullets continued with his speech, describing his last days at the Cantina Deburga and his work routine, serving the burgers to the customers, bagging the fries, stocking the Coke machine, stuffing the potato chips into little plastic bags, and polishing the stainless steel counters. He always kept the place spotless, he said proudly.

"And then look at what these shits did to me. They kicked me out."

Bullets continued to speak for at least an hour and a half more. He said that he had worked his trade for many years and in many places but that his real commitment had been to the Cantina Deburga. That had been his real home. Behind the blank eyes in the front, a few flag-waving newcomers in the crowd clapped and cheered each time Bullets finished a full sentence. Since some of his sentences were short and some of them were long, the clapping was pretty noisy and unpredictable.

"I gotta tell ya," he went on, "turning burgers for people who want them is a spiritual experience. I don't ever need to be any more spiritual than getting my hands into that meat. Frankly, I wouldn't be surprised a bit if eatin' those little burgers gives you fellas the big shits. But I'll tell you, I know lots of guys who'll eat those burgers even if they know they're going to get a big case of the shits. That's how bad they want them. The burgers are totally addictive. And I love my job just as much as those guys love the burgers. It's all I know how to do. It's a mutual thing. The customers want the meat taste, and I want to serve the public. It's all I've ever done. It's all I've ever wanted.

"So, you guys, who are you anyway? Are you rat shit on the floor or fly shit on the walls? What are you going to do?" Bullets stood there glaring at the men. He had a disgusted look on his face. "I can't wait for you. I need action. I'm making my move now. I'm going back. Chief. Rupp. I'll see you at the Cantina."

The Chief could see that Bullets was angry and disgusted by the apathy of the crowd. He had tried to rouse them to action, to do something, to get their jobs back, to regain their self-respect. But it was obviously too late. America's steel doors had clanged shut on these guys. They were finished. The Chief, sickened as well, vowed to continue his work.

The crowd of men began to dissipate, just as their brain neurons started scattering all to hell.

After everyone had left, the Chief and Rupp went into the bar for a last one. Bill was mopping up the floor. It was pretty late, but Bill popped them a last couple of Spudkas. The Chief pulled out some loose change from his pockets, but Bill said that it was all on the house.

"That's very generous of you, Bill," said Rupp, "but you know the Chief can't accept gratuities or anything that might be construed as a bribe. We're running a clean campaign."

"Ruppert Waldo Emerson and Chief Shelldrake," said Bill, with obvoius disdain, "play your little clean campaign. Some of the guys have tried that before. It won't work. It won't cleave. Take the fucking Spudka; that's all you want anyway. All your pretenses, your massive land reform, all the pompous talk about de-nutting the corporations and eviscerating the military—it's all a pile of you know what. Horse poopies. At least there's some integrity in the Spudka. But you'll never get there. They won't let you. Take the goddamn Spudka. Will you, for christsake?"

Rupp, for one, was impressed by Bill's honesty and generosity. With Bill's condemnations still ringing in his ears, he turned to the Chief and said: "Take the vodka, Shell. And thanks, Bill, but I can't drink any more of the stuff today. It won't go down. I'm loaded. Thanks for thinking of me, though. But tell me this, why do you think that all we want is more vodka?"

"Rupp," Bill snorted, "that's a policy question for upstairs. We're not going to talk policy here. I know too many people on both sides. Remember, guys, bartenders don't tell."

Bill turned back to the bar sink and began rinsing the glasses and platters from the restaurant. It was a good thing that the crowd outside had finally subsided, Bill thought, since he was all out of nachos.

At Rupp's side, the Chief was contemplating the bottom of his vodka glass.

"Ya know, Rupp," said the Chief, "I think Bullets made some good points this afternoon. His humiliation and shame at losing his job may be the most important motivator in getting back to work. I don't think we should deify the burger work; we should see it as it is. But there could be enough substance there for a guy of Bullets's ambition to make it work. He's entitled to quality employment, and he should go for it."

Bill returned to the bar, wiped off the surface with his rag, and then poured two more double Spudkas. He spoke with authority.

"Chief Shelldrake," he said, handing over another tray of delectibles left over from the streetside wine mess, "I've got to know where you stand if you want want any more hors d'oeuvres and Spudka tonight, or any other night, for that matter, and if you expect to keep your legion of miserable failures supplied with crumbs from time to time."

Shelldrake downed the double in a gulp and handed the glass back to Bill. Frankly, he was a bit surprised by Bill's ferocity. This time, Bill didn't refill the Chief's drink, but instead bent down and stuffed the empty glass into the underbar bus tray.

"Stand on what, Bill?" queried the Chief.

"Well, Chief, they say you want to get rid of the white man. Is that true? Are you one of these wise guys who hates the white man? And are you going to say you were here before the white man? Yeah, and are you going to say the white man gave your native buddies smallpox and the syph?"

"Our goal is to make peace with the whiteys," said the Chief.

Bill said that his people had told him that the Chief and his band of warriors were just a smokescreen, just puppets in a bigger conspiracy. "You shouldn't even be running, Chief," he said. "We're never letting you in, asshole."

Chief Shelldrake showed no emotion. He wasn't going to give Bill a crumb to chew on.

Instead, he turned to Rupp and said: "See, Rupp, you're right; that's why we've got to go back to the nickel economy. You said it all the time. We've had it. It's time to watch these schmucks scream as we rip their balls off and their foreskins slide up over their faces."

Bill had turned away and was wiping his bar cloth across the counter near the register. In the mirror, the Chief could see his pale, impassive face. The Chief did his best to gauge Bill's reaction to what he was saying to Rupp, but he knew that Bill could be deceptive. Maybe he and Rupp had gone too far, let too much out of the bag. Maybe the oyster shooters and the Spudka that he'd just enjoyed with Rupp had been a bribe, after all. And now Bill would probably go public about all the free shit he'd given them. As they left Bill's place, the Chief shared his concerns with Rupp.

"No question, Chief," Rupp replied, "it could be a legal impediment and it could catch up with you someday. You've got to be careful. Bill is sure to start talking."

Heinreicha Helmsley

HEINREICHA HELMSLEY OPENED THE SLIM FILE on her desk and read through the reports. At first, she was shocked, then bewildered, then stupified. She cursed herself.

"You asshole," she said. "You total asshole."

They were already doing everything they could to stop Chief Shelldrake from getting to his destination.

"Get that sonofabitch Krakens up here pronto!" she screamed into the intercom.

Heinreicha waited for an answer from the outer office. She spun her chair around; through the dark, one-way mirror she was able to spy on lower Manhattan. On a clear day, she could see all the way to Bayonnne. There was no answer from the receptionist area, so she called again. This time, she pushed the alarm bells. The clanging resonated into the city. People should know by now that she meant business. Within ten seconds, the bells were turned off and Krakens had appeared at her office door.

Krakens stood before her king-sized desk, and Helmsley laid into him.

"You and your little pranks, dickhead. The word is that Chief Shelldrake's picture is on every telephone and power pole in the country. Why can't you stop him? That's all I asked of you."

"But Chella."

"Don't Chella me, Krakens. We expected more of you than this."

She picked a single sheet of paper off the desktop and waved it at Krakens.

"How do you explain this? From what I can tell, Bullets has defected from Cantina Deburga and has started to talk. He's doing a wake-up call. And what if they all wake up? Then we've really got trouble."

Krakens nodded in agreement. He tried another approach with Heinreicha.

"But, Madame, you've said all along that there may be some leakage in this. I'm doing my best to keep it all covered. I'm more concerned about Buzzozzi. When he gets to the fish lab, we've got a real problem. Our whole scientific establishment is at stake. I think Urbanchuk was put in there too quickly. He's not ready. He really hasn't been tested."

Heinreicha waved one of the reports in Krakens's face. "Listen, Krakens, forget Urbanchuk. He's one of the best we've done so far. Keep your focus on your own goddamn work. Your job, Krakens, is to hold the line, keep the status quo, prevent the Chief and his people from getting in there, at any cost. And, man, you ain't getting any gold stars for this one, even if you do stop him somehow. So you worry about the Chief; that's your department. Personally, I think we've got Dr. Buzzozzi right where we want him. He won't have a neuron left in his brain when we're finished with him.

"And if you can't stop the Chief yourself, then I'll have him arrested and brought here to my office, where I'll conduct my own interrogation. And you'll be history, Krakens."

Krakens noticed that Helmsley was starting to calm down. She could probably see that she had been a little rough with him. He had been through it all before. Her angry fits. She was always teeing off on people with her scathing criticisms and her horrifying judgments. Then a calm would prevail, at least until the next big blowup.

"If you must, kill that pusball Indian before he kills us. And take out that crazy agrarian boogie reformer Remus. And that Ruppert Emerson. Jesus, shit! I've had enough of their nonsense!"

She looked into a scanner on the edge of her desk. "By my reckoning, Buzziboy will be at the lab between 8 and 12 p.m. tonight."

"Well," said Krakens, still trying to find the right conversational niche with Helmsley, "I think we may have them on the run. There's some evidence that the tarbabies may be playing an important role, perhaps a decisive one. And I know for a fact that the hailstorms have been very effective."

"Krakens, that's a load of shit. I have a report right here." Helmsley opened the top drawer of her desk and pulled out another piece of paper. "It says that the Chief and his men, Remus and Sambo, have disabled the last sixteen tarbabies. What do you say to that? We sent out one that was six-hundred-feet tall, and Sambo talked it into heading back toward Chicago. We even tried the Carl Sandburg crap, and that didn't work. People just aren't falling for this stuff anymore."

Krakens hesitated. He knew that the tarbaby program had its

weaknesses. More and more people didn't seem to believe the messages designed to massage the masses. He definitely didn't want to tell Helmsley the latest news about that. God and country and Miss America. A real eighteen-wheeler that he pushed down the road himself. None of it was really catching on, even though the country was swamped for years in Barbie dolls. But the hailstorms; that was something else.

Krakens waited in silence for a few more moments, trying to decide which way to take the conversation.

"Chella," he finally began again, "I heard this morning that FEMA has declared the whole coast, from Wheeler on up, a disaster area, so that they can get in there on an emergency basis. Martial law. The droppas. I really think it's coming together."

"Admittedly," Heinreicha responded, "it's a sign of something, Krakens. But it's all happening after the barn door has already closed. You should know that better than anyone.

"So forget it, Krakens. Let's get down to business. I don't have time for any more of your fuckups. I want action. I have a board meeting in two hours, and the bosses want to know what's being accomplished to protect our country from these proletarian do-gooder hairshirt dogshits.

"I've got a report to make," said Heinreicha. "The FEMAs say that they want a full accounting of the Chief's activities as soon as possible. Right now I think FEMA is scared shitless of Shelldrake. They see him and his little band of bravos as the real cancer on society, as a real danger to what we're trying to accomplish here. And, frankly, Krakens, I believe that their concerns are well taken. And, Krakens, they've been telling me that they're getting a little anxious about where you're heading. A little more than anxious. They say that if you can't get your shit straight, I should can you and handle the matter myself.

"They're watching us closely. First off, Krakens, where's the stuff you say you have on Buzzozzi? How did Buzzozzi get to India in the first place? Carbide wants to know. They want to know where he got the photographs and how he wrote the report so quickly.

"And secondly, Krakens, you promised me that there would be no Diehard meeting this year. But now I hear one is scheduled for this weekend. It's billed as the biggest one ever, and Chief Shelldrake is giving the keynote. How can you explain this to me? You're giving off such a stench of failure, Krakens."

Chief Shelldrake

SHELLDRAKE VERY CAREFULLY DREW THE BLANKETS over Durka, who was sound asleep on the White House roof. He looked at her, the most courageous and beautiful woman he had ever known. And here they were, together on the verge of the great breakthrough. The electricity to the missile bases had been cut off. All naval vessels had been ordered to return to port immediately and discharge their crews. All missiles were disarmed. All military procurement had ended. All banks were closed. They had blocked the electronic circuits to Visa, and now trillions of little green rectangle proteins were dying on the vine, a testament to Rupp's economic brilliance.

The campfires lining the mall and the streets down below were a smokey sign that the strategy was working. Over by the front steps, just off of Pennsylvania Avenue, lay the body of a giant MX missile that Borker had coughed up. The Chief could see the Virginia and Maryland highlands leading down the gorge to the Potomac River. The early morning rush hour traffic snaked, bumper to bumper, over the vast network of highways leading into the city. The doors to all the departments of the government had been locked shut. No more paychecks. No more nothing. Soon, all the commuters would have to turn around and go back home, where they'd have to watch their televisions for news of the coup, if there was any television.

Before Shelldrake arrived, hundreds of helicopters had been parked on the White House lawns to take the former occupants away. As the Chief's followers hurled themselves over the fences to enforce their electoral victory, the whirlybirds quickly packed up the government officials, their spouses, their children, and their advisors, and soared west like giant flocks of vultures. It was a glorious moment. The outgoing administration had spent months trying in vain to conjure up a Constitutional crisis to overturn the Chief's inevitable victory. But now it was too late. Now, all their attention was focused on saving their own asses and stealing every last penny and possession they could grab before they left town.

Shelldrake shimmied down a White House drain pipe, waving at and shushing the tribe below to keep them from waking Durka. The tribes returned to their breakfast fires and to the task of straightening and burnishing their tools. A few scouts had left the south gate to check out Pennsylvania Avenue breakfast spots.

The Chief found an open window near the west gate and climbed unceremoniously into the White House. Stark and empty, the art, rugs, draperies, and furniture gone, the gloomy hallways looked more like a broken down mausoleum than the electrode central of modern political society proclaimed to the world daily by the schmageggies who ran the place. Shelldrake knew that this wasn't the real seat of power, but Durka had convinced him that it was important to occupy the symbol while they continued to chop away at the gangrenous, festering crud still layered on everything, everywhere. He had accepted this as his duty.

Every few moments, he crossed paths with palsied-looking secret service men, their heads bowed to avoid the Chief's greeting. One followed the other, steadily, but they all looked like the same man to the Chief. "Hi there, little fella," he would say, as they slithered silently away into the gloom in their little black suits, little black shoes, and little black socks. Whitey had been so utterly defeated, and it had been so much easier then he thought it would be. The conversion to Rupp's nickel economy had done the final trick. Whitey was in no mood to fight back. Pasturizing the country would be easier now. Restoring health and neurons to the people required immediate attention.

The Chief knew exactly where he was headed. Eventually, he took a few lefts, using his smeller to reach the outer offices of the inner sanctum. As he entered the Oval Office, he could see that everything was gone, the rugs and couches, the furnishings, all the imperial touches of the last administration. The President and his cronies had taken everything, not leaving even a single pencil or paper clip. It was a real mess, the Chief thought, but it could be used as an object lesson, a temporary showcase, to hold public attention while the real work of dismantling the old systems and old values was carried out.

The Chief went through a short, narrow corridor and into a bathroom to take a leak. A short cocktail-party dress hung above the toilet. Curiously, the Chief nosed a small whiff of DNA from a crotch-level stain on the fabric. Nothing else remained in the room, however, not even a towel or a single roll of toilet paper. They had taken everything but the dress. When he'd finished in the bathroom, the Chief wandered upstairs. The situation was the same up there. All the offices had been cleared of their furniture, drapes, rugs, art, artifacts. The place was totally stripped. They had stolen everything.

On his way to the upstairs east wing, the Chief heard commotions both in front of and behind him. He suddenly remembered Old Man Spoogie's warning about the long knives and the need to stay always in the middle of the corridors to guard against shadowy threats from the corners.

But it was too late. The Chief never saw the gang of men who grabbed him, threw a large potato sack over his head, and savagely beat him. The pounding was relentless. He knew he was at the very edge with each blow, but he did his best to hold on, to remain conscious. When the attack finally stopped, the Chief was somehow still alive. Who could be doing this? he wondered. He couldn't think clearly, however, and he didn't have the strength left to struggle against them. He felt himself being pulled and dragged down the stairs. When they reached the bottom floor, they tied and taped his arms and mouth. He heard a car engine starting up, just before he was shoved violently into the backseat of a waiting limousine.

"Ve finally got dis fukker," he heard someone say above the racing engine. There were no sirens. He figured that they must be heading west when he heard the car's tires crunching along the grates of the 14th Street Bridge as they crossed the Potomac River. Finally, they reached the smooth pavement of the parkway, and the car bulleted along through the suburbs and toward the open Virginia countryside. The Chief groaned when he realized that he had already missed his first meeting with the Joint Chiefs of Staff by now. He decided just to roll with the punches, since he didn't really have any other options. He continued to chew on a wad of lichen that he'd started on that morning. He'd get his strength back somehow. He had to.

Wake-up Call

WHEN THE CHIEF AWOKE sometime later, he was still chewing the wad of lichen. He noticed that he was in a gurney. His arms were pinned down in a model-16z straitjacket. His head was no longer covered by the potato sack, however, and he could look freely around the large lit room where his captors had left him. Through the windows, he could see blue skies, and as his eyesight adjusted to the bright light streaming through the glass, he noticed several dozen other gurneys parked in rows beside his own. The beds were filled with his people. Three rows over from the Chief, Nighthorse breathed heavily. They had really done such a job on him. There was Buzzozzi in the fourth row, sleeping like a baby. Durka was next to him, tied in tightly, her eyes closed in fierce determination. There were Barb, Cheryl, and the other office staff over in the corner. Rupp was there, too, in the front row. The Chief noticed Bullets a little further back, the third from the left in the fifth row. Millie, Rhoda, and some of the interns from the lab whom he didn't recognize were strapped down close beside him. Leon Henderson lay unconscious in the back. Reba was strapped down right next to the Chief, and what looked like the entire Spoogie family took up a row along the side. The Chief noticed the unmistakable bulk of Lillian Spoogie towering above her granddad. Everyone appeared to be unconcious, asleep, or at least too far gone to communicate. There were no sounds in the room, except the occasional snores and groans.

The room was completely antiseptic, equal parts white and stainless steel. The whole team had been neatly bedded down there, each with his or her own bedpan and reading light. Near a door leading out into a hallway, the Chief could make out a table piled high with huge hypodermic needles, some of them as long as two feet. He scanned the room further. He hadn't expected to see Elena, but there she was, hidden in part by Leon's bulk. Behind Elena, he saw in horror that Harry Teitel's corpse had been disinterred and lay bloated on its own gurney. Harry's presence in the room really confused the Chief; he thought that Harry had been incinerated and already spread as compost in Elena's garden.

The Chief seemed to have been the first to awaken, though Rupp had begun to show some signs of stirring. The Chief looked toward the windows again; a broad panorama of foothills gave him a new reference point. Those must be the Shenandoah, he thought. Obviously there had been a successful counter-coup, starting with his ambush in the east wing.

The Chief watched Reba, who was strapped down beside him. After a few minutes, she opened her eyes, and her gaze connected with his. She appeared to know what had happened. She signalled with her lips that he should continue to play dumb. The room was very quiet and still. The tribes were clearly on the defensive. We'll wait, he mused, as we have always waited. For a little while longer, at least.

Perhaps an hour passed. Shelldrake was beginning to hear murmurs around him. He strained to see who was up and who was still unconscious. He noticed that Barb and Millie were beginning to stirr.

Suddenly, he could hear the sound of trampling feet in the hallway. The swinging doors crashed open. The group that entered was led, the Chief was surprised to see, by a tall woman dressed in black, followed by numerous military brass with badges festooning every square inch of their clothing. At the front of their combat baseball hats was blazoned the word *"FEMA"* in blood-red letters. Behind them, a couple of squads of little soldier dwarfs marched in. The little guys were dressed in much the same way as the others had been dressed when Nighthorse brought them into the tribal offices. They carried weapons of every description, and their bandoliers dragged on the floor behind them, clanking like chains across the concrete. After the soldiers had deployed themselves around the room to cover all the beds, a hand motion was given by the tall woman in black. The little dwarf soldiers fell immediately into parade rest. They turned and rotated their bodies until they they were curled up on their sides on the floor with their thumbs in their mouths. A few used pacifiers. Clearly, they had learned their lessons well.

The racket in the room had really picked up now, and the Chief knew that everyone in the gurneys had to be awake. He looked around for signs. The tall woman in black approached him. She stared him in the eye. She wasn't bad looking, the Chief noticed. Not bad at all.

Before she addressed the Chief, the woman tapped a heavy metal pointer on his gurney, just above his head. He could feel the cold vibrations of steel against steel ripple through his entire body.

"I'm here because we're tired of your nonsense," the woman said, still staring right into the Chief's eyes. "I'm not happy today because of the damage you've done. We don't take it lightly; do we, boys? We're going to end this crap once and for all."

She snapped her fingers and the swinging café doors opened once again. An unusually short, extremely fat dwarf waddled into the room, dressed in an enormous white smock. A stethoscope hung between his legs and dragged on the floor behind him. There was no doubt about who he was. His hairy face and arms gave him the same ugly, fearful look that the Chief had heard about from Rupp and the girls at the lab. The insignia on his baseball cap, the dripping axe head of the ustashi, floated ominously above his deep, blackened eye sockets. The guy definitely looked like a real dick-do. The Chief could hear Millie and Rhoda whimpering in the back.

"Chief, I want you to meet the top scientist in the country, Dr. Bill Urbanchuk. He'll do the honors."

The Chief scanned the room again. Rupp was semi-conscious and trembling violently. Buzzozzi murmured something and Rupp quieted down.

"Before we start," announced Bill Urbanchuk, "there's some information that we need to get from the Chief and his cronies." Urbanchuk turned to the senior military officers and to Heinreicha. "We want the locations of the lichen stashes. We want the maps of the tribal land deeds you've been hiding from us. We want the Bhopal report. After that, Heinreicha, I can promise nothing but peace and tranquillity. There won't be a neuron left in this crowd that its mother could love."

The tall woman in black was preparing to distribute the giant syringes to the little soldiers lining the walls of the room. She commanded, *"Achtung! Achtung!"* and the little mercetemps soldiers jumped to their feet at the new command. "Yes, Chuky, is that all you need?"

"We want the Bhopal report, and we want it now," said Urbanchuk, who was standing over Buzzozzi. Buzzozzi gave no response. "We'll simply drill his brain out until we find it. When we caught him sneaking around the lab last night, he claimed he didn't have it."

Buzzozzi was resolute. He wasn't going to tell.

"Think of the Roto-Rooter, Buzziboy."

Shelldrake continued to search the gurney-laden faces of his people. He knew that something had to happen soon or everything would be lost. Durka was stirring slightly. Dr. Urbanchuk was assembling his Roto-Rooter syringe contraption; he had lined the top of Buzzozzi's head with a purple magic-marker to indicate the point of penetration.

Suddenly, the Chief heard ripping sounds. Durka was finally coming out of it, and she was mad; she had torn her arms free from the 16z restraints. She sat up with a roar, took several deep breaths, and then just let go of everything, all her fury, all her frustration, all her disappointment, once and for all. The gigantic flood of pus and gunk she promised for the Triple Revolution exploded from her body. The fluid crud rose majestically to the ceiling and poured down on everything below.

The mercetemps were screaming now, running for the windows and doors. Heinreicha Helmsley was quickly drenched with Durka's scapa flow. She screamed helplessly as she ran for the door with her FEMA people. The oozing pus was so deep now that Dr. Urbanchuk was up to his chest, trying to wade out of the primordial slime. Durka was still coughing away, giving off what the Chief estimated had to be the entire treasure house of her secret weapon. It had to stop soon, he thought. But the flow continued. The Chief and the others watched in delight as Urbanchuk was washed out the door and down the hill. Heinreicha and her people were nowhere to be seen. The mangled bodies of the little soldiers were splashed and splattered on the rocks down below.

The gurneys were starting to move now, swept along by the deepening flow of gook and floating one by one out the front bay doors. The Chief was in the lead. He looked back and saw that everyone was awake and accounted for. Durka rolled up beside him, and the pair looked out over the sun-drenched Shenandoah Valley.

"You did it, honey," he said, reaching fondly toward her with his free hand. The Chief looked up at the sun. "There's not too much time, Durka. You should take Millie and Barb and get the offices organized. Take Rupp and move the nickel economy. Take Cheryl and get the fax set up. Take Nighthorse and Sambo for security. Take Bullets; he's our new full-employment man. Reba will come with me. I've got to get to Skankerville to the Diehards."

Durka and the Chief caressed goodbye.

Still strapped to their gurneys, Shelldrake, Remus, Reba, and the Spoogies headed west. They rolled in formation along the superhighways of America. The people cheered them as they headed into the interior. A big, yellow Mashpee Moon rose steadily above them, smiling broadly, signalling their destiny.

Also from AKASHIC BOOKS

THE NAMES OF RIVERS by Daniel Buckman
197 pages, hardcover; $21.00, ISBN: 1-888451-29-7

"Let the word go out: There's a new Hemingway loose in America. Buckman's powers of observation are breathtaking, his lyricism continually puts a fresh face on the mundane things that usually pass unnoticed, and his prose rolls forward with a sure rhythm, concision and grace that make almost every paragraph a textbook model of how to write well." —*San Francisco Chronicle*

THE ICE-CREAM HEADACHE by James Jones
235 pages, trade paperback; $13.95, ISBN: 1-888451-35-1

"The thirteen stories are anything but dated . . . a compact social history of what it was like for Mr. Jones's generation to grow up, go to war, marry, and generally, to become people in America." —*The Nation*

SEED by Mustafa Mutabaruka
*Selected for the *Washington Post's* Best Novels of 2002 list.*

*Selected for *Library Journal's* Best First Novels of Spring/Summer 2002 list.*

178 pages, trade paperback; $14.95, ISBN: 1-888451-31-9

"Mutabaruka's deft maneuvering between past and present, Morocco and the United States, blurs distinctions and creates a mystical and frightening story . . . [P]lain prose and interesting characters keep this novel on its feet and make it dance." —*Library Journal*

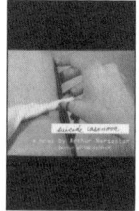

SUICIDE CASANOVA by Arthur Nersesian
370 pages, hardcover binding into hard-plastic videocassette; $25.00, ISBN: 1-888451-30-0

"Sick, depraved, and heartbreaking—in other words, a great read, a great book. *Suicide Casanova* is erotic noir and Nersesian's hard-boiled prose comes at you like a jailhouse confession." —Jonathan Ames, author of *The Extra Man*

ADIOS MUCHACHOS by Daniel Chavarría

Winner of a 2001 Edgar Award

245 pages, paperback; $13.95, ISBN: 1-888451-16-5

"Daniel Chavarría has long been recognized as one of Latin America's finest writers. Now he again proves why with *Adios Muchachos*, a comic mystery peopled by a delightfully mad band of miscreants, all of them led by a woman you will not soon forget—Alicia, the loveliest bicycle whore in all Havana."
—Edgar Award-winning author William Heffernan

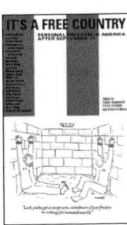

IT'S A FREE COUNTRY: Personal Freedom In America After September 11
Edited by Danny Goldberg, Victor Goldberg, and Robert Greenwald

Contributors include Cornel West, Michael Moore, five members of the US Congress, Howard Zinn, Ani DiFranco, Matt Groening, Tom Hayden, and many others

370 pages, hardcover; $19.95, ISBN: 0-971920-60-5

"A terrific collection about civil liberties in our society. We must never forget that we live in our faith and our many beliefs, but we also live under the law—and those legal rights must never be suspended or curtailed."
—Reverend Jesse Jackson

SOME OF THE PARTS by T Cooper

Selected for the Barnes & Noble Discover Great New Writers Program

264 pages, trade paperback; $14.95, ISBN: 1-888451-36-8

"Sweet and sad and funny, with more mirrors of recognition than a carnival funhouse, *Some of the Parts* is a wholly original love story for our wholly original age."
—Justin Cronin, author of *Mary and O'Neil*
(2002 PEN/Hemingway Award Winner)

These books are available at local bookstores. They can also be purchased with a credit card online through www.akashicbooks.com. To order by mail, send a check or money order to:

AKASHIC BOOKS, PO Box 1456, New York, NY 10009

(Prices include shipping. Outside the U.S., add $8 to each book ordered.)

EDWARD STONE COHEN, 1937–1999

When Edward Cohen first ran his fingers through earth, he returned to the beginnings. Discovering and building links, putting things back, tracing out the meanings of things through their connections— long before Italo Calvino wrote of it in his *Memos for a New Millennium*, Edward Cohen recognized the ultimate value and power of vectors as superseding the old structures, as producing something beyond structure.

Edward Cohen may have come out of the sea at his birth in Massachusetts in 1937. He surely returned to the sea at Nahcotta, Washington, on the rim of the Pacific, at his death in 1999. Some would say that, across the last decades of his life, Edward was amphibious. When the tides were out, he nurtured his oysters; when the tides were in, he drew organic greens and root crops out of the ground in a wonderful circular garden. Wherever you went in that garden, you always came back to the beginnings. Edward's hands connected the fate of the sea and the fate of the land, and he understood the relationship between the two.

Edward Cohen held on to things that mattered—especially language. He caught hold of the transient words that reflected an era—might he now from some deep place refer to these words themselves as "weenies"?—and he kept these words alive in his speech and in his writing. In his life and his work, he made these words work again and again, just as he makes them work within this novel. He loved unusual surnames, their poetics, as if the names drew out additional meanings from their owners. He could remember such surnames forever, invent them if need be, warp their pronunciation to his needs. Perhaps these names signalled a tribe apart, a tribe capable of exceptional, wonderful, and demonic arts, a tribe ready to produce, as in this novel, a presidential candidate. Names, words, language, for Edward, constituted a soil in which wonderful things could grow.

Edward was born a writer, and he meant to use writing to recognize, understand, and represent the connections—better, the conspiracies—of life. He had a keen eye for the unexpected and not-quite-proven, but surely convincing, associations among every realm of life—from the doomsday strategies of the Cold War to the simple life of a shellfish, from the hunger and needs of the poor to the sexual indiscipline of a nation's leaders. For Edward, it was these connections that defined his relationship, and the relationship of every individual, to the fate of the planet. His was a whimsical intelligence, an intelligence with no borderland. An earlier piece of writing reflected both this whimsy and his outrageous political sensibility: *Fellatio, the Boy Scout,* an unpublished novel that developed upon his call "to expose the Boy Scouts before they expose themselves."

Edward moved back and forth between two coasts and the two small, unique hotels of which he and his wife were proprietors, developing the properties from bare buildings and their given names as they found them—the Moby Dick in Washington State and the Tabard Inn in Washington, D.C. In toggling between coasts, Edward drew us back and forth between Melville and Chaucer. Edward dreamed of bigger whales than Melville and stayed to tell stories longer than Chaucer's. And when he left behind his wife and partner Fritzi, his children Sarah, Jeremiah, and Josh, his grandchildren Rosie and Henry James, his siblings, and his many, many charmed friends, he also left us with a veritable "green novel," a salute to the so remarkable and vexed world that he understood too, too well. Edward Stone Cohen: 1937–1999.

David William Cohen (a sibling)
Ann Arbor
May 2002